To Be Cherished
A Rutherford Novel

By R.C. Wynne

To Be Cherished
By R.C. Wynne

Second Edition
Copyright © 2020-2021 by R.C. Wynne
All rights reserved

Cover art by Beautiful Mess Graphics
Editing by CTS Editing & Weis Editing/Proofreading Services
Formatting by CJC Formatting

www.rcwynnebooks.com

ISBN: 978-1-944984-94-6
Library of Congress Control Number: 2021903491

This book is a work of fiction. All names, characters, locations, and incidents are strictly products of the author's imagination. Any resemblance to actual persons, living or dead, is entirely coincidental.

This book is licensed for your personal enjoyment only and may not be reproduced in any form, except in assisting in a review. This book may not be resold. Thank you for respecting the hard work of this author.

For up-to-date news on R.C. Wynne's latest releases, book signing events in your area, and giveaways, follow his newsletter -
https://landing.mailerlite.com/webforms/landing/l7q0q7

You can also join R.C. Wynne's reading group one Facebook, Wynne's Romance Hideaway, for more updates, extra giveaways, and even more fan involvement - https://www.facebook.com/groups/wynnesromancehideaway

PUBLISHING

To my sister, Laurie

Acknowledgments

Regardless of my name being on the cover, it takes a team to put these stories in your hands, and I'm surrounded by one of the best. Charleen Cox keeps this team running and organized, keeping our office records, taking care of my swag for each book, and building the things we need for shows and events. Teri Edney is amazing at my book covers and has even started her own graphics business with Beautiful Mess Graphics, which if you're an author, you truly need to check out. She also does my teasers, advertisements, and acts as my marketing manager. Sarah of SEA Creations does all my formatting, which would drive me absolutely crazy. All three of these ladies serve as beta readers, making sure I don't screw up characters or hand you a weak, slow story. Their input and ideas are invaluable in making each novel the best it can be before we allow it to reach your hands. Without these three wonderfully talented and patient ladies, there would never be a Robbie Cox in bookstores. I owe them an abundance of gratitude.

I also need to thank Katie Weisenberger who has been my editor from the start, making sure my tense, commas, and typos are caught before publication. She is awesome, and I appreciate all she does and how quickly she handles the manuscripts, since I'm usually pushing them at her last minute. I also need to thank her husband, Bill, for allowing her to work so many nights to make sure these stories are as perfect as we can make them.

There are so many components in being an Indie Author, and I could never figure it all out on my own, so I want to thank Linzi Baxter, Gracen Miller, C. L. Roman, and Violet Howe for always allowing me to bend there ear, run ideas by them and ask them questions as to where I'm going off the rails. From marketing to publishing to grammar to trends, these ladies and fellow authors have been a wealth of information, helping me along this journey. Thank you for your time, patience, and valuable advice.

There are more, many more, and each one is important and needed as we strive to bring you the steamiest, most adventurous tales to keep you entertained and returning to see what happens next.

One

"Are you fucking Edwin?" Glen Lansky stood in their kitchen, palms down on the Formica counter, his eyes begging Cherish to say no and just laugh it off.

She didn't laugh it off, however. Instead, she became pissed. Really pissed. "What the hell are you talking about? Faith's the one fucking Edwin. Not me. He barely talks to me anymore, too busy bending my sister over his desk more than likely. Where the hell did that come from, anyway?" How the hell did their evening escalate to him accusing her of having an affair? Glen came home just like always, played with Jordie for a bit, the two of them on the floor playing with plastic dinosaurs all over her living room, the living room she just finished cleaning, actually. Of course, they didn't clean up after themselves, assuming Mom would do it just like she always did. Not that Cherish didn't bust her ass all day at Rutherford Construction. Hell, she had to do twice the load at work with Faith on the West Coast with Morgan, not that Edwin or Faith cared for that matter. As long as Cherish's sister was off having fun, no one cared if Cherish got stuck doing all the work in the office. She turned back around, snatching the sponge out of the sink and grabbing the next plate. "That was a gutsy accusation."

Glen shrugged beside her, keeping his gaze fixed on her even though she refused to look at him. How could she after that accusation? "It's just you seem more on edge than normal, especially about work. You've done nothing except complain about Faith's trip and how Edwin doesn't seem to care about the effect it's had on you. All you've talked about over the last couple of weeks is how much time Edwin spends with your sister. It's *all* you talk about, actually. Faith and Edwin. I know it's not because you're worried about her."

"Hell no, I'm not worried about her. She can fuck whoever she wants." Cherish scrubbed the plate with vigor, releasing her anger onto the ceramic dish. "Faith's had her nose so far up Edwin's ass lately, she could probably tell you what his boss had for lunch."

"If you don't care, then why are you so angry about it? Why do you even care?" He took a deep breath, shaking his head. "I'm sorry, Cherish, but you sound jealous."

"Jealous? Of Faith? Why the hell would I be jealous? She's a timid little mouse who's finally broadened her experiences. I just hate that she's chosen to do it at work. Hell, she only has that job because of me."

He shrugged as he slipped his hands into his jeans pockets, turning and leaning back against the kitchen counter. "Because she went to Tampa with Morgan and you didn't. Because Edwin spends more time with her than with you these days. Because she seems to enjoy her life right now more than you're enjoying yours. To be honest, I really don't know why you're jealous. I thought you enjoyed your life. I'm just telling you how you're acting."

Cherish rolled her eyes. "If she wants to play house with Morgan in Tampa, what do I care? She's probably trying to sleep her way up the corporate ladder, and Morgan has a hard-on for anything with a vagina. She's already banged Edwin. It only makes sense that Morgan would be next. Hell, Neal might even get a shot."

Cherish could see the pain in Glen's eyes and knew he figured out the truth. He didn't have proof, of course, just his intuition. But he knew, and he reached out trying to get her to admit her affair so they could figure out what to do next. If she just stopped fighting and admitted she cheated on him, they probably could fix their marriage; she could keep her family together. Yet, she was too hurt, too damn angry. It wasn't just Glen's accusations or the fact he busted her. Those were actually small items she could fix if she would just take the time. No. What pissed her off so much was the fact that it was Wednesday night, the week half over, and Edwin had barely paid her any attention in Faith's absence. Cherish assumed—hoped, actually—with Faith out of the picture for a week, Edwin would need his itch scratched, and Cherish could work her way back into his life. Yet, he maintained the buffers between them, never allowing the two of them to be alone for her to attempt to regain his attention. It was obvious his mind remained on Faith. Cherish still had two days to make it work, and she wasn't about to give up and throw in the towel, confessing all to Glen. She started herself down this path, and there was no way she could back up and admit defeat now. Edwin just needed to realize he needed her more than he needed Faith.

Cherish just stared at Glen, her shoulders rising and falling with her heavy breathing, the tension twisting her gut, the conflicting worlds of work and home threatening to undo her.

Glen stared back at her, but whereas her eyes were daggers of fire daring him to challenge her, to accuse her once more, his resembled a kicked puppy who only wanted the pain to end, for someone to love him, to cherish him. He stood for a moment longer, staring at her, and then just nodded and walked out the door. "I need some air."

She should run after him, call him back, done something. Instead, she just watched him leave, listened as his car started and then faded off into the distance. Ten minutes passed before she realized she still stood in the same spot.

~ ~ ~ ~ ~

Glen's head hurt, his stomach a twisted mess, his heart... His heart broke. He kept taking deep breaths, doing his best to keep the tears from falling. Everything made sense now. All the time Cherish spent working late, the weekends where she had to go in suddenly, the texts and late-night phone calls. He should have known, should have seen it happening. Yet, he had closed his eyes and stuck his head in the sand, ignoring the signs and pretending his family wasn't falling apart. But it was falling apart, collapsing around him.

He turned down New Haven Avenue, heading to the one person he knew he could talk to about Rutherford Construction and the drama that was Edwin Coldwell and the Driscoll sisters—Selby Greer. Glen tried Selby's house first, but he wasn't there, so Glen assumed his brother-in-law stayed busy at the bookstore he owned while Faith was in Tampa. Glen stopped, bought a six-pack of Shock Top, and headed downtown for advice more than company.

Faith and Selby were the happiest couple Glen knew, and Selby did a great job keeping the Driscoll family from interfering with that happiness, something Glen had failed to do, especially with Valerie, the Driscoll matriarch. Instead, he permitted his mother-in-law to control more of their lives than he ever should have, because it seemed Cherish needed her mother's mothering. The woman even controlled their schedules too much, a mistake Glen now regretted deeply. If only Glen could have pushed Cherish to stand up to her mother, like Faith had, and loosen up some and have fun with him. Instead, Cherish decided to have fun without him, her adventures private and behind closed doors. He bit his lip, twisting the steering wheel in his hands as he did his best to keep his anger down.

Downtown Melbourne was lit up for a Wednesday night, the dinner crowds shifting to the mid-week bar-hoppers. Streetlamps illuminated the cobblestone sidewalks and streets as people walked from one bar to the next, browsing the store displays they passed. Pulling into a vacant spot in front of Selby's Downtown Books, Glen shifted his car into park and turned off the engine. He just sat there for a moment, staring at the front of the store, debating whether or not opening this part of his life up to Selby was a smart decision. He already talked to Selby about the jealousy between Cherish and Faith, Cherish's obsession with Edwin. Selby told him Faith and he had an open marriage, and he knew his wife screwed around with Edwin. It wasn't a secret. Or at least, Selby implied that's what was happening. He never came right out and said Faith slept with her boss, just that he knew she flirted around with other men, teased them, and allowed them to cop a feel once in a while. He even admitted it turned him on and suggested Glen talk to Cherish about opening up their marriage. Now Glen wished he had talked to her about it, maybe then she would just admit she cheated on him, maybe then they could be having fun and laughing, instead of him sitting in front of Selby's store with his heart torn out. If only she told him what she wanted…

Glen shoved his driver's door open and slid out of the car with a deep breath. Pushing the door open to Selby's bookstore, the cowbell gonging over his head, he called out, "Selby!" He watched as Selby weaved his way through the bookshelves to the front of the store. "I swung by your house, but obviously you weren't there. So, I thought I'd gamble you'd be hiding here." He held a beer out for Cherish's brother-in-law.

Selby took it, a curious expression on his face, and the two men clinked bottles. "Cherish doing better with Faith out of the office?"

Glen shook his head as he leaned back on the counter. "Yes and no. She's busting her ass and working overtime, bitching that Faith isn't there to do anything. I don't know if Cherish will ever be happy."

Selby just laughed. "They all have too much of their mother in them." He took a long swig from his Belgian white.

"Bite your tongue. Why would you wish that on us?" The one thing Glen didn't need was a miniature Valerie Driscoll. He didn't need the full-sized one, either, for that matter.

Selby shrugged. "Genetics. Arni's the only calm one." That itself was an understatement, and both men knew it. The entire time Glen knew the Driscolls, he never once heard Arni so much as raise his voice. The truth of the matter was the Driscoll children all possessed their selfish sides, and that was all Valerie, because Arni would give you the shirt right off his back. Valerie and the kids were every-man-for-himself, even Cherish, something which came out more and more over the past couple of weeks.

Glen watched as Selby stared at his beer bottle, obvious that his mind was somewhere else right then. As the other man lifted his bottle to take a drink, Glen said, "I asked Cherish if she was fucking Edwin."

Selby spit out some beer as he choked on what he managed to

swallow before Glen's abrupt announcement. Selby's eyes watered as he tried to get his coughing fit under control. "You timed that," he said, his voice strained.

Glen gave him a sheepish smile as he flipped through a children's book on the counter. "Sorry. I guess that was kind of random."

Selby took a deep breath as he said, "Don't worry about it. And?"

Glen shrugged. "She got pissed I even asked." Glen looked up, his chocolate eyes fighting back tears. "She's always laughed off comments like that before, but this time she actually got pissed."

"So she denied it?" Selby leaned back on the counter, his gaze focusing on something far away, even though he did his best to listen to Glen. Perhaps he was going through the same thing Glen was, wondering how much of the Driscoll sisters' exploits he actually knew.

"Have you heard anything? I mean, has Faith said anything that would indicate that Cherish was banging their boss?"

Selby shook his head, his shaggy blond hair swishing across his forehead. "No, Faith has only talked about herself lately." He shrugged. "You know how it is, any mention of the other and both sisters get ridiculous."

Glen sighed. "Yeah, I know. I really wish I knew what was up between the two of them. I don't think I've ever seen them get along."

"Faith's never said anything outside of Cherish being Val's precious baby. I just assumed it was sibling jealousy. Of course, Val is great at digging the trench between them deeper. As it sounds, Edwin is only adding fuel to the fire."

Glen lifted his beer bottle to his lips. *That's an understatement.*

~ ~ ~ ~ ~

Cherish sat on the couch, sipping wine, when Glen finally returned home. He said nothing, at first, just dropped his keys on the small table by the front door and went into the kitchen and pulled a beer from the fridge. She decided not to start any conversation, waiting to see where his mood was at the moment. She didn't want to start another fight.

She heard him pop the top and take a long swallow before he returned to the living room and plopped down into the recliner. He still said nothing, the silence deafening.

For a moment, Cherish debated asking where he went, but only for a moment. She didn't want to know, wasn't even sure she had a right to ask right then. Instead, she decided to just pretend nothing happened earlier and life was normal. Deny all accusations, even when the evidence stared you dead in the face. She took a sip of wine, and then said, "Mom called while you were out to talk about Jordie's birthday. She's offered her house for the party again."

"Now, there's a great idea," Glen rolled his eyes as he lifted his beer bottle to his lips for another swallow.

Her temper flared. "What's that supposed to mean? My mother loves Jordie. She's just trying her best to give him a great birthday, like she always does. We have the party there every year. I don't see what the problem is."

Glen held his beer with both hands, dangling it between his legs. "Yeah, it's just everyone else she hates. Every time we have his party at your parents' house, things get tense and awkward, and you know it. You know damn well she does her best to instigate my mother into a fight. Why do we always have the party at her house as opposed to neutral territory? I think it's time for a change."

Cherish's eyes went wide as she gawked over at Glen. "My mother does not hate your mother. That's pretty rude. How dare you!"

"What it is, is pretty damn honest. Your mom always tries to put on a show for my parents, doing her best to make them somehow feel inferior to her. She does it all the time, doing her best to one-up everyone. It's childish. No. We're not having the party at your parents' house. We can have it here or at a park, even the playroom at McDonald's for all I care, but not at your parents' house."

"Is this because of earlier? You think I'm screwing around behind your back, and so, you're taking it out on my mother?"

He blew out a sigh, shaking his head. "This has nothing to do with earlier and everything to do with how your mother treats my family. Treats everyone, actually. No. It's not happening."

"I'm not having Jordie's party at McDonald's. I'm not celebrating my son's birthday around a bunch of strangers."

"Fine, then we'll have it here," Glen said with a shrug. "It's two weeks away. I'm sure we can clean up the place by then and make it presentable. Do we have a list of who we're inviting?"

What the hell? "Wait. Are you saying our home isn't presentable for company? Excuse me, but I work for a living just like you. I'm not going to come home and spend all night working on the house after dealing with a bunch of idiots all day long."

"I never said you had to. What I said was, we had time to clean house before inviting people over. Do you really want people to see the house like this? It's a mess."

"And that's my fault?" She couldn't believe him.

"I never said it was anyone's fault. It just is what it is. Why are you arguing with me about the house? Now who's holding onto the angst of earlier?" He shoved himself to his feet, walking back toward the hallway. "I'm going to bed."

"We need to settle this about the birthday," she called out after him. She couldn't believe he just got up and walked away. What the hell was he thinking?

"It's settled," he called back over his shoulder, still walking away. "We're having the party here. We can clean this place up this weekend."

She felt her eyebrows pinch above her nose. She couldn't believe how stubborn he was. "My mother is not going to be happy."

"See, it's a party already."

"Glen!" Cherish shoved herself off the couch and started walking toward the bedroom. He popped his head back out of the hallway, his arm at his side, fingers around the top of the beer bottle. She stopped, her heart thudding in her chest with her frustration. And her worry, if she was honest with herself. "I just want Jordie's party to be perfect," she said, trying to rein in her frustration.

Glen stared at her, his expression unreadable. "I'm sure he'll have a great time wherever we have his party. He's turning five for crying out loud. Parties are still pretty simple at this age and rarely remembered. He'll be fine."

There was more she wanted to say and none of it about Jordie's birthday party, but three glasses of wine and two hours spent waiting for Glen to return home had not given her the courage yet to admit her infidelity. She didn't want to risk screwing up her family by admitting something before it was necessary. Jordie didn't need a broken family as his birthday present, and if she told Glen about her affair, she would hand him the ammunition to end their marriage. He had stepped up to the plate once; that didn't mean he'd keep running around the bases when the ball headed his way.

"Anything else?" Glen asked as he stood there staring at her.

There was quite a bit more, but she decided not to pursue it.

There was too much at risk. Besides, she still wasn't sure what she would do about Edwin. She was hurt by a man she had no commitment to while she devastated the man who stepped in and saved her life. She was torn, and she saw no way to repair the rip that was about to tear her life apart. She couldn't stop, even if she wanted to. She had to see how it all ended. Had to see how far she could go, keeping it all together.

Two

Thursday morning dawned just like every other morning. Glen had breakfast with his family, even if his mood was more sullen than usual, and then went off to work. Cherish played the dutiful wife, saying all the right things at all the right times, going through the motions, but her mind was anywhere but on what she did. Faith was due back tomorrow, and that only gave Cherish one day to get Edwin back in her grasp. So far, nothing she attempted that week had worked. She followed him around the office, brought him lunch, even stayed after work hoping to get him alone. Yet, he seemed to do everything in his power to avoid her. He went home early. Left the office for lunch on some trumped-up business meeting. Arrived to work late. He did everything he could to avoid her, and so far, it worked. Today would not differ from the looks of things, either.

By the time work was over, Edwin Coldwell was nowhere in sight, and she had no real reason to hang around. Nessa Sanchez, the part-time office help who filled in for Faith that week, was already packing up and heading out the front door, leaving Cherish alone in the room affectionately known as the Girls' Den.

Jed Jorrell, one of Edwin's main office managers, walked into the room about ready to flip the lights off when he saw Cherish sitting there in her chair, staring at her computer screen. "You okay?"

Cherish blew out a frustrated breath. "I'm fine. I just expected more than I should have." *The truth is, I shouldn't be expecting anything. I have a family.* Yet, she couldn't help it. Edwin became more than he should have in her life, and she just couldn't let him go. Not yet. "I'm going home. See you tomorrow."

"Only another day, and then the office returns to normal," Jed said as Cherish passed through the door.

"Oh goody," was all she said as she passed out of his sight. She didn't want her sister to come back. Faith could stay away forever for all Cherish cared. She wanted to scream. Why wasn't life going in her direction?

Once home, she picked Jordie up from her neighbor, Aubrey McDonald, and headed home to cook dinner. Glen came home from work, his mood still somber and distant. Obviously, what she told him the previous night still didn't satisfy him, but he didn't press the issue. For that, she was glad. She didn't need another evening of defending her actions, of which there was no defense.

Friday morning was much the same thing, only this time Cherish dropped Jordie off at preschool before going to work. Edwin was actually at the office this morning before her, which didn't surprise her, really. Faith was due back this morning. He'd want to make sure he didn't miss his precious piece of ass. Cherish's temper already boiled by the time she dropped her purse on her desk in the Girls' Den. Nessa walked right in behind her and offered her a good morning to which Cherish only offered a growl in return.

Glancing back at the office door, she decided it was time to push her advantage, and it didn't matter who was around. Faith was due back, and Cherish needed Edwin's attention before then. Saying nothing, she left the Girls' Den, heading for Edwin's office. Jed and he stood at the giant whiteboard in the hallway outside of Edwin's office, going over the list of jobs for Rutherford Construction. They both turned to look at her when she approached, Jed with a smile, Edwin with a tense frown. "Can I talk to you?" she asked Edwin. "Alone."

"Sure." He gestured toward his office as he turned to Jed. "Get Grady up to the Melbourne Medical Buildings. We need to push those guys a little more."

"Will do," Jed said as he turned to leave the two of them alone.

Cherish stood in Edwin's office by the corner of his desk, her arms across her chest, her foot tapping when he entered. He left the door open; she assumed he hoped she would be careful with what she said, worried others might overhear her. He was wrong. She was way past the point of others knowing her business.

She followed him with her gaze, turning so she always faced him as he made his way behind his desk and into his chair. Already, he acted protective of himself, putting a barrier between them whereas before he would usually sit on the edge of the desk, his jeans tight against his cock and thighs, tempting her. She had lost. She knew it. She just wanted to know why. "What happened to us?"

"Us?" He feigned ignorance with his expression, his brows

crinkled over the bridge of his nose. "Nothing happened to us. You're a great employee. You're doing a fine job."

"Don't be an ass, Edwin. And don't think just because that door's open, I won't shout out our business for the whole office to hear. Glen is already asking if I'm fucking you, so there isn't much else for me to risk now, is there?" Why did men always play stupid? Did they think it was their superpower? That by ignoring or pretending something never happened, it would just go away? "So again, let me ask, what happened to us?"

Edwin ran a hand through his dark hair, his gaze darting to the open door as he blew out a breath. "Nothing happened to us, Cherish. We were having fun, and now, we're not. That's all."

"But why not? What did I do? What does my sister do that I don't? Tell me, and I can do it. Tell me!"

Edwin held his hand up, gesturing for her to lower her voice as he glanced out the door again to see if anyone was there, listening. "Cherish, you didn't do anything. Look, the longer we went on, the more obvious it was you needed something I couldn't give you. You were looking for a relationship, something you're missing apparently in your marriage. I'm not wanting a relationship. I was just in it for the fun."

"Don't assume you know a damn thing about my marriage. And so what, my sister was more fun than me?"

"What makes you think anything is going on between your sister and me?"

"Because I know you. I was the one you were sleeping with, remember? I know what it looks like—what you look like—when you're screwing one of your employees. Don't even deny it." He'd deny it until his dying day, and she knew it, but it didn't matter. She knew the truth. She lived it.

"I won't be the one who comes between you and your husband, and it was obvious that's what was happening. You weren't just wanting to have fun anymore. You wanted a white knight, and I am far from that for anyone."

"That's for damn sure." She glared at him. "You're afraid of coming between Glen and me, but you have no problem coming between Faith and Selby."

He sighed. "I told you; there's nothing going on between your sister and me."

She knew he lied. She knew him. She knew her sister. Or, at least, she did at one time. Faith became someone totally different from the timid little church mouse she used to be a year ago. Now, she was more like some nymph on steroids.

Cherish said nothing else. She simply turned and walked out of the office. *This isn't over, Mr. Coldwell. I swear, this isn't over.*

The morning went by quickly, phones ringing off the hook as people prepared for their weekend, trying to get as much into the day as they could without really doing too much at all. When she finally allowed herself to glance up, Edwin stood in the doorway, a cigarette tucked behind his ear. "Join me for a smoke break?"

She nodded, scrounged in her purse for her own cigarettes and lighter, and then followed him through the office and out the back door. It used to be their daily ritual, a few moments when they could be alone and talk, flirt, talk about what they wanted to do to each other when the rest of the employees left. That is, until he started banging her sister. Then it all changed. Cherish couldn't get her cigarette lit fast enough. She needed the calming nicotine and action of smoking.

"Look, I'm sorry," he said after he had his own cancer stick lit. "I should have talked to you about it, instead of just dropping things like I did. I was wrong."

"You were an ass," she said. "And I don't doubt for a moment that your attention went somewhere else. If you weren't screwing my sister, you'd still be sniffing around my skirts. Men like you don't give up a piece of ass for no reason, and I highly doubt your pulling away had anything to do with your conscience and worrying about my husband. You were getting your jollies somewhere else, even if you don't want to admit it."

He sighed, blowing out a stream of smoke as he did. "You can believe what you want. I just wanted to clear the air and apologize."

The sound of tires on gravel drew their attention to the side of the building as Morgan Brewer drove into the back parking lot of Rutherford Construction. He parked his massive truck beside Faith's small Toyota, and Cherish could see the two of them talking as he turned off the engine. *Probably thanking my dear sister for playing house all week. She must be a lot better piece of ass than her personality dictates.*

When Cherish saw Faith come around Morgan's truck, Cherish took a step closer to Edwin, letting her sister think things were back to normal, even if they weren't. Cherish watched as Faith took a deep breath, shaking her head as she turned her attention to Edwin.

"How did it go?" Edwin tossed his Salem into the distance as he left Cherish's side and approached Morgan and Faith. "Ready to return my girl to me?"

Cherish wanted to scream. Not even back two minutes, and already, Faith had Edwin's undivided attention again, leaving Cherish behind. She glanced at Faith. "Welcome back," was all Cherish said as she dropped her cigarette and went back inside, leaving the two men alone with Faith. She refused to stay and watch them fawn all over her sister. Not when she stood right there wanting to be the object of at least one of their attentions.

She dropped into her desk chair with a growl. She had failed to get what she wanted this week. She lost. She swiped at her eyes with the back of her hand, keeping the tears from rolling down her cheeks. It had been a long time since someone dumped her. Almost six years, actually. This time hurt just as much, if not more, than that one because this time there wasn't someone stepping in to fill that void. This time, she was alone.

~ ~ ~ ~ ~

Glen spent all day trying to shake the feeling that his wife had betrayed him, sneaking around behind his back for some sexual adventure with her boss. Yet, the feeling never went away. The worse part was that since he arrived home, the feeling only grew into a nauseous knot in the pit of his stomach. All Cherish did was bitch about her sister and how Edwin immediately went all gooey when she returned. She didn't even care that Glen dropped Jordie off at his Grandma Lansky's for the night. Barely even noticed it, actually. She obsessed over Edwin and his infatuation with Faith. You just don't talk about someone that much unless there's something happening between you. Glen knew. He knew his wife cheated on him, even if she hadn't admitted it the other night, and now he just couldn't take hearing it anymore.

"You're fucking Edwin," he whispered. It wasn't an accusation. He didn't yell. He merely made a statement.

"Are we really going to do this again?" She glared at him.

He shrugged. "It's the only explanation as to why you won't stop talking about him. It's the only reason you're so obsessed about him and Faith. It's the only thing that makes sense. You're fucking him. You're jealous." The pain of the statement seared his chest, constricted his lungs forcing him to fight for each breath. He held out hope that his gut instinct was wrong. He prayed he was wrong, scolded himself for even contemplating such a thing. Cherish was not the same woman she had been almost six years ago. She settled down, turning her focus on raising Jordie and being a family, being a wife. She wouldn't just throw that away on a whim, would she?

He stood there in their kitchen and stared at her, silently begging her to deny his accusation, to laugh the notion off like she always did. He had dropped Jordie off at his mother's, not wanting his son around just in case his gut was right. It was a smart decision.

At first, he thought she would still deny it, starting another fight, instead, full of denials and false statements about how ridiculous he acted. He almost wished she had done that, kept denying it. Then, he could pretend as well. But she didn't deny it this time.

"Yes! I fucked him! Is that what you want to hear? I had an affair with Edwin. There. I said it." She stood there, her arms wrapped around her waist. Her face grew red with anger, but she shed no tears. She didn't apologize or say that it was a mistake she regretted. She said nothing like that. She wasn't sad at all. Instead, she was furious.

He should be furious as well. Perhaps that would come later. Right then, he only felt broken. "Why?" His voice came out as a distant whisper. This couldn't be happening. He had pulled her away from that lifestyle. Stood by her when others walked away. He gave up his life to create a new one with her, with Jordie. He covered her sins with his love, and his sacrifices weren't enough for her.

"Because it was exciting. It gave me a rush to sneak around with Edwin. I missed that excitement in my life." She squeezed herself tighter as she looked away. For just a moment, he thought he saw the glistening of tears in her eyes. "I grew bored with my life. Up until I had Jordie, my life was one giant party. I missed that feeling, the feeling of being chased and then of finally allowing someone to catch me." She turned her gaze back to him, and he saw the pain on her face. "Life had fallen into a rut, and

Edwin offered me an escape. I took it."

"So all this jealousy with your sister, all this...anger...is because he stopped fucking you?"

She turned her lips up in a sneer. "He's been fucking Faith, if you can believe it. The timid, little Faith Greer isn't the saint she pretends to be."

He gave a weak chuckle as he shook his head, his gaze looking at anything except her. "You're mad because the man you cheated on me with cheated on you? You don't see the hypocrisy in that? You don't even care that you cheated on your husband. Nice."

"Glen..."

"No!" Tears finally began to fall from his eyes, streaking his cheeks. He didn't wipe them away. He wanted her to see the pain she caused him. "No. There's nothing you can say. I'm sorry I bored you. Perhaps you'll be better off without me then." He nodded, decision made. "I'm leaving." He pushed past her toward his bedroom, their bedroom.

She grabbed his arm, attempting to jerk him back around. "What do you mean you're leaving? You can't leave. Hell, Faith fucked Edwin, and Selby didn't leave."

He spun around, and she collided into him. "I don't care what Faith and Selby do!" His voice was a snarl. Cherish took a step back, her eyes wide with the shock of his outburst. "He, at least, knew his wife was fucking Edwin. You were cheating on me! You're not even ashamed of being caught, only that Faith got to play with your toy." He took a menacing step forward. "You no longer get to have your cake and eat it, too. I loved you enough to come to your rescue once. I don't love you enough to allow you to cheat on me. I'm done."

"What about Jordie? What are you going to tell him?"

She stared at him with wide eyes, and he could tell she was

afraid. After all this time, after everything they've been through together, she still didn't know what type of man he was. It turned his stomach. "I'll figure that out when I get there, but don't worry. He's my son. I'll always protect him and take care of him. I'll drop him off in the morning, but I won't be staying with him."

She just stared, her lips moving, but nothing came out. She played her hand as long as she could, and now, Glen called her bluff. With all the cards on the table, there really wasn't a winner. Everyone lost this time.

He packed enough clothes for a couple of days. He'd stay at his parents' place until he figured out his next move, whatever that was. To be honest, he didn't know. He just knew he couldn't stay here. Not tonight. Maybe never.

He jerked his car door open and threw the quickly packed bag into the passenger seat. With one foot in the car, he stopped, his hand gripping the door as he turned back and stared at the front door of his house. She didn't chase after him, didn't beg him to stay and not leave her. She just stood there, watching in her stoic silence as he stormed past her, leaving her with the pain she caused him. His throat constricted as he stood there, staring, fighting back the tears that wanted so badly to burst from his eyes, shedding his pain. *Why hadn't she tried to stop me?* Not even once did she say, "Please don't go." He wasn't sure which hurt worse, the fact she slept with Edwin Coldwell or that she hadn't asked her husband not to leave her.

He slid into the driver's seat, shoving the key into the ignition. He needed to leave, to get out of her sight for a while. Yet, if she had just once asked him to stay, said she was sorry and for him not to leave, he would probably have caved right then. But she didn't. She just stood there, arms across her chest, and watched him walk out the door. He shoved the car into drive and hit the accelerator as he punched in his father's name on his cell phone.

"Glen? Hey, son. How's your night going?"

He took a deep breath. "I'm coming home for the night. Mind if I crash in the spare bedroom?"

Silence. Then, "No, no. Not at all. I'll put on some coffee."

"I may need something stronger."

He could hear the worry in his father's voice. "It'll be waiting for you when you get here."

Glen ended the call and tossed the phone in the seat beside him. He was going home.

~ ~ ~ ~ ~

She stood in the hallway, her arms wrapped around her stomach doing her best to keep her insides from spewing all over their living room floor. Cherish hadn't meant to hurt him, to say the vile excuses for what she did. Her words were hateful and hurtful. She didn't even apologize. She spewed her venom and watched the pain of her words dim the light in his eyes. If she was given time to cool off after her day with Edwin, she probably wouldn't have gone off on Glen the way she had. Yet, she still fumed, her body pumping with the adrenaline of her encounter with Edwin and then watching him go all puppy-eyed over Faith when she returned.

Glen didn't deserve what Cherish did. He was right. He had stepped in when everyone else had stepped out. He kept her secrets, gave her a life without shame. Yet, how did she repay him? She screwed around behind his back, betrayed him. And she didn't even show remorse.

She heard him shuffling around in the bedroom; drawers opening and slamming shut. She heard the bi-fold closet door jerked open. Hangers rattled as he ripped clothes from their place. She could hear the hurt in every movement, even though she couldn't see what Glen was doing. She fought the urge to throw up.

She was remorseful. Very. Yet, she was too hurt and angry to rein in her outbursts. She couldn't stop. She couldn't even stop him from walking out the door.

When the front door clicked closed and the car engine started, she crumbled to the floor, sobs wracking her body as her world fell apart.

Three

When she woke, still crumpled on the floor in the hallway, she had a text from Glen. *I dropped Jordie off at your parents' home. You can pick him up there. Don't worry. I didn't tell them anything.* But what did he tell Jordie? That was the question rattling around in her brain right then. She moved, every muscle screaming at her for the way she slept last night. She deserved the agony. She deserved worse. All she had wanted was to feel again, to have the adventures she used to have that made her feel alive, even those adventures in the end left her high and dry. She wasn't sure when she fell asleep. When Glen left, all she could do was crumble to the floor and cry until no more tears flowed. It felt like forever ago.

Cherish heard the front door open. "Anyone home?" It was Aubrey, their neighbor, which meant Cherish slept all night on the floor with the front door unlocked. Glen always made sure to lock the house up before he went to bed.

"I'm here," Cherish said as she forced herself into a standing position, her body screaming as she stretched out her cramped muscles, slipping her phone into her back pocket. She knew she had to look like a mess, but Aubrey had already seen her at her worst. The two women had been friends even before they lived next door to each other.

Apparently, Cherish looked worse than her worst. "Whoa, what in the hell happened to you?" Aubrey asked as she rounded the corner from the living room and saw Cherish leaning against the hallway wall. "Did you guys have a wild party last night and forget to invite me? I love wild parties."

Cherish gave the other woman a weak smile. "I wish that was why I look so glamorous. It was a rough night last night, and not in the *I was on my back for hours* kind of way." She sighed, the weight of the words she was about to utter like a lump threatening to choke her. "Glen left me last night and spent the night with his parents. Some things came out last night, and we need to regroup."

"Wait. Back up." Aubrey fell back against the doorframe, her arms crossed over her chest. "Glen slept at his parents' house? This seems rather sudden. When we grilled out last week, you both seemed the perfect, happy couple. What the hell happened?"

"I happened." Cherish tucked a strand of her strawberry-blond hair behind her ear as she took a deep breath. "I cheated on him with my boss at Rutherford. It all came out last night, although I'm pretty sure Glen guessed it a couple of weeks ago. Apparently, I wasn't as subtle as I thought."

It was obvious by Aubrey's face she didn't know how to react or what to say. That was okay. Cherish didn't know how to react, either, and had already said way too much last night. She felt the tears begin to well up again. So much for being all cried out. She wasn't sure she could say anymore, to speak out loud the wrongness of her actions. She was afraid to speak, even to Aubrey, who was the most non-judgmental person she knew. The dark-haired woman had been close to Cherish and her family since before Glen and her bought their house just over four years ago. The other woman was actually the reason they bought the house. Aubrey had always been the one person outside of Glen who Cherish could open up to about anything. Together, the three of them had shared meals, drinks, and even skinny dipped in Aubrey's pool. The only thing, outside of her husband, Cherish never shared with the other woman was her affair with Edwin.

So, now she did. She said it all while she stared at the opposite wall. She told Aubrey about the late nights at work, about decorating Edwin's new office when Rutherford moved locations, about the very first time she snuck over to his house on a Saturday afternoon, supposedly while out shopping while Glen went fishing with Jordie. Then, how Edwin began to pull away from her and started sleeping with her sister. Glen figured it out, of course, and left, and Cherish wasn't sure he would return.

"Do you think he'll forgive you and come back?" Aubrey asked.

Cherish shrugged. "I honestly don't know. He was pretty devastated when he left last night. He was supposed to bring Jordie home this morning, but he took him to my parents' house instead, which means he's still not ready to see me yet. Not that I can blame him." She blew out a tense breath. "I need some coffee. Do you want some?" She pushed herself off the wall and made her way to the kitchen, Aubrey right behind her.

"How did Glen find out? And why didn't you tell me all this was happening? I could have used some intrigue in my life." Aubrey entered the kitchen right behind Cherish and took a spot leaning on the counter by the sink.

Cherish shook her head at her friend's statement. The woman thrived on drama and sex. Cherish should have known her infidelity wouldn't shock her friend. "You don't tell other people you're having an affair. That's why it's an affair. The whole concept is to be secret." She dumped the old coffee grounds into the trash and reached into the cabinet for a new filter. "And, apparently, my mood hasn't been the best lately. Edwin started screwing Faith, and I couldn't keep my feelings about it from coming out." Cherish dumped three scoops of Eight O'Clock coffee into the little basket. "That sounds so asinine. I got pissed at Edwin for cheating on me while here I was cheating on Glen. What kind of level of crazy is that? The sad part was, Edwin and I weren't even in any type of relationship. I was just someone he slipped his dick in on occasion. Who knows how many others there were? I read more into it than there was, lost in how Edwin took control of me during our moments together." She pressed the brew button.

"Took control, huh?" Aubrey looked at Cherish with raised eyebrows and a smirk on her lips. "Should have known you were the little submissive type. Do you like to be spanked, too?"

Cherish rolled her eyes. "You're not spanking me, so get that thought out of your head."

Aubrey giggled. "Too late," she said with a bounce of her eyebrows. She then slid her arms over her chest. "So Faith was fucking your boss as well? She never struck me as the wild one. More the timid church mouse."

The aroma of fresh coffee wafted through the kitchen. "Faith is so not a timid church mouse anymore. She's been acting like a tramp at work, letting men play grab ass with her, the comments more than suggestive, and she even went to Tampa with one of our bosses for a week under the guise of putting an office back to rights. She probably fucked the man the whole time she was gone."

"Really?" Aubrey laughed as she pounded the counter with the palm of her hand. "That's awesome!"

Cherish turned and looked at her friend as if she were crazy. "How in the world is fucking around awesome?"

"I'm not even going to point out how hypocritical that statement is coming from you right now. Besides, with what you've told me of your past, can you really judge your sister?" Aubrey shrugged, her rounded shoulders thin under her flimsy top, her ample breasts rising and falling with the movements. "Sex is sex. As long as Faith and Selby are happy with what they're doing, more power to them. They're at least honest about it."

"Ouch. Thanks. Toss more salt in my wounds."

"I wasn't slamming you, Cherish," Aubrey said. "I was just impressed your sister had the guts to go after what she wanted. Most people just stay normal, bottling up what's inside of them in order to conform. Conformity is what's killing our nation, if you ask me."

Cherish couldn't disagree with her friend. Conformity had made her lose control, craving what she had before family life swallowed her. Of course, she couldn't use conforming as an excuse for what she did. There were other ways to get what she felt she needed. All she had to do was look at her sister to know that was true. Cherish had been selfish, and that selfishness cost her everything.

"What do you think would have happened if you told Glen you wanted to sleep around? This isn't the fifties anymore. People do it all the time. Hell, the Internet is full of swinger sites and hook-up sites. Maybe your sister is on to something."

Cherish shook her head. "No. Glen would never have gone for

it. He's too straitlaced, a family man through and through. You remember how father-like he got when Jordie was born. Besides, that wasn't the point." She took a deep breath before reaching into the cabinet for two coffee mugs. "This is going to sound so wrong, but here it is. Being a wife and a mother just became too overwhelming for me. I was suffocating. I didn't feel like I lived my life anymore. When Glen and I first met, I would go out all the time—dancing, shooting pool, drinking—I had fun. I wasn't tied down to a schedule or had to be home at a certain time. I miss that. I felt alive back then. I don't anymore."

"You regret getting married? Having a child?"

Cherish turned and leaned back on the counter. "Yes and no. I love Jordie. I wouldn't give him up for anything. And I love Glen. He's always been there for me, even when I wasn't there for myself. I just... I just missed some of what I had before and wanted to feel it again. There were things I explored back then I never finished exploring." She shrugged. "I guess I got lost in what I was doing."

Aubrey nodded. "I get that. Things were pretty wild back then, especially between you and Nick. So what now?"

Cherish just looked at her friend. "I wish I knew. I guess I wait and see what Glen wants to do. I don't want to lose my family, I know that. I just don't know how to keep us together after what I did."

"Glen's a pretty great guy. He'll come around. Just give him time. But don't keep hiding things from him, either. If you need something like this, tell him. He just might surprise you. He was just as wild back then, remember? He went to the same parties we did."

Cherish nodded as she turned to pour them both some coffee. Glen always did surprise her, especially when he asked her to marry him. Yet, while he saved her once, she didn't think he had it in him to save her again.

"What will you tell your parents?" Aubrey asked.

Cherish closed her eyes. She did not look forward to facing her mother and telling her what her precious baby girl did. Worse, she didn't want to see the look of disappointment in her father's eyes. That would be her undoing.

~ ~ ~ ~ ~

Glen dropped Jordie off at the Driscolls' and sent Cherish a note telling her she could pick him up there. He just didn't want to face her again, didn't want to listen to more of her justifications and hurtful words. He didn't think he could take any more pain. Not from the woman for whom he sacrificed everything.

Instead, he texted Brent Dodson, his partner at Melbourne Docks and Piers, and told him to meet him for a beer. Of course, Brent, always up for a cold one, said no problem, and thirty minutes later, they sat around a bar table at Grill's, overlooking the Indian River, Glen pouring his guts out to his friend. The night before, he gave his parents a quick synopsis of what transpired between Cherish and himself. Both said he was free to stay at their place as long as he needed, his mother seeming as if she knew this would happen and felt justified in her feelings toward Cherish, which had never been accepting. Glen spent the night sleeping next to Jordie, but not really sleeping. Instead, he just stared at his son, wondering what the future would hold, afraid of the answer.

When morning came, Glen still didn't have the guts to face Cherish, his stomach still a knot of Christmas tree lights. Instead, he called Arni and asked if he could drop Jordie off there for a little while. He made some excuse about having to work and Cherish needing to take care of something. Glen didn't even remember what he offered as the something she had to do. He figured he would give her the chance to tell her parents what she wanted. He wouldn't be the one to tell Valerie Driscoll her baby girl broke her family. That privilege belonged to Cherish. Arni could tell something was wrong when Glen dropped Jordie off but didn't ask about it. Arni was always the wise one of that family, knowing just when to push, and when to let his family work out their own issues.

"I can't believe it," Brent said, shaking his head as he twirled his beer bottle on the table in front of him. "I just can't... Are you sure?" He tilted his head, staring at Glen, disbelief masking his face.

"Yeah, I'm sure. She admitted it. Finally." Glen lifted his beer and took a long swallow as he glanced out at the river. "I don't believe it, either, as a matter of fact," he said as he lowered the beer bottle.

"What are you going to do?" Brent sipped his beer as he scanned the women who walked back and forth, his eyes raking them up and down as he smiled his approval.

Glen shook his head, chuckling at his friend. "You're supposed to be here for my support, not checking out the feminine scenery."

Brent turned back around, grinning at him. "Why can't I do both?"

Glen just laughed. At least one of them could have a good time. He sighed again as he dropped his gaze back to his beer. "I don't know what I'll do. This all went down last night. I've barely had time to process it all. For now, I'm staying with my folks."

"Nothing like going back home," Brent said as he lifted his beer bottle to his lips.

"Not my idea of progress." You weren't meant to go back home. A person was meant to move out of their parents' home and start their own life, raise a family, have a career. Moving back in with his parents was moving backward, not forward. It was a sign he failed. Sure, Cherish was the one who cheated on him, but ultimately, he failed as well. She said as much last night. She missed something in her life, something he didn't give her, and discovered it somewhere else with *someone* else.

The two men were silent for a while, Glen staring at the passing river, Brent staring at women's asses. When Brent finally turned back around to face Glen, a serious expression pulling at his features, he asked, "Are you going to leave her?"

That was the real question, one Glen struggled with since Cherish finally admitted her affair with Edwin. At first, he wanted to go and confront the man, take him to task for screwing Cherish. Glen even imagined it, his fist pounding into Edwin's face, turning the man into a bloody mess as he expended every ounce of rage at the betrayal. In the end, however, Glen decided against it. After all, what would it really accomplish other than a few moments of satisfaction? Instead, Glen just called Brent and decided it was time for a drink.

Glen took a long swallow, his eyes closed as he felt the coldness of the beer slide down his throat. When he finished, he glanced back out at the water, thinking over Brent's question some more. Would he leave her? Almost six years they'd been married. In that time, he witnessed Jordie's birth and given up his college years in order to raise a family. He regretted none of it, loved Jordie with everything he had. He loved his job, his life, the course he was on now, the course of taking care of his family. Sure there were things he missed about their past, the drunken parties out in the fields at Lake Washington, the nights shooting pool and dancing. There were nights he barely remembered getting home, and mornings he woke up with his head practicing a drum line inside. However, he gladly gave it all up when Cherish told him she was pregnant, and he decided to give her the family she needed to raise her son. He loved Cherish. Her infidelity didn't change that. But did he love her enough to forgive her? That was the question he struggled with at the moment. The problem was, he didn't know.

He took another long swallow of his beer. Cherish said she missed the days before they were a family. He understood that, but that's what came with starting a family, what came with the next phase of life. You had to stop acting like a teenager and grow up when children started entering the picture. You had to change the course, incorporate new goals, new ambitions. Your fun had to take a different direction. Didn't it?

Had he lost them by going too far? Could he have given Cherish what she said she needed and still remain the family they were? Glen sighed. Was it too late to find out? He closed his eyes, clutching the bottle with white knuckles. *God, Cherish, why didn't you just talk to me?*

Four

It didn't go well with her parents. Cherish stopped by their house to pick up Jordie, and her mother, ever the nosy one, was full of interrogating questions Cherish couldn't avoid. After all, Glen never dropped Jordie off on the weekend, and why wasn't Cherish with him when he did? After sending Jordie out to the backyard to play in the sandbox his grandpa made for him, she dumped everything on her parents in one lengthy monotone monologue. She screwed up, and she owned it. Her mother went hysterical at first, blaming Edwin for seducing her daughter and Glen for not satisfying Cherish. It was everyone's fault but Cherish's. Valerie Driscoll even managed to somehow make Cherish's affair Faith's fault. Cherish just shook her head, not saying a word. Her father, Arni Driscoll, just sat there, his hands on the top of his head as he stared into space. He said nothing. He didn't condemn her. He didn't join in his wife's rant against everyone else who failed his daughter. He just sat there. When Cherish finished her explanation, he nodded, patted his upper thighs as he stood to his feet, and just said, "Looks like you have some groveling to do to make this work." Then, he just stared at his daughter, and she saw the pain in his eyes. "For Jordie's sake, you need to fix this and pray Glen forgives you." Valerie only scoffed, blaming Glen once again for not being the man Cherish needed.

They kept Jordie overnight, Valerie saying she'd take him to church with them. "He always loves playing with the kids in the nursery." The hope was that without Jordie at home, perhaps Glen and Cherish could talk things out and repair their marriage. It didn't work, however. Glen still didn't want to talk to her and swore he never would as long as she still worked for "the dick who fucked his wife."

Cherish spent a restless night, tossing and turning on the couch, not wanting to sleep in the bed she shared with Glen for the last six years without him. When she woke up, her mouth dry and her head throbbing, it took her a moment to remember the chaos that was now her life. *How does Faith get away with it? How can she fuck around and Selby be okay with it?* Cherish showered and slipped into some baggy shorts and a loose T-shirt. *There's no way Selby knew what was happening. Impossible. Not Mr. Squeaky Clean.* It was time, she decided, that he found out.

When she reached Selby and Faith's house, no one answered the door. She let herself into their backyard, climbing the steps to their wooden deck so she could peer in the back doors. No movement. She sighed. Turning, she stared out at the Atlantic Ocean, the three-foot waves cresting at odd increments as a light breeze blew across the water. She envied her sister living directly on the beach. It had to be calming to listen to the waves pounding the shore all night long.

Cherish walked toward the ocean and took their stairs down to the sand. As she reached one of the middle steps, she sat down, hands clasped in front of her as she stared out at the water, surfers waiting for that perfect wave, which didn't appear to be arriving anytime soon. The more she sat there thinking about Faith's charmed life, the angrier she became. Her sister, the one who whined about everything, had it all. It wasn't fair.

She turned, sweeping her gaze over the beachgoers scattered along the sand. And there was Faith with Selby and another woman walking her way. She watched them walking for a while, both women flanking Selby as they laughed about something only they could hear. When Faith finally noticed Cherish, she stopped and just stared. The redhead said something to the others, probably asking who Cherish was. When they started walking again, the stranger moved to Faith's other side so that now Selby and she flanked Faith. Her protectors. People who would do anything for Faith always surrounded her. How in the hell did her sister demand such loyalty from people? Why did they never give that to Cherish?

Cherish sat there waiting, her arms wrapped around her chest, hugging herself as she bent over as if ready to puke at any moment. She knew she looked like a mess; she had seen herself in the mirror that morning before she left the house, and she wasn't a pretty sight: bloodshot eyes, hair a twisted mess, her whole appearance looking as if she hadn't slept in days. She hadn't, and she didn't care who knew it. Faith caused this by stealing Cherish's boyfriend. Faith could have had anyone she wanted, but oh no, she had to take Edwin, Cherish's fling.

Cherish watched as they approached, and Faith stopped at the base of the stairs, arms crossed over her chest. Cherish sat far enough up that the two of them were eye-to-eye. She said nothing. She just waited.

Selby was the one who finally broke the silence, his expression one of sympathy. She should have known they would know about Glen leaving her, probably had a party about it, laughing at her. "Hey, Cherish. Your mom told us what happened. I'm sorry to hear what's happening."

Cherish glanced at him and nodded. "Me, too. Thanks."

Faith continued to stare. "Why are you here?" Cherish's sister had really perfected her bitch face.

Cherish looked out at the breaking waves, then down at the beach. She struggled to hold it together, bouncing between being angry and just feeling lost. Finally, she stared down at her hands. "I don't know what to do. I've lost Glen. You've got Edwin. I …"

"I don't have Edwin." Faith's voice wasn't a shout, but it was cold and hard. "I have Selby."

Cherish snorted a short laugh. "You were fucking Edwin. I'm not stupid." She glanced at Selby. "He seduced your wife, too."

"No, he didn't," Selby said.

Were they really going to deny it? "Bullshit. Your wife isn't Miss Innocent. He got to her just like he got to me. She fucked him."

Faith started laughing. "You came out here to tell Selby I fucked your boyfriend? Your marriage is screwed, and your way of fixing it is to try to ruin mine? You cheated on your husband, Cherish."

"So did you!" Cherish stood to her feet in one quick motion, and as she did, both Selby and the woman who was with them took a step forward.

"No, I didn't," Faith said. "You are very much mistaken there."

"You fucked him!"

Selby placed his hand on Faith as he spoke. "Yes, she did, but she didn't cheat on me. As I said, Edwin didn't seduce Faith. She seduced him. She didn't cheat on me, because I knew what was happening."

"You knew? You *knew* she screwed our boss, and you were okay with it?" Cherish jerked a finger at Tracey. "Are you two fucking her, as well?"

"Probably not now, since you've shown up and ruined the mood," the redhead quipped. "Your family has lousy timing. First your mother, now you."

Cherish watched as Faith reached over and gave the other woman's arm a gentle squeeze. When the redhead turned her focus to Faith, Faith just gave a soft shake of the head as if to say, "Not now."

"Cherish, you can't blame Faith for what you did," Selby said. "I'm sorry your life is screwed up right now, but the way to fix your marriage isn't to come here trying to screw up ours. What we do is our business, and I assure you, we both know what the other is doing."

"How can you be okay with it? It's wrong." Cherish stood with her arms across her chest, all her assumptions about her sister being a slut finally proven true.

"No. You fucking Edwin behind Glen's back was wrong. Glen didn't deserve it, and he doesn't deserve you. He deserves better." Faith took two steps forward. "Now, get off my property." She walked past her sister, not looking back.

Selby watched his wife climb the stairs, arms still folded across her chest. He motioned for the redhead to follow, which she obediently did. Cherish watched Faith's departure, not believing the charmed life the middle Driscoll sibling lived. She gave a slight jump, startled when she turned around that Selby still stood there.

With a sheepish look, Cherish ducked her head. When she

spoke, her voice was a bare whisper against the ocean breeze. There was no use arguing any more. She would never win against her sister. "I'm sorry. I'll get out of your hair."

"Not yet." Selby stepped in front of her, blocking her from walking away, his face a knot of anger that seemed like he struggled to control. "I have tried to keep my mouth shut, but you and your mother have pushed too far. I don't know where either of you get off blaming Faith for you cheating on Glen, but it's total bullshit."

"My mother blamed Faith? When?" She didn't even know her mother had talked to Faith. It had to have been after she left their house yesterday.

"Last night. She was here when we got home. Seems none of you know to call first." Selby stood with his hands on his hips. "Faith has never done a damn thing to you or your mother to deserve the abuse you both give her. I don't care what you two do, but you won't hurt my wife anymore. What we do with our life and in our marriage is our business, and I don't care if you approve or not. I'm sorry your marriage is on the rocks, but that's your fault. Not Faith's. Own it and leave her the hell out of it."

Cherish just stared at him, shocked that Selby finally stood up to someone in Faith's family. Anger made her shake, and there was more she wanted to say, but not today, not now. Instead, she just turned and walked away, leaving Selby standing there staring after her.

~ ~ ~ ~ ~

Glen stood on his parents' back porch staring up at the clouds drifting by as his thoughts churned. Cherish called, telling him about her conversation with Faith and Selby, wanting him to know they were right, and Faith actually fucked Edwin. Selby even knew about it and was happy. All Glen could tell her was that at least Selby knew and wasn't blindsided. What the Greers did in their marriage was up to them. He didn't care. What he cared about was his wife cheating on him and knowing she would go to work tomorrow, side-by-side with her lover. "Ex-lover," Cherish reminded him, but he didn't care. She wanted him to come home, but he couldn't. Not yet. Not while she still worked at Rutherford Construction.

He heard footsteps behind him. "Here," his mother said as she stepped up beside him, a coffee mug with a rooster painted on the front in her hand. "I thought you could use a cup of coffee. A hot beverage always helps ease tense emotions."

Giving his mother a weak smile, he muttered his thanks as he took the steaming cup. The warmth caressed his face as he took a sip, the liquid scalding his lips as the first sip always did. He felt the heat spread through his chest and stomach. She had been right. It felt good.

His mother didn't leave. Instead, she wrapped her arms over her chest, rubbing her hands up and down her upper arms. There wasn't a chill in the air, so Glen assumed it was an attempt to strengthen her fortitude to speak her mind. However, he could tell something was on her mind.

He glanced over at his mother, the coffee cup held at waist level. His fifty-five-year-old mother had black hair that seemed faded as the gray began to sneak its way into her wavy locks. She refused to dye it. "Between you and your sister," she would say, "I've earned every streak of gray that I get. I'll wear it like a badge of honor." Robert Lansky, his father, was bald, and he blamed it on his wife. He would tease that her gray hair was karma for his baldness. Glen claimed his thinning hair was hereditary. Tanya, Glen's sister, just prayed she didn't get the hair loss gene and started dying her hair blond.

"No coffee for you?" Glen asked his mother, trying to break the silence.

"Nah. Two cups are my limit. I knew you liked it, though."

He took another sip while she answered. As he lowered the cup, he licked the coffee from his lips. "I probably drink too much coffee." Cherish always said he did, that all that caffeine would catch up with him one day. She was probably right.

"Your father would disagree with you." His mother shrugged, keeping her gaze out at the approaching storm.

Glen laughed. "The only person who drinks more coffee than me."

She laughed with him, and then the silence became heavy once again. He knew his mother had something on her mind, but he wasn't sure he wanted to know what it was. Brenda Lansky had strong opinions, which she usually kept to herself. When she did finally share them, it usually left someone stinging.

"You know you can stay here as long as you want, right?" She didn't look at him but kept her gaze on the falling rain.

"I appreciate it. I just need a little time to get my feet back under me." The truth was, he had no idea what he would do. He didn't want to stay there long, he knew that. Yet, he was afraid that if he rented a place, it would mean he gave up on his marriage. He wasn't ready to put the next nail in their coffin, yet.

"You know, now's your chance to make a clean break." His mother glanced over at him. "You can get your life back."

He took a deep breath. He should have known this was what it would be. "Mom…"

"No, Glen. I'm going to say this, and you're going to listen." She turned to face him, her voice a strained whisper. "You changed your entire life for Cherish. You dropped out of school, married her, gave her your name and a home. You gave her a life she would not have had without you. And how does she show you her appreciation? She sleeps with her boss! She tricked you into marrying her, and then, she cheats on you. You deserve better.

Now's your chance to claim your life back. She hasn't changed." His mother stood straighter as she took a deep breath. She looked up into his eyes, her face a mask of seriousness. "It's true, Glen. A leopard cannot change its spots. I warned you back then, and she's proven me right."

He stared into his mother's eyes. He knew his mother never cared for Cherish. He had hoped over the almost six years of their marriage, his mother would have softened and had a change of heart. After all, Cherish had been the dutiful wife for the past six years. By his mother's words, the passing of time hadn't changed her mind, however. She only became more adept at hiding her true feelings. The coffee turned in his stomach. "Mom, they're my family. Cherish is my family."

"But they weren't supposed to be," his mother said. "Haven't you sacrificed enough for a woman who obviously doesn't appreciate it? Look at how she repaid you. Jordie's your son. Fight for custody and raise him right, but now's your chance to shed yourself of Cherish and her craziness. Take it."

Glen wasn't sure what to say, so he said nothing. He knew he would never take Jordie from Cherish, but he couldn't tell his mother the reason. After a lengthy moment of silence hung in the air between them, his mother just nodded. "Just...think about it. Whatever you decide, I'll stand by you as I always have, and I'll love and support them. I just want what's best for you. I love you."

"I love you, too." He tried to give her a smile, but doubted he pulled it off.

She stared at him a moment and then nodded before looking away. "There's a full pot of coffee. Help yourself." She turned and walked back inside. He doubted she got what she wanted by coming out onto the porch.

He turned back to the afternoon sky, although his thoughts

were much further away. Everything his mother said was true. Basically, that is. He never saw the changes he made of his life as sacrifices. He merely saw them as a change in his journey. No one forced him to make those changes. He made them voluntarily for the woman he loved. They were important life alterations that gave him a purpose. And Cherish hadn't tricked him, either. She didn't ask him to marry her; he proposed. He had loved her. He loved her then, and he loved her now.

He moved to a wicker chair and sat, his back to the house, so he could continue to watch the drifting clouds. He rested the coffee cup on his knee, no longer wanting it. It was a theme with him, lately—not knowing what he wanted. He was hurting, he knew, and he didn't want to make any rash decisions while he still stung from Cherish's betrayal. Whatever he decided would affect not only Cherish and him but also Jordie as well, and he wouldn't do anything to hurt his son. Glen would do anything to keep that from happening. He took a deep breath. Almost anything. Living with Cherish's cheating may be just a little too much for him. He knew he couldn't handle it right now. He wasn't sure if he could ever get past it and put it behind them. He wasn't sure if he could give Cherish back what she thought she lost.

Five

Cherish pulled up in front of the Lansky home, the other Lansky home, her stomach a twisted knot ready to snap and send her hurling into the bushes. Faith and Selby's words haunted her with how accurate they were. She had screwed the pooch, being her typical selfish, bitchy self, and it was time for her to fix it. It was time to talk to Glen, and if she was honest with herself, she wasn't sure she had the guts for it. He didn't seem too willing to talk on the phone earlier.

She shifted the car into park and turned off the engine, but she didn't make a move to open her door. Instead, she stared at the front of her in-laws's house, dreading knocking on their door. She had thought about just texting Glen and asking him to meet her outside, so she could avoid the judgmental glares she knew Brenda Lansky would give her, but then decided against it. She deserved those glares.

Once Cherish left her sister's house, she drove around for a while, not even paying attention to where she drove. She just needed to meander, lose herself in the traffic as she screwed up the courage to face her husband again, her father's words echoing in her mind. *Looks like you have some groveling to do to make this work. For Jordie's sake, you need to fix this and pray Glen forgives you.* Would Glen forgive her? She wasn't an angel when they met; he knew that, but to betray him the way she did was unforgivable after everything he did for her.

With a deep breath, she opened her car door and slid out into the humid April air.

Each step to the front of the house felt as if she walked through water, her movements slow and heavy, as if she dragged herself to an unknown fate. She knocked on the door, praying anyone else but Brenda would answer. Karma, however, was not her friend.

Brenda Lansky opened the door, her glare firmly in place as she stood there, one eyebrow raised. "Cherish," she simply said.

What did I ever do to this lady to make her hate me so much? "Brenda," Cherish said. "Is Glen here?"

"Let the girl in, Brenda," Robert Lansky snapped as he moved up behind his wife, taking the door from her hand and opening it wider, gesturing for Cherish to come inside. "He's on the back porch."

Cherish thanked him as she walked past Brenda and made her way to the porch. She wrapped her arms over her waist, rubbing her upper arms to chase the chill of her nervousness away. Would Glen even talk to her? Or would he toss her out on her ass like she deserved?

Sliding the back door open, she stepped out onto the porch. Glen sat in a wicker chair off to the side, a beer bottle in one hand

and an empty bottle on the table in front of him. His face seemed worn, his eyes tired as he turned his gaze to her. If her appearance surprised him, he didn't show it. He also didn't bother saying hello to her. He just stared.

She took a deep breath, her body shaking as she moved to stand in front of him. "Can we talk?"

He just nodded.

She took another fortifying breath. She didn't expect him to make this easy on her, but she wished he would at least say something. "I need to know what I can do to fix this." Faith's words repeated in Cherish's mind. *You fucking Edwin behind Glen's back was wrong. Glen didn't deserve it, and he doesn't deserve you. He deserves better.* Faith was right. Glen did deserve better than Cherish. He always did, even when he asked her to marry him.

"Did you love him?" His voice was soft, almost a whisper when he asked the question.

"What?" She stared at Glen, her mouth open slightly, eyes wide. "I don't love Edwin, Glen. I love you. I screwed up." Tears threatened to erupt, so she clamped down on them, squeezing her arms in an attempt to hold the tears at bay. "What I did...What I said to you...Glen, I royally fucked up, and I know it. I hurt you in ways I can't imagine, and I'm sorry." She lost the control she held, and tears streamed from her eyes. "God, I'm so sorry." She didn't wipe the tears away. "I don't know when I became this bitch, but I want to fix it. I need you to help me fix it. Please, don't give up on me." She could hear shuffling inside the house. More than likely Brenda trying to hear what Glen and Cherish said, probably hoping Glen would scream at her, accuse her of being what Brenda always thought Cherish was. "Please. I need you. Jordie needs his father back home."

"Jordie will always have me," Glen assured her. "But I don't know if I can go back home, not while you still work at Rutherford with Edwin. And for the record, you've always been a bitch, just not to me."

She nodded, accepting his criticism. It was true, as Selby pointed out earlier. Cherish was a bitch, because she could get away with it. "I'll quit if that's what you want. I can find something else. No big deal. Just, come home."

Glen sighed as he shook his head. "It's not that easy, Cherish. I can't just forget what you did. I gave you everything, or at least, I thought I did, and you still went and spread your legs for someone else. Hell, if you wanted to explore, why didn't you just tell me? We've done crazier things before. I would have at least talked to you about it. But, no, you just had to go off and explore without me."

"You wanted me to come to you and tell you I wanted to fuck Edwin?" she asked, disbelief scrunching her features. "Glen, when did you ever even hint you would be open to that? Once we were married, you were determined to turn me into the dutiful little housewife. Outside of skinny dipping with Aubrey and some heavy flirting, you never gave me the idea you would want to explore sleeping with others."

"Neither did you," he said. "You could have at least brought the subject up. Hell, it seems to work for Selby and Faith well enough. They're having fun together. Didn't I at least deserve the opportunity to say yes or no? You never even gave me the chance."

She stared at him. "You want an open marriage? What my sister has? You would have agreed to that?"

He stood, setting his beer on the table in front of him. "You'll never know now, will you?"

She watched as he walked over to her, his hands in his pockets. There's no way her soft, quiet husband would have gone for her having sex with others. He wasn't Selby. Glen was a homebody, predictable, safe.

When he reached her, he shook his head. "The point is, you never gave me the chance to give you my thoughts on the matter, to choose one way or the other. You decided you knew what I would say, and then, you went ahead and did it on your own." He shrugged. "You made the decision for me. It might have been a fun adventure, seeing you loosen up like you did right before we were married. You've been so stiff since Jordie was born, I just assumed that's what you wanted."

She didn't know what to say. He was right, of course, and now, it was too late to see what he would have done if given the chance. "I'm sorry," she told him as she wiped the tears from her face. "You're right. I never gave you the chance or told you I even struggled with the way things were." She turned pleading eyes up at him. "I'm here now, though. Come home, so we can fix this. We need to fix this."

Glen shook his head. "I'm not so sure we can, Cherish. I'm sorry. There's no going backward. We can't erase what you did."

"Can't we, I don't know, start over?" Yet, she knew the answer even before she asked the question. The look on his face told her she lost, and she had no one to blame but herself.

Glen leaned forward, kissing her forehead. When he leaned back away from her, he shook his head again. "I'm sorry, Cherish. Right now, I just can't give you what you want. I just…" He took a deep breath. "I just can't."

She nodded, the lump in her throat keeping her from talking. Her heart shredded, she turned and left him standing there. She whispered a goodbye to his parents as she made her way to the front door and to her car. There was no use arguing about it anymore. Glen made up his mind. She would just have to wait him out, and in the meantime, she could start by giving him what he seemed to need. It was time for her to quit Rutherford Construction.

~ ~ ~ ~ ~

Glen watched Cherish slip through the doorway, her shoulders slumped, face downcast. He knew she hoped he would give in, return home, and pick up where they left off, but how did she expect him to forget what she did?

He walked back over to the table, picked up his beer bottle, and downed the rest of its contents. The coolness of the beer did nothing to assuage the burning in his heart, however. This was a frickin' nightmare.

He glanced down at his beer bottle—empty beer bottle, that is. He needed another one. With a shake of his head, he turned and walked back inside his parents' house. His mother sat in front of the television, watching a rerun of Wheel of Fortune while his father read the Sunday paper, something Glen didn't see many people do these days. As he walked through to the kitchen, his father glanced up at him, but said nothing. His mother, however, could never allow anything to go when it came to making a dig at Cherish.

"She didn't stay long," Glen's mother said as she glanced over at him. "Will you be here for dinner?"

Glen nodded. "I will. I'm just going to step out and get some fresh air."

His mother raised her eyebrows at him. "Air on the back porch stale?"

Glen just smiled at the woman but said nothing.

"Leave him be, Brenda," his father said, never lifting his eyes from the paper.

Glen just smiled at his father as he made his way to the front door. He'd get another beer later. Right now, he just needed to be outside.

He stepped out into the late afternoon, the sky a dusty gray as clouds started to float in from the west. Glen stared up at the sky for a moment, wondering if another storm would blow in to match his sour mood. He couldn't believe Cherish showed up like she did, all sad and begging to patch things up. Worse, he couldn't believe she thought he would just roll over and take it.

"Escaping?" his sister asked as she walked up the walkway toward the front porch. "Mom isn't going on about politics again, is she?"

Glen chuckled as he shook his head, crossing his arms and leaning back on the doorframe. "No, just being typical Mom. Cherish stopped by, and Mom wanted to make sure I knew Cherish was not wanted here." He shrugged. "She's never really liked Cherish."

Tanya stood in front of him, hands in her pockets. "Well, Mom blames her for you quitting college. She thinks you gave up your future for Cherish." Tanya shrugged. "Kind of puts a mother in a grumpy mood. You can't really blame her."

"She's never been so vocal about it before, though," he said. "And, it's been over five years. You'd think she would have realized I was happy with my life and lightened up. I didn't realize she held this grudge so long. It makes no sense."

Tanya laughed as she brushed her blond hair out of her eyes. "You've met our mother, right? She still despises Aunt Peggy for daring to wear the same dress as her at Christmas twenty years ago. The woman never forgives anyone for anything."

Glen sighed as he shook his head. "It's ridiculous. And stupid."

Tanya glanced at him, her head cocked to the side a little. "Cherish did hurt her baby, you know? Even if Mom did forgive Cherish at one point, the fact that she cheated on you only reinforces our mother's preconceived notion that you deserve someone better. It doesn't matter whether or not you're happy. Mom has her opinion of what she wants for your life, and Cherish never factored into it. I don't know if she ever will as far as our mother is concerned. She can fake it, but she will never change her mind." She took a deep breath, glancing out at the street for a moment before turning her gaze back to Glen. He could tell she was about to say something he really didn't want to hear. "Are you sure Mom's not right? Look what Cherish did to you after you gave up everything for her. Seems rather selfish to me."

"Now, you sound like Mom," he sighed as he shook his head. "This is my life; I loved Cherish back then, and I still love her today. That hasn't changed, no matter what she did."

"Then why are you sulking here, instead of at home with her?" Tanya asked. She blew out a breath as she shook her head. "Look, I don't care what you do. Cherish has always been a wild child. I thought that's what you liked about her. It always confused me when you turned her into this little domesticated housewife. Maybe it just became too much for her, and she wanted a taste of what she gave up. Take her to some wild party out in the woods like you used to do. Let her get crazy."

He chuckled as he eyed his sister. "You think a life of debauchery is what she needs to keep her faithful? We still have a kid, you know?"

Tanya shrugged. "Big deal. You don't think those couples who swing don't have kids? They still manage to bed hop from time to time, getting their rocks off, and being all naked and shit. Don't make it an all-time thing but give her some of what she wants."

"And just how do you know what swingers do?" He couldn't believe he was even having this conversation with his sister. Sex was never something the two of them talked about, and now he knew why.

"Remember Derek? Well, when we dated, we kind of did some fooling around with others and even found a site where people could connect and hookup. There's a ton of swingers in this area. You should look into it."

Glen ran a hand through his dark hair as he took a slow breath. "So, you think the answer to Cherish cheating on me is to let her fuck more men? Doesn't that sound a little...odd?" He shook his head, remembering when Selby told him about his open marriage with Faith. Glen wondered if the two of them were on that site, and if they were, then Glen definitely didn't want to be on it. How awkward would it be to make a meeting and then realize it was with Cherish's sister and her husband? He shook his head. "I don't think that's the answer for us."

"How do you know if you don't try?" Tanya pressed. "I remember the two of you back then. You were practically swingers then; you just didn't call it that. Hell, don't you go skinny dipping with that neighbor of yours? Maybe something she had back then is what she needs now. Have you even asked her?"

Glen gave his sister a puzzled look. "And just how did you know about Aubrey?"

Tanya chuckled again. "Cherish isn't as close-lipped as you think she is. Besides, I can tell there's something between the three of you every time I go over there, and it's not just flirting. Have you three ever...you know, done the dirty deed together?"

"No, we haven't, thanks," Glen said, blowing out a frustrated breath as he shook his head. "There's a difference between nudity and sex."

Tanya laughed even harder. "Yeah, one usually leads to the other. Maybe that's what Cherish wants, for you to push the boundaries of polite society and take your nudity to another level. You should give it a shot. What can it hurt?"

Glen just stared at his sister. Now, he really needed another beer. He couldn't believe he stood there, taking sex advice disguised as marital advice from his younger sister. Life definitely had a funny way of twisting things.

Tanya shook her head as she patted his arm, moving toward the front door. "Just think about it. You've become a little too straitlaced for your own good. Loosen up, and maybe, you can salvage that marriage of yours."

Glen watched as his sister opened the front door and disappeared inside, choosing to say nothing about her suggestion. Still, that didn't mean he didn't think about it. Could opening their marriage up like Selby and Faith did be the answer Glen needed? Was Cherish wanting to sleep around with others? Was that the excitement she missed? And if it was, could he handle it?

He turned his gaze out to the quiet street, his brows pinched over his nose. He had to admit, looking at Aubrey's body had left him stirred more times than he ever admitted. He just never made a move to act on those stirrings. Nor had he ever brought it up to Cherish, even in a fantasy-type scenario. Of course, there was also Rachel at the Royal Chef who continued to flirt with him. He knew she would sleep with him if given the chance; Brent made that perfectly clear.

He shook his head, blowing out a frustrated breath. *Why am I even thinking like this? Normal people don't sleep around with everyone they meet.* He sighed as he pushed himself off the doorframe. *But if this is what Cherish needed, should he not at least give it a shot? Could it do more damage than she had already done?* God, he wished he knew what to do. He couldn't stop thinking that by opening up their marriage, he would in essence be rewarding Cherish for what she did. But, would it be worth it if that reward saved their marriage? How the hell does one even go about opening up their marriage? It just seemed so...so...weird.

He ran his hand over his scalp again. *Can I handle weird?* He wasn't so sure.

Six

If Glen would ever forgive her, she needed to get out of Rutherford Construction and stay away from Edwin. Tears streamed down her cheeks as she drove, her mind repeating the look in her father's eyes when she told him of her affair, a look that was like a knife in her gut that wouldn't stop twisting. She lost it all, her husband, the respect of her parents, and now, the job she loved, and the sad part was she should have seen it all coming. She was such an idiot! She wasn't sure how she never saw Edwin's betrayal coming, except for the fact she was too preoccupied committing her own betrayal. She knew Faith's behavior was odd but Cherish never connected it with Edwin. It was right under her nose the entire time, though. How could she have been so blind?

The sun started to dip in the west as she weaved through the

Sunday traffic on her way to the offices of Rutherford Construction, ready to give Glen what he needed. It was time to quit Rutherford Construction. Jed said he'd meet her there so she could clear out her desk, although he wasn't exactly happy about it. She knew she could have come in while the office was open earlier, but she wasn't in the mood to deal with Grady, who was in charge of the office this Sunday, and his leering comments. In her mood, she'd probably kill him, not that that would be a great loss. It was one of the few things Cherish agreed with her sister on lately.

That and Edwin Coldwell.

Just the thought of Edwin with her sister sent Cherish's temper into a boil again. She fell for Edwin's charm all too easily, fell for him more than she ever expected to, and what started out as a fun office fling became a humiliating heartbreak. *I'm such an idiot!*

The shocking part wasn't necessarily that Edwin had cheated on her, which Cherish realized sounded hypocritical since she cheated on her husband while Edwin had no commitments to anyone, including her. No, the shocking part was, he did it with her sister, Faith, Mrs. Goody Two Shoes, the rule follower. Even with Faith's newfound zest for life busting through the walls of her timidity, Cherish never would have thought her sister would actually stray from her marital bed. It seemed like too far of a stretch. Yet, Edwin tossed Cherish to the side so he could sleep with Faith, working his way through the Driscoll women. At least with Grady, everyone knew he was an outright snake. Edwin hid his deceptive side well.

Cherish thought—no, hoped—that when Faith was on the West Coast with Morgan for a week, Edwin would start paying attention to her again. Yet, all he did was mope around for the entire week, even after she practically threw herself at him, grabbing his cock with one hand while shoving his hands onto her breasts with the other in a last-ditch effort to regain his attention, letting him know she was still a willing participant. All he said was that he was busy and work was going crazy. Of course, that never stopped him from playing grab ass with her before, so she knew he just wanted nothing to do with her, not like he had before, not like he wanted with Faith. Cherish should have known then that her life was about to go over a cliff.

When Faith returned to the offices Friday, Cherish could tell by the look on Edwin's face exactly who he wanted, and it wasn't Cherish. She clutched at the steering wheel with white knuckles as she swiped at a lone tear that snailed its way down her cheek with her other hand. So angry with Edwin's betrayal, she had been blind to the devastation she wrecked on her own family. By trying to have it all, she lost everything. Her job at Rutherford Construction was the final piece of failure, the final price she had to pay in the hopes Glen would come home.

She sighed, feeling the invisible hand that clutched her heart, squeezing it. She didn't even know if quitting the job she loved would be enough, but at least, it would show Glen she was serious about making things right. It was a step toward the groveling her father told her she needed to do to save her family. The first of many steps, she knew.

The next would consist of altering her way of thinking. She wasn't sure she could, having been the cold-hearted bitch most of her life, but she needed to try. She needed to do whatever was necessary for Jordie's sake.

Glen was the perfect excuse she needed to get out of Rutherford Construction, even though part of her truly didn't want to leave. She loved her job. Well, she had loved it up until the last month. The truth was, Cherish couldn't take it anymore. She was through. There was no way she would stay and watch Edwin and her sister play kissy face all over the office. It was time for her to leave.

When she pulled into the back parking lot of Rutherford Construction, Jed was just getting out of his truck. *Good. I can make this quick.* She pulled in beside him, ignoring the unhappy look on his face. She didn't care. She would no longer work for Edwin Coldwell knowing what he did to her. Behind her back. With her own sister. Cherish threw her car into park and popped her door open. She would get in, get her stuff, and get out. Quick and easy.

As she stepped out into the darkening day, she heard another set of tires on the gravel coming around the building. A sinking feeling pulled at her stomach. *If Jed...* A red Ford F150 turned the corner, Edwin not even bothering to slow down.

Cherish shot Jed a dirty look. He only shrugged, a sympathetic look on his face. She should have known better than to trust him. The boys club protected themselves. She started walking faster toward the back door of the offices. Jed stood there, hands stuffed in his pockets, looking like he wished he was anywhere else but there right then.

"Cherish!" Edwin called from his truck. He slammed on the brakes, not even parking, the driver's door open before his truck even stopped. "Cherish, don't do this." The engine of his truck still idling, his door left open, as he crossed the parking lot to try to head her off. She paid no attention to him as she continued toward Jed. "Cherish, stop!"

"Fuck you, Edwin," she screamed, still not turning around. "Go away. You're not needed—or wanted—here." She reached Jed and stopped, pointing a finger at his face. "You're a son-of-a-bitch for calling him."

"He's the boss, Cherish," Jed said, his expression one of hope that she would understand. She didn't. "I had to call him to tell him his employee was quitting."

"You could've waited."

"Cherish, you don't have to go out like this," Edwin said, reaching them. "We can talk; we need to talk."

"We don't *need* to do anything," Cherish said, still not looking at him. "I'm quitting. Jed is going to let me in so I can get my stuff. You're going to leave me alone." She finally turned and stared at him. "If I were you, Edwin, I'd *really* leave me alone."

Edwin glanced at Jed, desperation in his eyes. "I got this," he said. "You can go. Give Cherish and I some time to...sort this out."

Cherish shook her head. "There's nothing to sort out. Jed's the one I called, so he stays. Besides, you may need a witness, anyway, if you keep talking." She turned, continuing toward the back door.

"C'mon, Cherish," Edwin pleaded. "There's no need for this. We can talk it out and fix things."

She spun on him, her brows furrowed in confusion. "What exactly are you wanting to fix? If you think I'm going to bend over the desk for you again after you fucked my sister, you're crazier than I thought."

Jed's eyes went wide at her statement as he glanced at his boss. He opened his mouth to say something but changed his mind. He just bounced his gaze between the two in front of him, curious, Cherish knew, but she ignored him. Edwin closed his eyes, taking a deep breath, realizing now that Cherish couldn't care less about what people knew any more. He made a fool out of her, and the only recompense she had was to make one out of him. Cherish knew how the rumor mill worked at a construction company. The entire office would know what happened before the day ended. She'd ruin Edwin's reputation as well as her precious sister's. Cherish did not believe in suffering alone.

Edwin took a deep breath. "I'm not talking about any of that.

I'm talking about you staying on and continuing to work here."

Cherish felt the anger building within her again. "I won't keep working here, watching you and Faith play kissy-face. I won't cover for her while you two sneak off to the warehouse for a booty-call."

Edwin glanced at Jed again, and Cherish knew she twisted the knife in Edwin's gut and, if she was lucky, into his career. He turned back to Cherish, his expression softening. "Cherish, I never meant for any of this to happen, for you to get hurt. What we had…" He gestured between them, and she could see the struggle on his face. "What we had was supposed to just be fun, remember? You wanted to break out of your monotonous life, you said. It was never meant to get emotional. I wasn't looking for a relationship and neither were you. It was just fun."

She took a step toward him, her hand on his chest. Edwin flinched, but didn't move away. "And that gave you the right to go after my sister? You don't think I at least deserved to know?"

Edwin gazed into her eyes, and Cherish knew she wouldn't like what he said next. His eyes pleaded with her to understand as they glistened with tears he fought to keep from falling. "Faith is different. What the two of us have… Cherish, I care about your sister. With her, it's more than just sex. Much more."

Cherish grinned. "And here I thought what we had was more than just sex. You let me decorate your office, used me to get your rocks off, and this whole time you panted after my sister?" She gripped his shirt, squeezing it with white knuckles, as she lifted her knee, driving it into his groin.

Edwin screamed—as did Jed—and then he doubled over, his hands cupping his family jewels. He scrunched his eyes up, tears now falling freely as he did his best to keep from toppling over.

Cherish snarled at him and then turned to Jed, the man's face scrunched up feeling the pain instinctively that Edwin suffered.

"Now, can I get my things, or should I call Neal?"

Jed glanced at Edwin, his boss still doubled over, and just shook his head. With a wave of his hand, Jed gestured for Cherish to follow him. What he would do with Edwin, she had no idea. She was sure Edwin's pride would take a greater hit than his balls just did. She didn't care. He deserved so much more than what she gave him, and she hoped he got it. She hoped he received everything he had coming to him.

She didn't want to be the only person who lost everything. She would *not* be the only one who lost everything. Edwin Coldwell would lose as well, and she would make sure of it.

~ ~ ~ ~ ~

The glass sliding door opened, and Robert Lansky stepped out, two beers in his hands. When he noticed the bottle resting on Glen's knee, he just shrugged. "More for me, unless you're ready for a refill."

"I'm good, thanks," Glen said, a slight smile pushing up the corners of his mouth.

Glen's father sat on the wicker sofa that formed a part of the L of porch furniture. He set one bottle on the glass table that sat between them and held the other in his hands as he crossed his legs. "Hope you don't mind me crashing your quietness. Those damn game shows drive me crazy. Your mother gets all pissed off when she gets the answer wrong. I want to put her on one of those shows and record it just so I can show her how idiotic she looks." He rolled his dark eyes.

Glen laughed. He went to sip his beer. Empty. He made a scrunched-up face and then swapped the bottles out. "On second thought…"

"Help yourself," his father said with a slight chuckle.

Glen really didn't need another beer, having had three already, but it at least gave him something to hold in his hands.

"So, what's the plan?" Robert took a deep breath as he rubbed his hand over his slight paunch. Life behind a desk had done little to keep the man trim, and the nightly bouts of ice cream didn't help.

"Plan for what?" Glen asked.

"For the future. What's your plan for the future? You've been here all weekend. My coffee bill has gone up drastically."

The third wave. First, his mother yesterday, then his sister this afternoon, and now his father today. "I'm not really sure." Glen felt himself slumping in his chair. "Mom said I should make a clean break."

"Is that what you want to do, though?"

"Yes. No. I don't know." Glen laid his head back and stared at the wooden ceiling, the ceiling fan a mesmerizing swirl above them. "My heart is breaking, but I don't know if it's because of what she did or because I just miss her."

"Well, I'll tell you one thing, you won't figure it out here." His father lifted his beer to his lips and took a small swallow.

Glen glanced at his father. "Am I really drinking that much coffee? I'll buy some tomorrow if I am."

His father waved off his statement. "It has nothing to do with coffee. And you're welcome to stay here as long as you want." He took another swallow of his beer, shaking his head when he finished. "That's not what I mean. What I'm saying is, if you're still debating it in your head, then you need to go home and fix it."

Glen stared at his father. "She cheated on me."

Robert nodded, his expression sympathetic but not pitying. "She did."

"I don't know if I can forgive that."

"Then get a divorce. Figure out custody and child support. Get a place or fix up the spare room. Move on."

"And here I thought Mom was the blunt one," Glen said with a soft chuckle.

"She is." Robert shrugged. "I just give fatherly advice. My advice for you is to go home. I've watched you. You've walked around like one of those dead people on TV…"

"Zombies?"

"Yeah, those. You keep checking your cell phone. You're up late at night, and you wake up early in the morning. You're not smiling. You're miserable, and I don't blame you. The woman you love betrayed you. Broke your heart. That hurts like hell. Can you forgive her, though? Can you move past it? The two of you have waded through deep waters before. Is this ocean too deep? If not, you won't fix it here. You need to be home with your family, in bed with your wife. That's how you fix it. Scream. Yell. Cry. Then talk it out. Together."

His father's words bounced around in his head. Cherish and Glen barely spoke since he walked out. She tried, but he shut her down every time, even when she showed up on his parents' back porch. He knew she was just as miserable as he was. She apologized, tears streaming down her face as she begged him to come home. Pain gripped his heart like a crushing fist as he remembered the scene in his kitchen Friday night when she finally admitted her affair. She may show remorse now, but only hate filled her then. Her words would always echo in his mind.

His cell phone rang beside him. Selby. *And now to hear from the other side.* He asked his father to excuse him as he stood and answered his phone. "Hey, Selby. What's up?"

"Cherish stopped by earlier and told us what's happening. I wanted to check on you and see how you were holding up, if there was anything we could do. I'm always here if you need to talk."

Cherish did nothing subtly. "Thanks. I may take you up on

that at some point. Right now, I'm just going moment-by-moment. Still kind of in shock."

"I can understand that. I'm sorry it happened. Have you decided whether or not you'll stick it out?"

The main question on everyone's mind, even Glen's. "I don't know what I'll do yet, to be honest."

"Well, if you need us to watch Jordie for a few days, just let us know," Selby offered. "My schedule's pretty flexible, and we have no problem watching him to give you two some time alone to work through things. Might be easier without him there to overhear everything."

Glen stared out at the late afternoon, the anxiety in his gut a twisted knot. Jordie would be the one who suffered in all this if Glen wasn't careful, and he didn't want that. "Thanks. I might take you up on that if needed."

"Anytime. Just let us know."

"I will. Thanks." They said their goodbyes, and Glen just stood there, staring out at the darkening day, a perfect symbol to the way he felt. It was the same question from everyone. What would he do? He took a deep breath. He wished he knew.

Seven

"Here's the hammer," Brent Dresden said as he held the tool by the head, offering the handle to Glen, who simply reached up and grabbed it. Brent squatted down on the deck as he looked down on Glen who was in the middle of adding more supports to the base of the dock they were installing for a Mrs. Patterson, soon to be Miss Patterson. Brent glanced back at the house, a smirk creasing his lips. "I bet she has an extra room. She may even cut you a deal on the rent. Obviously, she has some major alimony coming in from the divorce." He turned, his eyebrows raised, eyes wide. "Hey, maybe she'll take the rent out in trade. Women have needs, you know?"

Glen shook his head. "You're a pig."

Brent shrugged his thick shoulders as he ran a hand through his walnut hair, the bangs once again falling back into his hazelgreen eyes. "So I've been told. I'm just trying to help you out. You'll never get lucky living at your parents' house."

Glen handed the hammer back up to Brent as he rolled his eyes. The two men had been partners since Jordie's birth. When Cherish and Glen found out she was pregnant, he offered to marry her, quit college, and went to work for Melbourne Docks & Piers. He had been teamed up with the single man ever since, listening to Brent's constant womanizing and dirty exploits.

Glen climbed out of the Indian River and onto the dock they just finished shoring up as he said, "I'm not looking to get lucky. I want my family back." Of course, with everything Tanya said yesterday, Glen wondered if he should start rethinking his philosophy.

Brent tossed Glen a towel. "Then why are you at your parents' place?"

Glen dried himself off. *Not him, too.* "Because I'm not ready to go home, yet." He tossed the towel over his shoulder as he stood back up with a heavy sigh. "But I'm not ready to walk away, either." He wished he knew what he wanted, or even what direction he needed to go to make either direction work. The problem was, he hurt too damn much to make a smart decision. He didn't want to just react. He needed to think of Jordie, as well.

Glen took a deep breath of the river air. He had been doing nothing except think since he left Cherish on Friday night. He grew tired of thinking, because he didn't have any answers, just more questions. His thoughts just kept going in circles. "I need a beer."

"See. You're thinking like a single man already." Brent slapped Glen on the back. "C'mon. I'll buy."

They quickly cleaned everything up and put away their tools, and Glen slid into the passenger seat of Brent's truck, losing himself in the surroundings that passed by the open window. He knew he made a lousy conversationalist right then, but he couldn't help it. Too many things weighed on his mind with no real signs of them lifting. Brent had been right. Glen couldn't stay at his parents' forever. First, it would drive him crazy. Besides that, he knew the longer he stayed away from Cherish, the harder it would be to return. Yet, could he take her back? Could he trust her again?

Brent pulled the truck into the Royal Chef along Harbor City Boulevard. It was an ancient diner that remained open twenty-four hours to service the after-hours inebriated crowd. Patrons could purchase breakfast at all hours, and the burgers were some of the greasiest around, just what drunks needed in their intoxicated bellies. The waitresses wore blue uniforms that stopped at mid-thigh and white, frilly aprons. The counters and booths needed some major repairs, but it was that ancient feeling that gave the place its appeal. For Brent, it was a waitress named Bonnie.

Glen just looked at his partner as Brent threw the truck into park and cut off the ignition. "Really? I said beer. This place doesn't serve beer."

"You don't need a beer. However, I do need a date." Brent opened his truck door, grinning.

"Fine, but you're still buying."

"Well, well, well, look what the cat dragged in," a blond behind the counter said as they passed through the open door. Her uniform blouse was unbuttoned enough that the creamy tops of her breasts poked through, making it hard for people to focus on her eyes—at least the men, that is.

Brent leaned over the counter, his hands clasped in front of him as he gave the waitress his best leer. "Hey Bonnie. What's cooking?"

She leaned toward him, holding herself up by her palms. "Not me. That menu's not open during the Tuesday lunch crowd. Come back at six, and just maybe, I'll have a treat for you." She winked, and Glen imagined the giant, pink bubble that should have popped on her lips right about then as she smiled.

Glen just shook his head as he pounded Brent's back before walking off in search of a booth.

"I see your friend isn't here for the burgers." He turned as Rachel Nolan stepped up to his table, placing napkins down on the chipped table, one on each side.

Glen laughed. "Well, after having your burgers..." Brent and he always ate at Royal Chef at least three times a week, mainly so Brent could flirt with Bonnie, but Glen had done his own fair share of teasing with Rachel, who always seemed to make sure she served their table right along with Bonnie.

Rachel arched an eyebrow. "Are you saying you've had the dish he's ordering?"

"Please. Glen isn't ordering off any menu," Brent said as he slid into the opposite side of the booth. "He'll be eating alone for a while, if you catch my drift. I keep telling him to venture out and live a little."

Rachel pulled a pencil from behind her ear, pulling a few strands of her dark hair with it. "Too bad. I was looking forward to a treat at six myself." She winked at Glen, her smile luring.

Brent grinned at her. "You could always join Bonnie and me. I've always got a sweet tooth that needs a fix."

Rachel rolled her eyes. "I'd hate for you to develop a cavity. Now, what can I get you boys?"

They ordered, and Rachael walked off with Brent making a show of gawking at her round ass as she sashayed away. "Why in the world are you turning that down?"

"You know damn well why." Glen shook his head at his friend, but inwardly, he wondered the same thing. If Cherish wanted to open up their marriage, would he have the balls to take Rachel up on her advances?

"Yeah, yeah. You're married. Correct me if I'm wrong, but that little fact didn't keep Cherish from playing house with someone else."

"So tit for tat? She screwed around, and that gives me the right to do the same thing?" Glen refused to cheat. If Cherish wanted an open marriage, everything would have to be out in the open. But again, did he trust her to tell him everything after she had already kept so many secrets?

"Damn straight. What's sauce for the goose is sauce for the gander as my dear sweet granny would say."

"So, if your grandfather cheated on your dear sweet granny, she would've had an affair herself?"

"Oh, hell no," Brent said, laughing. "She would've shot Granddad's pecker off with his own shotgun."

"That's what I thought."

Glen didn't want to get back at Cherish. Having sex with anyone except his wife didn't interest him; at least, that's what he told himself during their marriage so far, ending all dalliances the minute she said yes to his proposal. He pledged her his heart, body, and soul, and he meant it. She may have strayed, but he had no desire to follow her path. If he climbed into bed with anyone else right now without the two of them agreeing to anything, he knew their marriage would be over. He wasn't sure he was ready to make that call, yet. However, he didn't know if he wanted to continue, either. She cheated on him, after all. Something made her stray. And while Tanya may think she knew the reason, he wished he knew what that something was for real.

Rachael returned with their sweet tea. Glen dropped a straw into his, using it as a stirrer. *Why did you do it, Cherish? What did Edwin have that I didn't give you?* God, Glen wished he knew.

Cherish parked her car in front of Selby's Downtown Books and stared at the front door. Jordie was at preschool, and she wanted to take this time to start her apologies. It was time to switch her way of thinking, to cease being the self-absorbed person everyone came to expect. She was the one who screwed up, and Selby had been right yesterday in calling her out on it. Of course, it turned her stomach to admit it, but if she was ever going to fix her family, she needed to start making some positive changes in her life. Selby was the safest place to start.

With a deep breath, Cherish left the safety of her car and stepped into the responsible thing to do. She wasn't really a fan, too used to being the selfish one. It was easy being selfish.

Pushing the front door open, the bell over the door announcing her arrival, she looked around for her brother-in-law. He appeared down one of the rows of shelves, a coffee mug emblazoned with #1 Husband on it in his hand, sipping it as he walked. When he noticed her, it appeared as if he almost choked on his coffee. She couldn't blame him. She knew she was the last person he ever expected to see in his store. He glanced at her but said nothing as he walked back around the glass counter to his chair.

Cherish fidgeted with her hands as she warred within herself about whatever brought her to his store. Suddenly, being there didn't seem like a good idea.

Selby took another sip of his coffee and just waited, not even offering her a greeting. She knew she really didn't deserve one, not after the way she behaved yesterday.

Cherish took a deep breath that lifted her tired shoulders, determined to see this through. "I'm sorry for yesterday. I was hurt and angry and took it out on Faith and you. I was wrong for doing that." Her nerves churned in the pit of her stomach, and she fought not to cry or throw up; she wasn't sure which.

Selby just stared at her for a moment and then nodded. "Faith's the one you should apologize to."

"I know. And I will." She stood still for a minute, hoping he would say something else. He didn't. "Anyway," she went on after the silence dragged, "I just wanted to come by and apologize."

"Thank you." Short. Curt. He was definitely not going to make this easy on her.

She gave him a weak smile and then left, having done what she set out to do. As she pushed open the door, stepping outside, another hand grabbed the edge of the door. Cherish recognized the redhead who had been with Selby and Faith yesterday morning, a shocked expression on her face at seeing Cherish. She nodded at the redhead and kept walking.

"What the hell was she doing here? Surely, not buying books," Cherish heard the other woman say as the door drifted closed. Obviously, Faith had told the other woman all about Cherish.

Sliding back into her car, Cherish sat there, staring into space, not a clue as to where to go next or what to do. She was always at work on Mondays, well most Mondays. She always had something to do either way. Never before had she felt so lost. All she really wanted to do was curl up into a ball and cry, and the part that really pissed her off was that she wasn't sure whether it was over Glen or Edwin.

She started her car, slipped it into reverse, and backed out of her parking spot. Heading east on New Haven Avenue, she turned right into the small park right before the Melbourne Causeway. Picnic tables dappled the area interspersed between towering pine trees as fisherman tried their luck in the Indian River. She drove to the back of the small park, the most southern point, and stared at the river as it floated by the small jetty. If ever there was a calming place for her in this city, it was this park. Glen used to bring her here when she was pregnant with Jordie, right after she screwed up her life the first time. Glen had always been her savior. It was even at this park, five and a half years ago, he asked her to marry him, making her bad decisions his responsibility.

When she first met Glen in high school, she dated one loser after another, but her last one before him, Nick Pepper, was the slimiest of them all. For a year, the two of them lived together, Cherish paying most of the bills to make sure they ate and the lights remained on and a roof stayed over their head. Her father helped out occasionally, but only because he worried Cherish would starve or be out on the street if he didn't. She played house, it was true, but she did all she could to succeed at it while Nick smoked his dope, drank his beer, and waved goodbye as Cherish went to work. Cherish thought she was so in love. Glen watched from a distance, attending the same parties, frequenting the same bars and hangouts, praying, he told her later, that she wizened up at some point. She never had the chance. Nick walked out on her one night at a bar, another blond on his arm.

But it was too late.

And that was when Glen stepped in, holding her, letting her cry her eyes out over the pig who left her high and dry.

And pregnant.

"Oh god, Glen, how stupid could I have been?" Her tears streamed down her cheeks and into his shirt as he cradled her head against his chest. "I should have been smarter. I knew he never would have taken care of a family; I knew it! So why wasn't I more careful?"

Glen rocked her, his hand stroking the back of her head. "It'll be all right. We can get through this. I promise." Glen loved her, had loved her for years he told her. Once Nick was out of the picture, Glen stepped in before Cherish distracted herself with someone else. The two partied and eventually wound up in bed, bodies intertwined. The night she told him she was pregnant, he told her later, was the night he knew he needed her in his life no matter what, his course of action determined. He told her it was right then he decided he would quit school, move back home, and get a job in order to take care of Cherish and her baby.

"My dad is going to kill me," she whined into his shoulder.

"Does anyone know yet?" Glen asked.

She shook her head against his chest, her tears staining his shirt. "Just you. I was too afraid to tell anyone else."

"Not even Nick?"

She shook her head again. There was no way she would go to Nick and have him just laugh at her. That son-of-a-bitch would never be involved in her life again. Or the baby's. She gave him enough, and all he ever gave her was heartbreak.

Glen gripped her shoulders, pulling her away from him so he could look into her bloodshot eyes. "Then let's get married. Tomorrow. We'll go to the courthouse and do it. No one needs to know this happened. A couple of weeks from now, we'll say you're pregnant as if we just found out."

She stared at him, her mouth moving slightly although no words came out. She blinked as if trying to focus on his words. "Glen, I..."

"Don't say it." *He leaned forward, kissing her forehead.* "Cherish, I've loved you since I can't remember when. Truth is, I don't remember a time I wasn't in love with you. I don't care that this baby isn't mine. I'll love him or her as if they were my own flesh and blood, and they'll never know they aren't. Marry me. Let me take care of you and the baby. Let me show you how much I love you."

She just stared at him. His heart beat in his chest so hard she could actually see his chest bounce with it. He held her, afraid of letting go for fear she'd run away.

"Glen, I don't know what to say. I mean, these past two weeks together have been awesome, but why would you want to take care of someone else's child?"

"Because that child is a part of you, and I adore you."

"But everything I've done..."

"Is what you've done, and not who you are. I know you, Cherish. I know we can make this work. Let me prove it."

She swiped at the tears along her cheeks, leaving dirty smears. She nodded.

"You'll marry me?"

"Yes," she said, bursting out into tears again as she covered her mouth with her hand.

They told no one the baby wasn't his. It had been his idea, to protect her and the child. He would rather people think they were both careless, that her family think he was the one who had ruined their daughter as opposed to ever thinking poorly of Cherish. She went along with it, not knowing what else to do and afraid of what her father would say to her. Glen offered her an escape, and she was too scared to refuse.

Cherish stared out at the river as a pelican floated by, the afternoon sun beating down on his back. Glen came in and saved her from shame and disgrace when she didn't deserve it. She needed him to come in and do it again; she needed Glen to save her.

Eight

Her father pounded away on the roof as the rain continued to pour down upon the city of Melbourne. The thunderstorm pummeled them for over an hour, and a leak developed in the kitchen of the Lansky home. Cherish hadn't even noticed it until she walked in to put a dirty plate in the sink, hit the puddle of water unaware, and just about broke her tailbone hitting the floor as her feet slid out from under her. Jordie came in after hearing her scream and, not knowing what else to do, called his grandparents. Arni Driscoll was now on the roof, covering the area that leaked, and her mother, Valerie, sat in Cherish's kitchen stirring her fourth spoonful of sugar into her coffee and grumbled about how Glen should be the one on the roof and not her husband.

Her body screaming at her from where she hit the hard tile

floor, Cherish stood by her kitchen counter scooping fresh coffee grounds into the filter while her mother grumbled behind her. Cherish really needed something stronger. A lot stronger. She'd even put it in her coffee to hide what she drank from her mother if she could figure out how to pour it in without her mother seeing. Valerie Driscoll didn't drink, and Cherish's father wouldn't drink around his wife, not wanting to hear the lectures. Cherish would have to wait until her mother left before reaching for the bottle of Captain Morgan under the counter and fixing a real drink. For now, coffee would have to do. At least, it would warm her father after his drenching repair job.

"Did you even try calling your absent husband?" Valerie leaned on the table, staring at Cherish's back. "He should be the one here taking care of his family. Your stubborn father is too old to be up on a roof, even in sunny weather."

"Is Daddy coming home?" Jordie stood in the kitchen doorway, staring at Cherish with hopeful eyes.

Cherish hit the power button on the coffeemaker and then went to where Jordie stood. She avoided looking at her mother, afraid she wouldn't be able to control her facial expression. "No, sweetheart. Daddy isn't coming home tonight. He's still working. Now, why don't you go get ready for bed."

The little boy looked heartbroken—for the hundredth time since Glen disappeared. Cherish's heart ached as she watched him walk away, tiny shoulders slumped. She took a deep breath, forcing herself to turn around. "I would appreciate you not making negative comments about Glen while Jordie is around." She reached into the cupboard and pulled out another mug for her father. "This is still Glen's house, and I won't have him disrespected in his own home, especially in front of his son."

"His house? Then, where is he? If it's his house, then he should be the one here fixing it."

Cherish poured her father a cup of coffee and placed it on the table for when he came back inside, moving slowly as she crossed the room, one hand pressed to her lower back. She didn't answer her mother. Glen wasn't there taking care of his home, because Cherish wasn't a good wife, and her mother knew it. Cherish's affair with Edwin cost her—and Jordie—everything. She didn't need to repeat it. Her mother knew why Glen wasn't there. She just couldn't put the blame where it belonged—on Cherish.

"Your sister apparently has your old job now," Valerie said. "Apparently, she did such a great job in Tampa, they just slid her into your position before your chair was even cold." Valerie didn't sound impressed, but then again, she never did, especially with her middle child. "And, from what she says, that boss of yours is being transferred. Savannah, I think."

A couple of weeks ago, Faith traveled to Tampa with Morgan Brewer to assist in the reorganizing of the Rutherford office there. From everything Cherish heard, and she had heard quite a bit, her sister did a fantastic job. Morgan even wanted her to travel more, helping them set up offices or fixing trouble spots in other areas. Faith said no the last Cherish heard, but who knew what Faith would decide now that Rutherford transferred Edwin to Savannah. Cherish hated that they gave Faith her position. Cherish enjoyed what she did and only became frustrated with her job when that two-timing bastard turned his back on her. Now, he wasn't even there. She quit for nothing!

Cherish refilled her coffee and then sat at the table, her hands wrapped around the steaming mug, warming them. Life wasn't always fair, but she couldn't begrudge Faith her successes. It was part of the whole changing her mindset course she needed to travel. "Faith was good at her job. She loves it, actually."

Valerie stared at Cherish with narrowed eyes. "With everything that's been going on at that place, I'm just sure Faith loves her job."

Cherish sighed, tired of listening to her mother's negativity. Normally, she wouldn't care how her mother talked shit about Faith, but Cherish knew she needed to change her way of thinking if she would ever fix her family. "She's not cheating on Selby." She couldn't believe she defended her sister. It had been years since the two of them got along, and the fact that Edwin left her for Faith was the card that brought Cherish's house down. She hated her sister, but, as much as she despised admitting it, she envied Faith as well. Her sister stood up for herself and went after life on her own terms. Selby and she had explored together sexually, opening their marriage up to different physical adventures. All Cherish did was fuck around on her husband. Yet, their mother would defend Cherish while condemning Faith. It never made sense to Cherish, but she had capitalized on it all she could. Now, however, seeing Jordie's slumped shoulders, her mother's words only made her stomach turn. Cherish didn't deserve defending.

"I'll take a cup of that." Arni stood in the kitchen doorway, dripping on the floor as he pointed to the steaming cup in Cherish's hands. "And a towel."

Cherish pointed to the extra cup of coffee on the table as she hopped up to grab a towel. "Thank you for fixing the roof," she said, tossing him the towel. "I really appreciate it."

"Oh, it's not fixed." Arni dried himself off. "It's just covered. You'll need to get someone out here to look at it, but it should be okay for now." He picked up the coffee cup and took a tentative sip. "Now, I'll change real quick, and we can enjoy a cup of coffee." After setting the cup back on the table, he disappeared down the hall. Cherish heard Jordie call out to his grandfather and had to smile at the fact the little boy was still awake. Jordie loved his Arni.

Cherish remained quiet until her father returned. She didn't want to stir up her mother's negativity again. She understood why Faith tried to avoid their mother now. Luckily, Arni didn't take long to dry off and change clothes. He slid into one of the empty chairs and took a sip of his coffee. As he sat back in his chair, he reiterated that she would need to get someone out there to fix it.

"I'll call someone first thing in the morning," she assured him. "Thanks again for coming out and taking care of it."

He licked his lips after taking a swallow of his coffee. Setting his mug back on the table, he nodded. "No problem. It's not like I get up early in the morning anymore." He smiled as he said it. Valerie just rolled her eyes. Obviously, the fact her husband quit teaching and followed his dream of being a writer didn't thrill Valerie. By the looks of it, Cherish's father enjoyed his new role quite a bit.

"Been sleeping in much?" Cherish laughed as she watched her father. He had always been the happy one, the counterbalance to their mother's sullen demeanor. Now, however, he seemed downright jovial. Obviously, he loved the new path he followed with his life. Cherish envied him. Of course, at first, she hadn't been in agreement with his decision. She had even blamed Faith and her "grab life while you can" attitude about living for their father quitting his steady job with benefits for something he had no idea would succeed. Cherish thought he bailed out on her mother and was being reckless with his life. Yet, watching him since then had been the only bright spot to the chaos her life became.

"I'm enjoying some time with no real structure—sleeping in, staying up late, walks on the beach. It's been refreshing to change things up from my normal routine."

"Routines are important," Valerie Driscoll snapped. "They help us stay on track."

He nodded. "They do. Yet, they can also make us stagnant." He turned so he faced Cherish. "Sometimes, we need to have our routines shaken up to remind us what's important."

Cherish swallowed the lump in her throat. She knew he spoke to her without being blunt, a fact she appreciated right then. That was her father. Subtle. Her mother always did things with an iron fist. She made her kids obey by bullying and manipulation. They obeyed their father because he earned their respect. They obeyed their mother out of fear. They loved their father.

That wasn't fair. They loved their mother, as well. They just adored their father more.

Cherish nodded. Message received.

~ ~ ~ ~ ~

Dinner over, Glen helped his younger sister, Tanya, clear the table. While he had only been staying at his parents' place for the past week, Tanya had been there since birth with no sign of moving out anytime soon. Together, they scraped and stacked the dishes while Brenda Lansky already scrubbed away at them. Their father shifted from the kitchen table to his recliner, flipping through the channels on the television. It was a normal Monday night in the Lansky home. It just wasn't Glen's home.

Once he finished his share of the after-dinner chores, Glen stepped out onto the back porch, the rain peppering the wooden roof. The wind rustled the banana palms along the fence line, making the evening storm seem worse than it was. He stood along the screen wall, arms crossed over his chest, staring out at the pouring rain.

Lightning cracked the night air. Glen counted. One. Two. Three. Thunder then rumbled through the turbulent night. Three miles away. He smiled as he thought about how he would have been counting the seconds between the lightning and thunder with Jordie. Would be, that is, if he was at *his* home and not intruding upon his parents. He sighed heavily, his shoulders rising and falling with his frustration. He missed his son. While it was true he gave up a lot to become a father, there was never a day that passed where he didn't think it was all worth it, even now after Cherish cheated on him. He would do it all again if given the opportunity. *Then why am I not home?* He sighed, his heart still torn in two different directions.

Thunder rattled the night sky, but Glen didn't hear it, his mind already lost in the past.

Ten hours. Ten hours and seventeen minutes to be exact. The fact Cherish made it amazed him. There were a few times when exhaustion seemed to sap every ounce of energy she had in reserves out of her, the pain too much to bear, her screams ricocheting off the walls of the delivery room. He held her hand, or rather, she held his, squeezing the hell out of it. He thought he would have to get it put in a cast if she kept it up. Still, even with the pain screaming through his fingers, he smiled, telling her she could do it, helping her to breathe like they learned in Lamaze class. Dr. Patton sat between his wife's legs, coaxing her to push or telling her not to push, reminding her to breathe. Valerie Driscoll stood on the other side of her daughter, reminding her how much pain she had been in when Cherish was born, how she was in labor for twelve hours, twenty-two minutes and fifteen seconds. If she could do that, so could Cherish. Brenda Lansky just stood behind her son, staying quiet.

Then, with an ear-splitting scream ripping from Cherish, Jordie was born. He wailed right away, his dark hair slick against his scalp, his body a bluish mess that needed cleaning. Glen still held his wife's hand, but his focus was on Jordie, his son, with his closed eyes and wide-open mouth, his tiny nose and tiny fingers and tiny toes, his legs bent up against his stomach as he continued to wail. Glen's heart pounded in his ears, his chest puffed out with the pride of seeing his child brought into the world, the life he sacrificed all to take care of, to raise. A grin spread across his face as he watched the nurse carry the baby over to a table to weigh him and clean him up. Brenda Lansky gripped her son's shoulders, squeezing and shaking him softly, telling him what a great job they did. This wasn't a sacrifice. This was a privilege.

Once the nurse finished cleaning and swaddling Jordie, she carried him over and laid him gently on Cherish's chest, who, even though exhausted, beamed with joy as she took her newborn and cradled him against her chest. She then glanced up at Glen, the same look of pride mirrored in her eyes he knew resided in his. "Thank you," she said, her voice a harsh, raspy whisper.

Glen ran his hand over the top of her head, smoothing her rumpled, sweaty hair, his smile busting across his face. "No, thank you. He's gorgeous. I'm one lucky guy."

Cherish pressed her head back into his hand, her eyes closed with satisfaction. "That he is," she said, and at that moment, Cherish never looked so beautiful to him.

After a while, the nurse took Jordie to the hospital nursery and ushered everyone except the two of them from the room. Dr. Patton stood at the doorway, smiling at them. "Enjoy the quietness of being just the two of you for a bit. You may not get it again for a while."

"Thank you, Doctor," Glen said, "for everything."

"All I did was catch him. Cherish there did the hard part." *She then winked at them as she closed the door behind her, leaving them alone.*

"Thank you," Cherish said, "for being here, for wanting to be a father. I don't think I could have done this without you."

"I'm sure you could have, but I'm so glad you didn't. We have so much to be grateful for, so much to be happy about." He could

feel the pride and excitement course through him, making his heart pound in his ears as well as his chest. "It's going to be fun."

"It already is," Cherish said, her eyes half-closed as exhaustion started to claim her. "It already is."

He watched as sleep finally overtook her, her head slumping slightly to the side. He just sat there and stared at her, soaking in his wife, the woman he had loved since she was a teenager. He would do anything for her, he knew. All she ever had to do was ask him. He would deny her nothing.

Another rumble in the distance shook Glen from his thoughts, scaring him just a little back into the present. He would still do anything in the world for her, even as heartbroken as he was at the moment. All she ever had to do was ask, so why hadn't she asked? Why didn't she tell him something was wrong, that something was missing from her life? He would have done everything to fix it. He sighed as he leaned on the frame of the back porch with his hand, his other hand combing through his dark hair. *Why didn't she just ask me?*

He thought back to his conversation with his sister yesterday. What if Cherish had asked him if she could sleep with Edwin? Would he have been able to say yes? Could they have made that particular journey together? He sighed, not really knowing. He would have appreciated the chance to find out, however, even not knowing what he would have said then. Now, he would never know which direction they would have taken if she had just told him what she needed. He felt as if by opening their marriage up, he would be playing catchup, reacting instead of figuring it out together. That wasn't fair of her to do to him, and now he wasn't sure if he could move forward or not with such a drastic lifestyle change.

The lightning streaked the sky again followed shortly by a

rippling peal of thunder. Glen looked out at the churning sky. *Yeah, my thoughts exactly.*

Nine

"I'm hungry." Jordie Lansky draped himself over the arm of the couch, upside down, his pouty face staring at his mother. "Can we have pancakes?"

Cherish looked over at her four-year-old. She wore a pair of Glen's old pajama pants and a baggy T-shirt with an old Mountain Dew logo faded across the front. She had skipped the bra, hairbrush, and toothpaste. It didn't matter. Who did she have to get dressed up for? Glen made it known several days ago he wasn't ready to come home yet; he wasn't sure he *could* come home yet. She didn't have a job to get dressed for either, so what was the point in even trying. She even kept Jordie out of preschool, so she didn't have to see anyone. She had no interaction with anyone since Tuesday morning when the roofer arrived to patch the leak in her roof. She cried her eyes out every night while sleeping on the couch and watched as Jordie played around the house. She knew she should get him back in school, but it was Friday, so what harm could one more day off do? Besides, she didn't have the energy to face others.

She placed her hand on Jordie's tummy and gave a soft nod. "I suppose one of us still gets hungry." She tried to give him a smile but had to take a deep breath to keep herself from crying. Again. Her son didn't need what he was being forced to endure. He didn't deserve what was happening. He didn't deserve her for a mother.

She forced herself to take another deep breath. *But he's stuck with me, so I need to get off my ass and take care of him.* "Sure thing. Pancakes sound great."

She shoved herself off the couch and weaved through the mess that became her home to the kitchen, Jordie trailing behind her. After searching the cabinets as well as the refrigerator, she had to fight harder to keep from crying yet again. She had allowed the cupboard to become bare. Now, she would have to get dressed and face the outside world. She didn't *want* to get dressed. She didn't want to face people. She went four days in the same outfit, wearing Glen's old clothes just to feel like she was a part of him still. *That reminds me. I need deodorant.*

Jordie stared at the empty refrigerator with her. "We need to go grocery shopping, Mommy," the little boy said. "Did Daddy not get money for working?"

She placed her hand on his head and tousled his dark hair. *He needs a haircut.* "C'mon, Slugger. Let's get some breakfast at Betsy's." It was a small Mom and Pop diner that Jordie loved. They made the best chocolate milk, he would always say. They also put bananas on the pancakes. He deserved bananas on his pancakes. He deserved a healthy family.

But you screwed that up, didn't you? She told him his father and her were just struggling with some things right now. None of it had to do with him. Daddy loved him. Mommy loved him. Now, she offered him another day off from school and breakfast out because she hadn't even thought to put food in the house. *Some mother I am.*

Jordie screamed, "Yay!" as he did a fist pump.

She turned him toward his room. "Go get dressed."

"You get dressed, too!" he yelled as he ran down the hallway.

Cherish watched him go, her throat tight at the changes in his life, changes she had caused.

Putting the self-pity and guilt aside for a bit, she made her way to her bedroom to peel herself out of her stale clothes. Looking at herself in the mirror—the first time in four days—she realized how far she allowed her depression to sink her. Her strawberry-blond hair was a knotted mess that rivaled any stored set of Christmas lights. Dark circles made her eyes look puffy and, while she probably hadn't gained any weight in just a week, she felt like she had gained fifty pounds. It had to be because she just sat around on her ass, because she sure as hell couldn't stomach eating anything. Her eyes were bloodshot, tired. Her whole body—her mind—was tired. She needed to get out of her funk, but how? *Jordie. First focus on Jordie.*

She spun the faucet of the shower to scalding. Perhaps the hot water would shock her system. Perhaps, just taking the shower would, since she hadn't taken one in a few days. She shook her head as she stepped into the pounding stream of water. She had definitely let herself go. Her life was falling apart and none of it was her fault. Okay, it was *all* her fault, but why wasn't her sister, Faith, suffering just as much as she was? They both fucked the same boss. Yet, Cherish had lost her job and her husband while Faith and Selby were sugary sweet. They even promoted Faith to Cherish's position at Rutherford Construction. How was that anywhere close to being fair? Forget what Cherish told their mother at the beginning of the week. Cherish wanted someone besides herself to suffer as well, but no one was. They even transferred Edwin to a new city, instead of firing him. They protected the man who created the whirlwind around them, but not Cherish. Of course, she hadn't actually given anyone a chance to protect her once she drove her knee into Edwin's crotch on her way out of Rutherford's workforce. Would it have been different if she had remained? She shook her head. She didn't quit because of Edwin, though. She quit because Glen needed her to quit, and so far, it didn't seem like it did any good whatsoever. He still hadn't returned home.

Valerie Driscoll, however, wasn't ready to drop the matter. One of the last calls Cherish took from her mother included the news that her mother called Faith and tried to get her to do something about Cherish's job, threatening to sue the company for ruining her daughter's life. Faith was the one to pass on all the changes to the company and told her mother to grow up and stop trying to protect her precious baby daughter. Cherish laughed slightly when her mother told her all that over the phone. Faith had developed a backbone. It was about damn time, even if it was the wrong time. Cherish needed Faith to be the weak, timid girl she had always been.

Cherish rubbed the hot water into her body, hoping it would scald away her bad decisions. If she had known Neal Rutherford would transfer Edwin, she probably would have convinced Glen to allow her to stay put. Yet, she still didn't want to face her sister day-after-day knowing they both fell for the same man, and that man chose Faith over her. Cherish allowed her head to hang under the shower. Her head pounded as a knot formed in her stomach at the thought of Edwin. She could still see his smartass smirk and seductive eyes as he stood in the doorway of the Girls'

Den, the office she shared with her sister, a cigarette tucked behind his right ear. He captured her heart and took her body. He ruined her family.

No, I ruined my family. As much as she wanted to blame Edwin, nothing forced her to spread her legs for him. No, she did that willingly. To Edwin, it had merely been a fun game, a piece of ass at work. Cherish, however, had fallen for the man. She hadn't meant to, of course. To be honest, she hadn't realized she had until he started pulling away from her and began fucking her sister. Cherish had not been ready for the void left in her heart when he ceased spending time with her. She should have just walked away, but she didn't. Couldn't. She was determined she would not lose Edwin to her sister.

But she did.

She lost it all. Even Glen.

She sighed as the shower pounded her flesh. This was not the life she expected, not the life she planned and dreamed. She was only thirty years old for crying out loud! She shouldn't be suffering this madness and chaos in her daily existence. She should still be having fun, living life to its fullest. Yet, because of her poor choices, her life took a serious turn she never meant for it to take. She stared at the tile wall in front of her without seeing it. Instead, she fixated her gaze on a life she planned versus the one thrust upon her. This was not the way it was supposed to happen. Her life was to be one giant party, filled with nightclubs and adventures. She wanted to travel, wanted to spend nights sleeping on the beach in the arms of someone she just met. Where was the adventure now? In doing dishes and laundry, scrubbing pots and pans while wiping runny noses? That wasn't life; it was a prison sentence.

She took a deep breath. Edwin had been her one spot of adventure, showing her life was still there for those with the guts to grab it. And she proved she had the guts.

"Doesn't it get old? Playing house all the time?" Edwin stood at the tailgate of his truck, his foot up on the bumper, his Salem cigarette dangling between his fingers. "Hell, I tried the relationships without kids and found it stifling. Life is too short to be tied down in one spot. There's too much adventure to experience out there."

Cherish stared at him, her smirk pushing up one side of her face. "You mean no one could tolerate your childishness for too long without going insane."

He chuckled as he took a long pull from his cigarette. Finally, he shrugged. "Perhaps. What can I say? Life is about having fun. From what you say, that was your motto for a long time as well."

She nodded, her own Marlboro Red dangling between her fingers. Glen had been after her to quit smoking, saying how bad it was for Jordie. Yet, she gave up enough of her vices as it was. She wasn't ready or willing to surrender more of what she enjoyed. "That was pre-family. Life doesn't tend to allow for that type of fun anymore."

He shifted closer to her, his body angling, so she had a perfect view of the outline of his cock in his jeans. She couldn't help but stare and notice how, even flaccid, it was prominent through his pants. "And what if life did allow for that type of fun? What if you could have that distraction without it derailing your life? Wouldn't that be worth it?"

It was a regular question of his lately. He tempted her to surrender to his charm for a few weeks, promising fun beyond her boring routine of what became her life. And the sad part was, she wanted it. Wanted it more than she wanted anything else right then. Five years ago, she would have taken it, throwing concern of workplace gossip to the winds and allowed him to bend her over his desk and have his way with her. She wouldn't have cared, and it pissed her off now that she did care. She wasn't supposed to be concerned about hurting people or getting caught. She never cared what people thought until she found herself married with a child, and then that was all she thought about. She hated it.

She ran her gaze up the length of his body, her tongue gliding across her top lip as she stared at his cock. "And you think you have this adventure I've been craving?"

He shifted even closer. "I promise I can scratch the itch that has you squirming lately."

Her eyebrows arched, the smirk back on her face. "Promising. I may just have to take you up on that."

"Oh, please do." His salacious grin told her he could definitely deliver on his promise. She never doubted it really. Cherish heard the rumors about Edwin Coldwell and how hard he liked to play. She could use a little of his roughness in her life.

She nodded. "I have to get back inside before Faith has a hissy fit about me taking too long out here, but we definitely need to talk about this some more." She walked around him, patting his ass as she passed him. "Definitely."

She didn't glance back as she sashayed her way toward the back door of Rutherford Construction, but she knew he watched her walk away, his eyes glued to her ass. She couldn't stop grinning. Someone wanted her, wanted to strip her naked and take her. Perhaps there was life in her yet.

Her body shivered. The water turned cold as she stood there lost in the past. She wrapped an arm around her naked breasts as she reached for the faucet to turn off the water. Did she wash her hair? She couldn't remember. It was wet, so she would go with yes. Reaching for a towel, she knew not all the water drops on her face were from the shower. She had handled everything wrong and had no idea how to fix it. Glen stopped answering her calls and texts unless it pertained to Jordie. She closed her eyes as she pressed the towel to her face, forcing the tears not to fall. She missed the adventure in her life, but did she miss it enough to give up on her family? Her heart ripped inside of her, torn between wondering how she could get Glen back and why Edwin didn't want her.

~ ~ ~ ~ ~

Glen scraped the leftover food into the trash and slipped his plate into the sink. He needed to get to work, but his mother wouldn't hear of him leaving the house until he had breakfast. "Most important meal of the day," she always said.

"Every meal is important," Glen's father would counter. "Who can live off one meal a day?" He would then make a big show of rubbing his paunch belly, grinning as he slid another piece of bacon into his mouth.

Glen just surrendered and ate what was in front of him. It was easier than listening to his mother whine. Brenda Lansky could whine better than any toddler.

"I know you're going through a lot right now, but have you thought about what you're going to do about Jordie's birthday?" Brenda asked before Glen could get away from her. "It's coming up quick."

Guilt filled Glen as he realized, with so much on his mind, he had forgotten about his son's birthday. He had ignored most of Cherish's texts and calls, not wanting to deal with her since he told her he wasn't sure yet what he would do. His father's words still echoed in his mind, about not being able to fix things if he wasn't home to fix them. He couldn't fix them with talking to her, either. He took a deep breath. He really didn't want to talk to her.

Turning to face his mother, he leaned back on the kitchen counter. "Valerie offered to have a party at her house, but I said no."

"Good. That woman is a snob for no reason. I swear she has a stick so far up her ass I'm surprised we don't see the tip of it whenever she opens her mouth." His mother shook her head as she lifted her cup of coffee and took a sip. Putting the cup back on the table, she asked, "So, what have you decided to do? Can you put all this to the side long enough for Jordie to enjoy his birthday?"

Glen nodded. "I will. There's no reason Jordie should suffer because of what Cherish and I are going through."

"You're here and not at home. Jordie is already suffering." His mother pursed her lips as she shook her head. "At least give him a day where he can pretend life is normal for a while."

Glen nodded, not able to say anything. What could he say? She was right. Jordie went a week without the benefit of his parents working together to make his life whole. The little boy was bounced from one to the other on a daily basis, his conversations reduced to snippets here and there on the phone at times. He didn't deserve that. Yet, could Glen forgive Cherish enough to give Jordie back his family?

Glen would never know unless he went home and tried. He nodded, decision made. Pushing himself off the counter with a bump of his ass, he said, "I won't be here for dinner." He would at least talk to Cherish. It was the only way to determine where they were headed, whether they got back together, figuring out how to make it work, or separating for good.

His mother didn't smile. Her face a mask of neutral. She would wait to see what his final plans were before she offered an opinion now that she had already stated what was on her mind. Cherish had been too much of a wild child for her tastes, and she believed her baby boy deserved better. Cherish was also too much like her mother—cold and distant—for his mother's taste, and that always put a roadblock up between them. Still, Cherish was his wife, and he owed it to them to see if he could make it work. Figuring out what she missed in her life and if he was able to give it to her was the key. Was it time to step back into the past? Could he handle it? He sighed, not sure of the answer.

Ten

Jordie had a great time at Betsy's, even asking for three chocolate milks. They were such regulars there that Tina Rogers, "Betsy," made sure Jordie was kept satisfied with pancakes until he couldn't eat any more. She even brought out a washcloth to wipe away the syrup that didn't make it into his mouth. Cherish sat there, smiling, as the older woman doted all over Jordie as if he was the king of the world. Jordie just laughed and ate it up.

Once they finished breakfast, Cherish decided it was a good idea to take Jordie to the park and allow him to run off some of the energy all that syrup pumped into him. Besides, it was a beautiful day, and her misery had cooped them up inside too long, wallowing in her self-pity. Today called for wallowing outside.

There were two other moms there with their children, so

Jordie at least had someone else to run around with, giving Cherish time to herself to sit and wonder where she went wrong. She knew she should focus on Glen and repairing her marriage, but she couldn't stop wondering why Edwin stopped seeing her. What did she do that finally drove him away? There was no way Faith was better in bed than she was. Not boring, timid Faith, the girl who didn't lose her virginity until twelfth grade. So what was it? *Why did you stop seeing me, Edwin?*

As she watched Jordie sliding down the slide, arms up in the air, she pulled her cell phone out of her purse, sliding the screen unlocked. She scrolled through the gallery, until she found it, a picture of Edwin standing in his office just after she finished decorating it, his dark hair fading to gray at the temples, his smile pushing up his bronze cheeks. It felt as if, even in the picture, his dark eyes stared right at her, penetrating her. It wasn't the only thing that had penetrated her.

Without realizing she did it, she opened up her contacts and scrolled down to Edwin's phone number. She stared at it, her thumb poised over the call button. *Why wasn't I enough?* Not knowing drove her crazy. She pushed the button as she took a deep breath.

Three rings. "What now?" His voice was terse, curt. "Didn't you give me enough hell already?"

"I... I'm surprised you answered." She could feel the lump that used to be her heart in her throat, pulsating as she spoke.

"So am I, to be honest." She heard him take a deep breath, could imagine him running his hand through his hair as he stared up at the sky or ceiling, depending on where he was. "What do you want, Cherish? I have a new office to get accustomed to thanks to you."

"I heard. I'm sorry Neal sent you away. Beats being fired, I guess."

"That remains to be seen. Look, I highly doubt you called to wish me luck, so why *did* you call?"

She deserved his anger just as much as he had deserved her knee. "Why wasn't I enough? I mean, when did I push you away?"

"Really? This is why you're calling me? Shouldn't you be worrying about Glen and your family?"

"I need to know."

"Why? What does it matter now?" She could hear the confusion and annoyance in his voice. She should have known he wouldn't understand. It had all been a game to him while with her it was all too real.

"It just does," she snapped. Better than whining, she supposed. "Please, Edwin. I need to know. I thought you enjoyed us being together. I tried to give you everything you wanted. Why wasn't I enough? What did Faith have that I didn't? What did she give you that I couldn't?" The questions felt odd coming from her mouth, the same questions Glen asked her a few days ago.

"You didn't do anything." She heard him take a deep breath. "Cherish, what we had wasn't supposed to be serious. We were just having fun. I was enjoying it, but you... You started needing something I wasn't ready to give. You started acting like my girlfriend at work, and it was just too much."

She felt the anger start to simmer. She had smothered him; he just about said she did. "And Faith? Why did you go to my sister?"

Another deep breath. "Faith *was* just wanting fun. She wasn't looking to leave her husband. They just wanted to open up their marriage to sexual adventures, and I was her adventure. But..." Silence. She could hear him breathing, so she knew they hadn't lost connection. After a couple of moments, he started speaking again. "But things changed on my end. I asked her to come to

Savannah with me, but she turned me down. I'm not sure when my heart got involved, probably just like you don't know when you started caring for me, but I crossed a line and broke one of her rules. It was just supposed to be fun, but I tried to make it more than that. It's probably good for both of us I'm in Savannah. I need to work on my career, and you need to work on your marriage. Trust me, this if for the best."

"I don't think Glen wants me back," she said, the realization of everything she lost hitting her again. "I've lost everything."

"No, Cherish, you haven't. You just need to work at holding onto everything. Besides, you still have that little boy to take care of. He needs you."

She said nothing as a tear jerked its way down her cheek. She glanced over at Jordie climbing the steps to the slide again.

"I'm sorry, Cherish," Edwin said. "For everything. I was wrong in a lot of things, but I promise, I never meant to hurt you or cause problems with your family. I'm sorry."

She nodded, doing her best not to break down. "Yeah, so am I. Goodbye, Edwin." Pulling the phone away from her ear, she hit the END button and swiped the tears off her cheek. *Well, at least now I know where I screwed up. Apparently, I'm good to fuck, but not to give your heart to, or to run away with.* She couldn't believe he asked Faith to run away with him, although the fact Faith turned him down didn't surprise Cherish. Faith was too ga-ga over Selby to stray too far. Obviously, she'd sleep with other people, but, just as Edwin said, it was only for fun and not emotional.

Jordie jumped from the steps leading up to the slide, screaming as a small blond girl chased him. That was where Cherish went wrong; she gave Edwin her heart without even meaning to do it. But why? Why didn't she just keep it fun? A fling? Because, she grew tired of the way her life went, that's why. She didn't regret having Jordie or even marrying Glen. She regretted her life becoming a monotonous rut. Edwin was her escape; he was never meant to be her life. That's where she lost focus.

She sighed. *Wrong. My focus should have been on fixing what I thought was broken, instead of looking elsewhere for my excitement. At least, Faith and Selby went after their adventures together.* Cherish sat back on the bench, slumped forward slightly. What would Glen have done if she asked him to open their marriage up like Faith and Selby did? Cherish couldn't picture Glen going for it. After all, he pulled her from that life when he asked her to marry him. No more parties. No more crazy nights. No more fun. *But, I never even gave him a chance to say no.* Yet, how do you ask your partner something like that? How had the topic even come up in her sister's house? That had to be the weirdest night ever, or they had to be drunk as hell. Yet, they made it work. They did it the right way and succeeded where Cherish cheated on her husband and failed.

Cherish slid her phone into her purse with a sigh. Maybe she should have tried it Faith's way first. Was it too late?

~ ~ ~ ~ ~

Having made his decision that morning, Glen couldn't focus on work, so he took off for the rest of the day. The jobs were light, and Brent could handle them himself. Glen's thoughts were a recycling of what his father told him Sunday night, Tanya's unwanted advice, and his mother's conversation with him that morning. *You're miserable, and I don't blame you. The woman you love betrayed you. Broke your heart. That hurts like hell. Can you forgive her, though? Can you move past it? The two of you waded through deep waters before. Is this ocean too deep? If not, you won't fix it here. You need to be home with your family, in bed with your wife.* His father was right; Glen wouldn't be able to move past it if he was away from Cherish. To fix the mess, they needed to be together. Did he want a divorce? No. Definitely not. He knew that even as he walked out the door a week ago. He just needed space to think, to move past what he felt right then. It didn't work, however. He still felt miserable. He missed his son, his home. He missed his wife. He wasn't sure how to make it work or how to fix it, but he knew he had to give it a shot. He'd hate himself forever if he didn't at least try. Hopefully, Cherish wanted to try as well. She asked him to come home already, but did she still want him back?

"Rachel's going to be highly disappointed," Brent said as Glen told him he was heading home. "She was looking forward to hooking up."

Glen shook his head. "I highly doubt that, since I never told her we were hooking up. You just need someone to keep her from telling Bonnie to avoid your ass."

"Isn't that part of a wingman's job?" Then Brent's face turned serious as he put a hand on his friend's shoulder. "Go on. Go save your family."

Glen whispered a thanks, his voice caught in his throat. He only hoped there was still time to save it.

Pulling into the driveway of his house, he noticed the absence of Cherish's car. Taking a deep breath, he thanked the universe for a few more minutes before he had to face whatever he was about to face. He had role-played several conversations in his head since that morning, but nothing seemed like it made sense.

As he stepped inside the house, he stopped just inside the front door, taking a moment to look around. The place was a mess, and from what he could tell, it seemed like Cherish had slept on the couch a few nights. Did that mean she hurt as much as he did? Did she regret hurting him or losing Edwin? He sighed, wishing he knew. Taking a couple of steps forward, he stepped on one of

Jordie's toy cars, making him stumble a bit. He reached down and picked it up, a smile on his face. *How can I give this up?* He determined within himself he would do whatever was necessary to make his marriage work. Cherish needed something, and he would find out what that something was and make sure she had it. Nothing would destroy what he spent the past six years building. Nothing.

He glanced at his watch. 2:15. He wasn't sure where they were. Possibly at her mother's house. It didn't matter; he'd be here when they got home. He went into the kitchen and opened the refrigerator, staring inside. He wasn't hungry. Or thirsty. Just bored.

And worried.

What if this was a mistake? What if he should have just stayed gone and waited for Cherish to return to him? Maybe she didn't want him back anymore. Maybe it was already too late.

Was it too late?

He closed the refrigerator door; there was nothing inside, anyway, and turned back to the living room window and the day he wasted by standing around waiting for his wife to come home. He let out a sigh as he ran his hand through his dark hair. Once again, he started to debate the wisdom of his decision to return home again, then stopped. The decision was already made. He was there. He wasn't sure how it would work, or how long it would take him to get past the betrayal he felt every time he thought about what she did to him, but he was determined to see it through—for Jordie's sake.

Just as he was about to turn back around for a glass of water, a beer, or just to stare at the refrigerator again, he heard her car pull up into the circular drive. His chest became a sudden compression of nerves as he suddenly felt like throwing up. As much as he paced around their living room, he would have hoped to have screwed up some courage for what he was about to face. However, he was as scared now as he was when he first made the decision.

He stood in front of the door, his hands stuffed in his pockets as he waited for Cherish to come inside. No sense giving the neighbors even more to gossip about. They had enough as it was, he was sure, especially with Aubrey in the know.

The car door slammed, and he heard her jingling keys as she approached, heard Jordie scream out about seeing Daddy's car in the driveway. That scream, the excitement it held, made Glen smile.

Cherish opened the door and stood, staring at him, her hand still on the door handle, while Jordie screamed out, "Daddy," and raced into his arms. He could see Cherish take a deep breath as she finished entering their home, closing the door behind her, bracing for the attack she assumed was coming. He wasn't going to attack her. He was too tired.

With her arms across her chest, she tried to look everywhere but at him. "What brings you by?"

"We need to talk if we're ever going to fix this." He took a step toward her, his hands back in his pockets, afraid of making a wrong move or sending the wrong signal. "I've stayed away too long as it is. I miss Jordie and want to be here for him," he said, glancing back at his son. Then, he took a deep breath and looked up at her. "I miss you."

She glanced at him, and he could see the tears beginning in her eyes. "Glen…"

He told Jordie to go play in his room to give Mommy and Daddy a chance to talk.

"Will you be here when I come out?" his son asked, and it broke Glen's heart to hear the concern in his son's voice.

Leaning down, he kissed Jordie's forehead. "I'll be here. I

promise. I wouldn't leave without a hug and a kiss from my boy." He gave his son a hug and then watched as he ran into the hall, skipping more than running. Once Jordie was out of sight, Glen stood and moved closer to Cherish, reaching out and taking her upper arms in his hands. He touched her chin with his index finger, forcing her to look up at him. "We can fix this, Cher. I know we can. If you still want to try, that is." That was the real question, he knew. Did Cherish still love him and want their relationship to work?

She nodded, returning her gaze back to him. "No work today?"

He could see the struggle in her eyes, knew she waged a battle within her he would have to help her win. He didn't blame her for wanting to avoid the subject. Every time the topic came up, all they did was fight and hurt each other. "I took the day off."

"Look, I don't want to fight." He watched as she took a deep breath, her chest rising and falling with the motion.

"I didn't think we were fighting. This is talking."

"Glen, I'm tired of living the way we've been living. I miss things." She took a deep breath. "It's taken me all week to realize why I did what I did. I miss being able to just cut loose and have fun. I miss having the fun we used to have." She shrugged. "I know you and I only had a couple of weeks before our lives changed, and I feel like we just got started before it was all shut down."

He nodded, doing his best to ignore the vise that gripped his heart. "All right. I can understand that. We can fix it, though. We take it day-by-day and see what happens. I think after six years, we at least owe that much to ourselves. We owe it to Jordie to try."

"Glen, you should never have…"

"But I did," he said, cutting her off before she could finish her sentence. "And I don't regret any of it." He took a step toward her. "Look, I'm here still, fighting for us, for our family. All I ask is that you fight with me, and we see what happens. Who knows? We might just find what you're missing. We could finish that first adventure we started almost six years ago." He gave her a weak shrug. "To be honest, I kind of miss it, too."

"And if we don't?" She crossed her arms over her chest, the fatigue of the past week clear in her posture.

"Then, we'll have to figure that out as well. Whatever we do, we have to protect that little guy in there. He doesn't need to get hurt because we can't make things work."

She nodded, and he wasn't sure if she agreed with him or just nodded her head for lack of anything else to say. "Okay."

"Okay, you'll try? Or Okay we won't let him get hurt?"

"Just okay. That's all I have right now."

"Then, that's where we'll start." He tried to force a smile onto his face, but he wasn't sure if he managed it or not. He knew he didn't feel like smiling. He felt like throwing up. "How about I fix us some coffee, and we can just…you know…talk?"

She nodded, her lips a thin line. He didn't push. He knew this wouldn't be easy, but he also knew he had to try. He owed their family that much, no matter what Cherish did.

Turning toward the kitchen, he left her standing there as he went to make coffee. He could only open the door. Cherish would have to be the one to walk through it. If their relationship would survive, they would both have to make it work, both make the sacrifices that would heal their family. They could have their cake and eat it, too. Glen would make her realize adventures never really ended.

Eleven

Glen pulled up along the front of his parents' house, shifting his car into park and turning the ignition off. He didn't rush to get out of the car however, choosing to sit there a bit longer in the silence. He even drove with the radio off as his mind continued to replay his conversation with Cherish after she tucked Jordie into bed. That had been tough, telling Jordie he was going back to his parents' house to sleep, that he wasn't sleeping in their home just yet. Jordie just hugged him, saying he missed him, before asking if his daddy could tuck him into bed.

Once Jordie was out, the real conversation began around the kitchen table and over coffee.

"You've been awfully quiet tonight. Would you rather I hadn't come over?"

Her hands wrapped around her coffee mug, Cherish shrugged. "I'm sorry. I'm glad you came over. Jordie loved seeing you. To be honest, it felt nice to act like a normal family again. I just have so much on my mind; I can't get it to turn off."

"So, talk about it. That's the only way we'll work this out or at least see if we *can* work it out."

"Glen, I don't think…"

He reached out, placing a hand on top of her wrist. "Cherish, it doesn't matter how bad it sounds or what it is. Sooner or later, we have to discuss it, or we can never move forward. This isn't something we can just sweep under the rug and ignore. I don't know how to fix this unless you talk to me."

She stared at him for a moment, wanting so badly to trust what he said, but also knowing what she would sound like once it all came out. Turning her gaze back to her coffee mug, she finally went for broke and unloaded her cluster of chaotic thoughts on him, not holding anything back, no matter how horrible it sounded. And it sounded horrible. Real horrible. But, he asked for it, and he listened to every word without interrupting. It was the only way they would ever move forward.

When she finished laying her cards out on the table, letting him know everything she felt, the real reason she slept with Edwin, her doubts of their future, she just stared at the table, waiting for him to unload on her. He said nothing. Not right away, anyway. It wouldn't do to rush a reply with pious words. Besides, it was a lot to absorb. The way their life played out had obviously frustrated her for a long time with her saying nothing about it.

He shifted in his chair, his hands holding his own coffee mug as he took a deep breath. She just sat there, her body tense, biting her lower lip. He knew she was ready for him to explode on her, for a storm of emotions to erupt from him. It never came. "I admit, life has definitely been different since Jordie was born. Neither of us expected it, and it changed everything. I guess I just didn't understand how much."

"I never meant to hurt you," she said, her voice soft, barely a whisper. "Or Jordie. I just...I just needed to feel again."

"I know you didn't mean to hurt us," he said. "I don't think either of us meant for our lives to take the paths they took. Still, here we are. We need to figure out what we're going to do about it. That's all."

"What can we do?"

He didn't answer right away, his mind trying hard to come up with an answer. Yet, he didn't have one. Instead, he slid out of his chair, walking around the table to where Cherish sat. He knelt down on one knee, took her hands off the mug she held and kissed her knuckles. When he spoke, his voice was as soft as hers had been just a moment ago. "We can take it one day at a time, just like we do everything else. We'll find an answer to this. Together."

She smiled, reaching over and squeezing his arm. He could see a wide range of emotions flitting across her face, but at least she smiled. "One day at a time," she whispered.

He pulled her to him, his arms wrapped around her as she laid her head on his chest. He didn't know how they would fix their marriage, or how he would give her back what she said she needed or what she felt she was missing, but he knew she was worth the effort to figure it out.

But it wasn't time for him to move back in, not unless they knew it would work, and with her doubts still, nothing was certain. He didn't want Jordie to go through seeing him move out a second time. He wouldn't hurt his son that way again.

Opening his car door, Glen stepped out into the cool April night. As he started making his way to the front door, another set of lights pulled up behind him as his sister returned from her date. He stood, his hands in his pockets, and waited for her to get out of her car, wondering if this boyfriend was as wild as the one she told him about this weekend.

"What are you doing here, brother dear?" Tanya asked as she shut her car door. "I thought Mom said you were going back home?"

He shrugged, glancing back at the front of his parents' house. "Not yet. I want to make sure I'll be staying before going back. I don't want to put Jordie through that again."

She walked up to him and put her arm around his waist as they started toward the house. "Makes sense. How are you holding up?"

"As well as I can, I guess. This sucks. I just don't know how to give her what she needs."

Tanya laughed. "What she needs is a swift kick in the ass. Glen, she cheated on you. She needs to be the one trying to figure out how to make it right with you, not the other way around. You've done nothing but bend over backward for that woman."

He glanced over at his sister, digging his keys back out of his pocket to unlock the front door. "You sound like Mom, now."

"Nah, Mom's nicer than I am. No one hurts my brother and gets away with it."

He unlocked the front door and opened it, but before stepping through the doorway, he stopped and turned to his sister. "Thanks, Tan. I appreciate it, but I have to figure this out if I'm going to make my family work. I agree, she needs to do some things as well, but I apparently wasn't giving her something she felt she needed. I need to know what that is."

Tanya just winked at him. "Then do as I said, and instead of kicking her in the ass, give her a spanking. That always works."

He held up a hand, stopping her from saying more. "I don't

need to hear anything else. C'mon, the beer's on Dad."

"Lead the way, brother dear."

~ ~ ~ ~ ~

Cherish just laid there, the night a dark blanket around her as she contemplated everything Glen said to her earlier. It was the first time she slept in her marriage bed since Glen walked out of the house over a week ago. It felt weird, lying there, alone. It had been his suggestion to try to make things as normal as possible for Jordie until they figured out their next move.

They had spent the night focusing on Jordie because neither of them knew how to talk about the other. When they did talk, it was all casual chitchat about everything other than the two of them and where their marriage headed. Neither wanted to go down that road just yet, and the walking on eggshells drove her crazy. It was hard just being in the same room at times. He couldn't keep the hurt from his eyes, no matter how hard he tried, and she couldn't get past what she did, waiting for him to explode at any moment. It was always at the forefront of her mind.

Yet, he came back. She really didn't think he would. Not after she screwed up so much. True, it wasn't to live back in his own home, but he at least wanted to talk it out, figure out a way to fix it. But why? Why did he come back? Cherish really didn't understand it. It wasn't like any of this was his responsibility. He didn't deserve what she put him through.

He loved her, he said. She loved him as well, but... Well, something was missing. She needed more than just love. She knew how shitty that sounded, but it was true. She missed the excitement her life was before a child, before marriage, before... Just before.

She stared at the ceiling, the nightlight in the bathroom sending a dim glow to the white paint. She saw the parties she used to attend, the games of pool she used to shoot, the nights where she could just leave without worrying about babysitters or answering to a husband, the freedom she had at one time in her life. She told Glen all of it, everything she felt. He still didn't walk out on her, instead choosing to continue and try to work through it all. It wasn't his place to work through it. She was the one who screwed up. She was the one who stepped out on her marriage. She should be the one to fix it, but... She didn't know how to even begin.

I sound like such a selfish bitch. Yet, was it wrong to be honest about what she missed? It's not like she wished she never gave birth to Jordie. He was the pride of her life. She would have preferred different circumstances, but she wouldn't wish her son out of her life for anything. Did that mean, however, she couldn't still want the things she gave up to raise him?

She lay there in the stifling silence for a while, her mind numb. After a moment, she glanced over at Glen's side of the bed, running her hand over the empty sheets. She felt her chest constrict as a sob escaped her throat. It felt weird not having him there. She needed to get up. She eased out of the covers and off the bed, making her way out of the room.

The hallway was a little brighter, the nightlight they left in the bathroom for Jordie casting shadows along the walls. She shuffled her way down the hall to Jordie's door, which was cracked enough for the nightlight to creep inside. She eased the door open until she could see her son's outline in the bed, all curled up in a tight fetal position. She didn't enter. Instead, she leaned against the doorframe, watching the slight rise and fall of the blankets as he breathed in his sleep, her arms crossed over her chest, her head leaning on the doorframe. She had always been a selfish woman. She was a selfish teenager as well. She pushed every boundary, broke every rule anyone tried to force upon her. She saw them as restrictions to her life, things others just didn't want her to have that she deserved. It was a wonder her father didn't kill her long ago or send her off to some faraway boarding school. Her mother, on the other hand, well, Cherish was her baby and could do no wrong to tarnish that shiny halo. Cherish took full advantage of that every chance she could. She sighed. *Have I always been a bitch?* She knew what her siblings would say, especially Faith.

Cherish's older sister always towed the line, obeyed everyone who ever had any type of authority over her. She was the good girl. Cherish had no desire to be the good girl. Or to obey; at least, not that way. Oh, she wasn't mean for the sake of being mean. Well, to anyone other than Faith, that is, but Cherish refused to fit inside a box. She partied, drank, dabbled in drugs, had been having sex since she was a sophomore in high school, and even lived with a guy for a year before realizing what a douche he was. Through it all, she was still her mother's angel. Her father just shook his head.

Why didn't her mother ever get onto her about her actions? Valerie Driscoll was always quick to judge and criticize Faith for every little thing the matriarch thought her middle child did wrong. Why did their mother never criticize Cherish? Why were there no lectures on drinking and drugs? After all, her mother was the faithful churchgoer. Cherish should have received constant lectures on the sins she committed. But nothing. Not one word. Not one tsk tsk. Why? Would her life have been different if her parents brought the hammer down on her more? Or at all? Her father tried in the beginning, but soon just surrendered to Valerie's coddling of her youngest daughter. To this day, Faith was his favorite child. It was obvious. But then, Faith never did anything to break her father's heart, either. Cherish broke it weekly with her actions, if not daily.

Cherish knew she took it out on Faith as well, berating her, bullying her, giving her the cold shoulder, just because Cherish didn't want to own up to her own terrible behavior. That would mean she had to take responsibility for her actions. It was easier to be angry at Faith for being such a goody-goody than for Cherish to alter the way she behaved. Criticizing her sister meant Cherish never had to take a real close look at her own behavior. Until now. Until her world crashed down around her. Until she practically ruined her son's life.

Jordie shifted in his bed, turning over in his sleep. The blanket slid off his tiny body, one arm plopping to the side. She smiled as she watched him. Her lack of control brought Jordie into her life. She didn't regret having him. He truly was her world. She would do anything for him, anything at all.

She would even make an effort to make her marriage work. Jordie deserved a family.

She swiped at a tear that trickled down her cheek she hadn't even realized was there. Her mind was made up. She would give it everything she had to make it work with Glen. Jordie deserved it. After all he did for her, Glen deserved it, as well.

Her stomach twisted in a nauseous knot, making her squeeze herself tighter, her doubts battling against her determination. What else was there to do, really?

She wished she knew.

~ ~ ~ ~ ~

As he slid between his sheets, Glen knew that, while telling Tanya Jordie was the real reason he didn't move back home, he knew the truth. Neither Cherish nor he was really ready. She needed to think, and Glen understood that. He needed time, as well. He knew she held some things back, but what she shared was enough to make him know they had a long road ahead of them if they were to make their marriage work. And he wanted it to work. His family was his entire world, and he didn't want to lose them. Yet, how far was he willing to go in order to give Cherish what she wanted? Was it even possible to give her what she said she was missing?

He stared at the ceiling, one hand under his head, the other resting on his stomach. She said she missed the parties, the crazy nights of going out and not worrying about when they had to be home or whether they had to wake up the next morning. He knew she wasn't saying she regretted having Jordie. That little boy was her world, and she would never wish him out of her life, even if she didn't want Glen in it anymore. No. She wasn't saying that at all. She was merely expressing her nostalgia for the days when life was more carefree and simpler.

He sighed. He remembered those days as well. He remembered when they met their junior year of high school at some party out west of I-95 on someone's property no one developed yet. Cars pulled up, people stacked cases of beer onto tailgates, and passed bottles of Jack Daniels around. Music blared, and a giant bonfire raged in the middle of the field. They were younger, without real responsibilities, and curfews were really nonexistent. They could do whatever they wanted, and they usually did.

He watched her from a distance for a long time, since high school, really. They shared classes, lunch hours, and even mutual friends. He was always on the edge of her friends up until that party, never in her line of sight, but close enough that he could get to know her. Everything he learned about her made him fall in love with her. She wasn't an angel by any stretch. She was her own woman, even as a teenager, and he liked that about her. He tried to get to know her better, but she always wound up with some idiot who never knew the great woman he dated. Even Nick Pepper turned out to be an ass, using Cherish when no one else was around to entertain or act tough in front of. He treated her poorly, but she tolerated it. It hadn't even been her idea to end their relationship. Instead, Nick found someone else who gained him more attention and left Cherish at a bar alone while he went off with the new girl. Glen had been there that night. He had hidden enough in the shadows and decided to be the knight she needed, even though she didn't realize it yet. It took him a while to make her see what a great guy he was. He smiled at the memory as he laid there. She attempted to push him away, but he won her over, enough so that she agreed to marry him when she found out she was pregnant just a couple of weeks later. She allowed him to prove to her they were great together and would make a fantastic family, and they did for almost six years.

Yet, here he was, once again asking her to allow him to prove it to her. He would do it, make her see the two of them were better together than they were alone. He wasn't sure how to give her what she wanted, but he knew he would figure it out. He had no other choice, not if he would save his family, and his family was all that mattered to him. He saved Cherish once, he would do so again. She'd see.

Twelve

Cherish had just finished brushing her hair when the knock came at the door. She dropped the brush on the counter as she took a deep breath.

"Oh, Cher!" Aubrey called out as she entered the Lansky home.

"In here!" Cherish stared at herself in the mirror, her hair a waterfall along her shoulders. She wore her business finest, straight gray skirt, burgundy button-down blouse conservatively buttoned. She thought about revealing the swell of her breasts just a little, but sex had cost her the last job, and she didn't need it infecting this one. She decided to play it safe.

Aubrey popped her head through Cherish's doorway. "You decent? Tell me you're not decent."

Cherish saw her friend's dark hair as Aubrey peeked around

the door. She forced a smile onto her face. "Sorry to disappoint. Maybe later if you're good."

Entering the room, Aubrey let out a dramatic sigh. "Ah, well. Story of my life." She collapsed onto the bed, bouncing a couple of times before sitting still. "You all set for your interview?"

"Not really, but what choice do I have?" She turned and leaned back on the bathroom vanity. "I wasn't exactly happy at Rutherford that last month, but if I'm honest, I didn't really have to do much. I made good money. It was a dream job. One that I loved before the bullshit."

"No offense, but how much of that was due to you boinking the boss?" Aubrey bounced her eyebrows at Cherish.

"That was rude." Cherish grabbed a white sweater—*Where the hell did I get a white sweater?*—and slipped her arms through it. "More than likely true, but still rude. You're supposed to be my friend, remember?"

"Which is why I can be truthfully rude. How long are you going to be gone?" She folded her hands between her knees. "Not that I have anything to do. Hey, speaking of which, we should go out and get a drink. Have some fun."

"I'm going for a job, because I need money. I can't spend the little I do have on booze." She stepped out of the bedroom and into the hall on her way to the living room. "Until I have this all figured out, my nights out are over for a while." She heard Aubrey following her.

"But I want to go out. I *need* to go out," Aubrey said in a whiny voice. "Please."

Cherish knelt down beside Jordie, who sat on the floor in front of the television. She glanced at Aubrey before talking to Jordie. "You're worse than my son. Stop pouting." She then kissed Jordie's forehead. "You listen to Aubrey while Mommy's gone. I'll be back soon." Standing, she snatched up her purse and keys on her way to the door. "Call me if you need anything. Wish me luck."

"Luck!"

Cherish didn't want to do this. She didn't like starting over and, right now, it felt like that was all she did. Start over. She weaved through the Thursday morning traffic, turning east on New Haven and then north once she hit Harbor City Boulevard. Her interview was with Harbor City Carpet. Through the friend of a friend, she heard their office manager was about to resign due to pregnancy. Rutherford Construction subcontracted them out on several jobs, so she knew the owner and hoped that would gain her a foothold in the interview. She would take any advantage she could get, since it had been eight years since she had to even apply for a job. She let out a nervous breath. She hated this part of the process.

Harbor City Carpet wasn't a giant building. The business set directly off Harbor City Boulevard, their parking lot only big enough to hold seven vehicles while employees parked around back. The front was all tinted glass with rolls of carpet displayed from the inside. Concrete steps led up to a glass door with a giant welcome sign hanging from the middle handlebar on the inside. With a deep breath, Cherish pulled open the door—then realized she should have pushed. *This is a great start.* She pushed the door open and stepped into the air-conditioned showroom.

"Hello, welcome to Harbor City Carpet," a middle-aged woman with dirty-blond hair said, stepping around a pile of carpet samples. "How can I help you today?"

"Hi. I'm Cherish Lansky. I was told to come in to discuss the office opening."

The woman stopped, and her smile turned sour. "Right this way." The woman turned, her skirt twirling around her legs in her rush as she marched her way to the back of the showroom, her heels punching the tile floor. Her arms didn't swing as she walked, nor did her ass sway. Cherish thought it was like watching a stick walk. *Something has this lady perturbed. Maybe I should rethink this position.*

The stiff woman led Cherish through the showroom into the warehouse area with a small office tucked off to the left. The woman knocked twice before opening the door, turned, and walked away—making sure to leave the door open. Wide open.

Before entering, Cherish turned and watched the woman walk away without so much as a good luck or kiss my ass. Cherish just shook her head, took a deep breath, and entered the small office. She never thought she would need to go through this process again. She hated it.

A balding man, thin, with round glasses perched on his forehead, sat behind a desk overloaded with bulging file folders, carpet samples, and a cold cup of coffee. He smiled at her as she walked in, arm extended to shake her hand as he stood. "Hi, hi. Come in, please."

She took the man's clammy hand and only held it as long as necessary. He was a squirrely looking man and set Cherish's nerves on end. Still, it was the only opening she had found so far, and she needed the job. With a fake smile on her face and determination pumping through her, she returned his handshake and introduced herself.

He waved it off. "I know full well who you are, Cherish, and the quality of work you do." He gestured for her to sit down in a chair in front of his desk as he took his own seat. "It's nice to put a face to a name finally. I'm Bernie. We've talked over the phone several times. These days, I get calls from your sister, Faith." He leaned back in his chair, a smile on his face, but Cherish knew he studied her. She did her best to seem neutral about it all.

"It was time for a change." She quit Rutherford Construction, albeit in a blaze of ball-racking glory, but nevertheless, nowhere could it be said Rutherford Construction fired her. She was sure there was gossip, however. It flowed throughout the construction field. Yet, she wouldn't surrender to it and allow her fear of what others said dictate her course. "If you know my work at Rutherford, then you know I can be a great asset to your company. I'd love the opportunity to show you."

His smile widened as he nodded. "I am quite familiar with your work ethic and the great job you did for Edwin at Rutherford." He leaned forward with a deep breath, his lips pressed into a thin line before he spoke. "I'll be honest, Cherish. The lady who escorted you in is my wife, Mary. She's the one giving me a hard time about bringing you on board. With the rumors of how you left Rutherford, she doesn't want to see that transfer over to us. We've had a great partnership with Rutherford Construction, and I need to know it will continue, and you'll be able to handle working with them. Even with your sister."

Seems the news has been more detailed than I thought. Ah well, people love to talk. "Mr. Overton, I assure you, all I want is a fresh start and to be able to work. I'm sure we can all be professional, and my sister and I have always worked well together."

The look he gave her told her he knew better, but he wouldn't call her out on it. She watched as he debated within himself for a moment, and then he nodded. "Very well. We'll give it a shot. Be here Monday at eight, and we'll get you settled in." He stood, his hand out again for another shake she wished she could avoid. "Welcome aboard," he said with a smile.

She took the offered hand, returning his smile. "Thank you for the opportunity." She only hoped she would survive it.

~ ~ ~ ~ ~

Three days. It had been three days since he told Cherish he

wanted to make their marriage work, and yet, they had barely even talked since then. He knew what she needed. Adventure. To feel desired. To be chased. However, he had no idea how to do that. How do you date someone you already married? How was he supposed to give her what she wanted? What had Edwin given her that she felt she needed?

"You know, the hammer, the one in the bucket, next to your leg, right there, beside you…"

Glen turned his gaze away from the Indian River and stared at Brent. "What?"

Brent shook his head. "Where the hell have you gone in that mind of yours? I've asked you three times to hand me a hammer."

Glen gave himself a mental shake, jerking the fog out of his head. "Oh, sorry. I guess I was lost in thought." He reached into the tool bucket beside him and pulled out a hammer. Handing it to his partner, he said, "Sorry," again and leaned over the dock to see what Brent worked on below.

Brent took the hammer with another shake of his head. "You've been like this since the breakup. You going to make it?"

That was a good question. "I'm fine. I just need to figure out what to give her that she wasn't getting."

"Dude, you're totally looking at this the wrong way." Brent started hammering away at the plank he replaced underneath the dock. When he finished, he paused and stared at his friend. "My sister went through something similar a few years ago. She gave birth to my nephew four years prior, and for a while, everything seemed normal. She was happy, a great mother, good wife, still a pain in the ass sister, though." He smiled at that last part. Then his face grew serious. "Then, out of nowhere, she just went through some deep depression. No one could understand it. She didn't want to go out, the house went to pot, she barely even talked to her family."

"What happened?" Glen sat on the edge of the dock, his legs dangling over the side as he stared down at his friend.

"Depression. Some mothers get hit with it right after they give birth; some suffer it later on, usually about the four-year mark. My mother figured out what was happening, and they got her help. Now, she's even more of a pain in the ass."

"How did they get her through it?" Could that really be all it was and not that Cherish pined away for a past from which she turned away?

Brent handed Glen back the hammer and other tools as they talked. "Made sure she talked to someone, made her get out and exercise, hang out with friends. Pretty soon, my sister pushed through it."

"You really think this depression would cause Cherish to have an affair?" As much as Glen hoped that was the case, relieving him of failing to meet Cherish's needs, it still seemed farfetched.

Brent hauled himself onto the dock, taking a seat beside Glen, water dripping from his legs and feet. "Depression hits people in different ways and causes them to do different things. It may be Cherish's way of coping. I don't know and don't take my word for anything. I just know what happened to my sister. Cherish went through a lot of changes since you two got together from what you've told me. Maybe her depression made her long for those things she did way back when before she had her own family." He found a rock on the dock and picked it up, bouncing it in his hand. "Maybe that's your answer as to what to do. Treat her like she was treated back then. If she wants to regress, regress with her."

Glen nodded his head as he thought over what his friend said. He wasn't the only one saying it, either. Could Glen do it, though? Go back to the wild nights and parties? How would that even work with Jordie in their life now? There would have to be a balance somehow. Yet, if this is what Cherish needed, he would find that balance. Somehow.

"C'mon. Your turn to get in the water," Brent said as he slapped Glen on the back. "We still need to shore up that other side. Mr. Jenkins is getting heavier and says his dock is feeling wobbly when he walks on it." He laughed as he said it. "I don't think the boards are weak. I think Mr. Jenkins needs to lay off the sweets."

Glen laughed as he slid down into the murky water, tape measure in hand.

"You know, Rachel is pretty keen on you," Brent said to the open air as Glen slid under the dock to measure the boards he would need. "Bonnie told me last night that if you were to ask Rachel out, you'd get a definite yes. Just sayin'."

"She told you last night, huh?" Glen repeated as he worked, the Indian River up to his chest. "I didn't know you went out with her last night. Why would you waste time with her talking about me?" It hadn't surprised him that Brent and Bonnie talked about him, however. Most days, they wound up at the Royal Chef for lunch, and each time, it was the same thing—Glen took a seat while Brent huddled around the blond waitress like a lovesick puppy waiting for a treat. Brent must have finally gotten his reward for persistence.

"Not a waste of time to look out for a buddy. Besides, Rachel and Bonnie are best friends, too. Bonnie worries about her. Seems she thinks you'd be good for Rachel."

"I'm married, Brent, and she knows it. How on earth would she think I would be good for her?" *Hell, I wasn't good enough for Cher.*

"Why not go out with her and find out? It's not like you're going after Cherish right now. Besides, if you're going to go back to the wild days, wouldn't this count? I bet Rachel could make you feel nostalgic."

"I'm not the one needing to feel nostalgic." Glen swam back out to the edge of the dock, holding the tape measure out for his partner. "I need a plank six-feet long. And I'm going to be taking Cher out. I just need to figure out where to take her is all."

Brent hopped up, walking over to the sawhorses they made into a makeshift worktable. "Where did the two of you used to hang out?" He measured the length of two-by-six and marked it for cutting.

"A bar called Crocket's up on Wickham. We were there so often before Jordie was born we became great friends with the owner, Jerry." Glen paused in his talking while Brent cut the board. When the skill saw was off, he continued. "We used to shoot pool, dance, and drink until closing. Sometimes even after closing. Hell, I can't remember how many times we did it in the parking lot when everyone else went home." It was his turn to stare out into the afternoon. He smiled as he thought of all the late nights in the back of his car, the two of them in too much of a horny hurry to wait to get to one of their houses or to their own house once they were married. It had been a long time since they did anything sexual in a car. The past couple of years, Cherish preferred the comfort of her own bed. Glen's mood soured. *Except with Edwin, of course. I wonder how many times they did it in a car or at the office.* He gave himself a mental shake, refusing to go down that road. It wouldn't help.

Brent handed him the plank, and Glen made his way back under the dock. *Yet, is that what she needs? Going back to the crazy adventures we had before Jordie was born?* His mind went through the friskiness they shared, not able to keep their hands off each other for safer environments. Cherish never cared about getting caught. *Hell, half the time, I think she wanted to get caught. It was all part of the thrill for her.* And that was what hit him. They were safe, too safe from where they had been when they met. They became the conservative couple, always playing it safe before having any fun, making sure they were quiet, in their own bed, an empty house or a sleeping child. Boring. They became boring in less than six years, and he never saw it happening.

As he pounded the plank into place, he decided that if he would get Cherish back, he would have to shake their lives up some and recapture their adventures and daring. *It's time to take our sex out of the bedroom. Who knows? This may actually be fun.*

Thirteen

The interview took less time than Cherish thought it would, so she decided to leave Jordie in Aubrey's care a bit longer while she took a much-needed break and enjoyed one of those chain coffee shops for some peace and quiet. She needed to clear her head a bit and unwind a little. On a positive note, she had a job now and wouldn't starve, not that she thought Glen would allow that, anyway. Or at least, the Glen she knew before she cheated on him wouldn't have allowed it. The new, devastated Glen she wasn't so sure about.

She parked in a spot almost too small for her car, grabbed her purse, and headed inside the coffee shop that rested between Harbor City Carpet and home. The Tuesday crowd was busy, but she wasn't in any hurry, so it didn't matter. She just needed to sit for a while without Jordie hanging onto her, asking when his father was coming home. She never realized how much going to work gave her a break before this. She loved her son, but she wasn't sure she had ever been ready for the bundle of energy he turned out to be and what it would require to be a mother. Glen, however, always took it in stride, calm, relaxed, always ready to give Jordie his full attention. Glen was always Mr. Patience when it came to their son.

And with her. Until last week, that is.

She purchased her mocha latte and headed for the outside chairs. This coffee shop possessed a covered patio area with cushioned chairs and couches around small coffee tables. The north and east sides were ringed with flora that protected those sitting there enjoying their overpriced beverages from sucking in the car fumes from those in the drive-thru. She took one of the chairs sitting off by itself and settled in to stare at the ever-filling parking lot. She sat in the chair, her legs tucked up under her ass as she blew out a breath she didn't know she held, hoping to release some of her pent-up tension as well.

She sighed as she swallowed her mocha latte. There had been life in her for a brief time, and that life just about wrecked her world as well as her son's. She surrendered to the urges of a woman nearing thirty and feeling desperate, and the aftermath was more than she expected. She was selfish, and she found her behavior loathsome. Yet, she had to admit, even after the chaos she brought to her world, she hungered for more of it, and if it hadn't been for her damn sister getting involved in Edwin's pants, Cherish would still be seeing him. She hadn't been finished having her fun when it ended. The adventure had been ripped away from her grasp, and she desperately craved it back.

God, I'm pathetic. She glanced at her cell phone, noticing the time. She needed to get back home, she knew, but she wasn't ready to face the chaos of her life again. Glen left her. Their talk

Friday night gave her every indication he would try to make their marriage work. He wanted to find out what she needed and give it to her. Yet, how on earth would he do that when she didn't even know what she needed?

She sighed. That wasn't true. She knew what she needed. Or, rather, what she wanted. To feel alive again. To recapture the way things used to be when she didn't have a care in the world. Now was her chance to move on with the life she had planned before everything changed. She could do both, have her adventure as well as take care of her son. She never needed Glen's help. It had been panic that made her get married once she found out she was pregnant. Cherish Lansky was not a weak woman. She could make it work. She *would* make it work.

Life was too short for a person to give up on what they wanted. She would get all she could out of life and damn anyone who didn't like her choices. She pushed herself out of her chair, determination filling her as she tossed her cup into the trash bin. It was time to take her life back.

Yet, she didn't get far. "Cherish? Is that you? Wow, what's it been? Five? Six years?"

Cherish stood there as panic made a nauseous knot in her stomach, her breathing ragged as her flight mode kicked into high gear. With all that pep talk about being a strong woman, all she could do was stand there, staring. "Um, hi, Nick."

~ ~ ~ ~ ~

"Selby!" Glen called out as the bell over his head sounded, announcing his arrival inside Selby's Downtown Books. Once they finished Mr. Jenkins' dock, the day was over, and Glen decided a visit to his wife's brother-in-law might help him get steered in the right direction.

"Be right there!" came the reply from the back of the store.

Glen heard some shuffling in the back, and a few minutes

later, Selby came out followed by a short redhead with a very satisfied smile on her face. Suddenly, Glen felt as if he should have called first. "Um, sorry, I should have…" He didn't know what to say. Selby had left the door unlocked, the OPEN sign still facing out. How was Glen supposed to know Selby was getting busy in the back?

"Glen, good to see you. I don't think you've met Tracey yet. Tracey, this is Cherish's husband, Glen." Selby introduced the two as if nothing had just happened in the back room or that Glen hadn't busted them acting out a scene from an erotic novel. Well, he didn't actually catch them *in* the act, but it sure sounded like they were screwing around in the back room. They're heavy breathing and flushed faces kind of gave it all away as well.

Tracey didn't seem to care either, the smile proving she wasn't the least bit embarrassed. She stretched her arm out, hand ready to shake. "Hey, Selby's told me you're going through some things. I hope it's getting better."

"I hope so, too," Glen said. He turned to Selby. "That's actually why I'm here. I was hoping the offer to talk still stood."

"Of course." Selby said as he turned to the small redhead. "Talk to you later?"

"Dinner at your place," Tracey said. "Faith's already told me what to pick up on the way out of the shop." She pushed up on her tiptoes as Selby leaned down, the two exchanging a quick kiss before Tracey said goodbye to Glen and left.

Glen just stared, not sure what to say or do. He knew Faith and Selby opened their marriage up to include swinging, but this seemed more intimate. This wasn't a goodbye after a quickie. This was more like a couple saying goodbye until later. There was definitely something more, something deeper, going on between the two.

Selby walked around the glass display counter at the front of his store and took a seat on the desk chair. "So, what brings you by?"

Glen glanced at him and then at the front door and then back at him. "She is..?" He pointed at the door.

Selby chuckled. "She is a mess, but if you're asking what's going on with us, Tracey's become part of our family. It's complicated, but then again, it's not." He waved off that part of the conversation. "But you didn't come here to ask about my home life. I'm guessing you're here to ask about yours."

Glen sighed as he leaned on the counter, his hands clasped in front of him. He pushed thoughts of Selby's love life out of his mind as he brought his own to the forefront. "Cher and I have talked, and we want to make a go of things, or at least, I want to make a go of it. She says she misses the way things were in her life before we got married and started a family." He shrugged. "I guess partying is more of a priority to her than I thought."

Selby nodded, swaying in his desk chair a little as he stared at Glen. "Cherish was pretty wild in those days. I remember it quite vividly. I also remember how Faith used to envy her and hate her for it all at the same time, because Valerie never got onto Cherish the way she got onto Faith about anything. So, Cherish just wants to go out and have a good time now and then?"

Glen shook his head. "I think she wants it all. The crazy nights, the wild sex, the spontaneity of it all. Brent, my partner at work, seems to think she's going through some sort of postnatal depression. I think she just misses sleeping around. My sister seems to think swinging is the answer to our woes."

Selby cocked his head, one eyebrow raised. "And how do you feel about that? What if that is exactly what she misses? You willing to travel down that road? It's not for everyone, so I get it if you're not."

Glen took a deep breath as he shook his head. "I don't know. I mean, I knew Cher wasn't an angel by any stretch of the word when we met. I watched her through high school and even after, saw the different guys she dated, and knew about her reputation. I guess I just thought all that faded when Jordie came into the world. Seems she had only postponed it. How do you do it? Watch Faith go off with another man?"

"I find it hot as hell, that's how. We don't see sex the same as love. One is an emotional commitment. The other is just fun. She comes home to me every night, no matter who she spreads her legs for during the day. Besides, we do a lot of talking and reconnecting. The relationship comes first, but we have fun exploring the different things that turns each of us on."

Glen pointed outside with a tilt of his head. "And Tracey?"

Selby's gaze flitted to the front window as a smile crossed his face. "Trace is a little bit of all of it wrapped into one tiny firecracker of a package." He turned back to Glen. "You knew all about Cherish before you married her, so I'm guessing her past doesn't bother you. What if it became her present? What if you gave her the freedom to go out and play with others while adhering to certain ground rules you both can adhere to in order to feel safe? Maybe you both find someone new to explore with."

Glen shook his head. "I don't want anyone else. I'm happy with just her." Of course, he wasn't entirely sure that was true, either. Oh, he knew he didn't want anyone else in his heart. The bedroom, however, well, he couldn't deny the thought intrigued him just a little.

"But what if she wants someone else?" Selby pressed, pushing home the crux of the matter.

Glen said nothing at first as he mulled it over in his head. Selby just sat there, watching and waiting, giving Glen time to process the questions. *She said she missed the adventures, so that's what I have to give her. Adventures. But will I be able to handle it? What if I give her everything she wants, and it's still not enough?* "I guess I need to ask her." They did a lot of talking, but not enough of figuring out what they needed to do to fix Cherish and their marriage.

"Honest, open communication," Selby said, staring at him. "Granted, you deal with some trust issues right now, but if you can get past that, make sure she knows you discuss anything and everything. You have to both be open and honest if it's going to work."

Glen tapped the countertop as he pushed himself away from it. "Thanks. Not sure which path we'll take, but at least I have an idea of what I might be facing."

"We're always here if you need anything. Just make sure you both want it before you do it. If you're only doing this for her, or hoping this saves your marriage, it won't work. Swinging isn't the answer to saving a marriage. It's merely something fun to enhance it." He shrugged. "You still may have a lot to work through, and nothing will change overnight."

"Thanks," Glen said, nodding. "I'm sure we do, but I have to start somewhere, and this is the only idea of where to start."

"Just be careful," Selby warned him, his expression serious. "Learn from the past and avoid the mistakes of youth."

Glen nodded again.

They said their goodbyes, and Glen stepped back out into the afternoon sun. He wasn't sure whether he received the answers he wanted, but at least he possessed more information with which to make a decision. Between everything Brent and Selby said, it boiled down to whether or not Glen could give Cher the sexual adventures she seemed to crave. Yet, how would that change their relationship? He knew he could give her some of what they had before, returning to that friskiness that kept them touching each other no matter where they were. It was the additional partners he would need to come to grips with if that was what she wanted. How would he feel if she slept with another man? One he knew about this time?

He needed to talk to her and find out.

~ ~ ~ ~ ~

"How have you been?" Nick stood there, his hands in his pockets, as the afternoon breeze tugged at his wavy dark hair. "I think I heard you and Glen tied the knot and started a family, right? I bet that's wild. I never even pictured the two of you together. He always seemed so tame compared to you."

She stared, her mouth opening and closing, but no words coming out. Finally, she shook the panic that gripped her and forced words out of her mouth. "Yeah, we did. Little Jordie." *Your son.* "He's great. Almost five now. Glen's a great father."

"Man, I just never thought of you as a mom. That's wild." He kept smiling, shaking his head.

"Yeah, pretty wild. How about you? Any family?" Was she really just standing there talking to her ex? He had left her standing there while he walked off with some dirty-blond. Left her high and dry after she took care of him for a year.

He laughed as he shook his head, his bangs swishing across his forehead. "Me? No way. Too many hot chicks out there who need some Nick loving for me to pick just one. You two still doing the party scene or is it purely home life and diapers now?" He shook his head. "Definitely not something I could do."

She stared at him. *Was he always this...stupid?* "Jordie's four, almost five, actually. He's been out of diapers for years. And life is pretty good. No complaints." *None that I'm telling you, anyway.* Nick was thirty years old; he should have grown up by now, she thought. Then, standing there, staring at him, the man she had lived with for a year before Glen came along, it all came back to her, his laziness, his self-indulgent behavior, his proneness to wander. She gave him everything, even went out to work, so he could stay home and sit on the couch playing his damn video games. All he ever did was party. *I wonder how much he did behind my back before I caught him.*

Nick shrugged. "Well, I haven't been around too many kids. I have no idea when they stop all that needing a diaper stuff. I'm glad things are going well, though. Glen was a pretty cool guy if I remember right. Always struck me as a family man. You needed someone like that."

She nodded, just wanting to get away from the mistake in front of her. "Yeah, I did. Well, I need to scoot. I left Jordie with a babysitter, and it's time I was getting back. Good luck with…whatever it is you do." She waved and started to walk off, but he called out and halted her a moment.

He slipped a business card into her hand before she could refuse. "Don't be a stranger. It'd be nice to talk and catch up some more. If you two ever need a party, I know where they're all at. Give me a yell."

"Gee, thanks." She held the card up so he could see she had it, smiling. "I'll be sure to hold on to this. Take care." She turned and walked off, tossing his business card into the center console of her car as she shut the door, putting it quickly out of her mind. *No way in hell am I calling him.* Nick Pepper wasn't a good time; he was a nightmare.

Fourteen

"Hello! Where's everyone at?" Aubrey's voice followed the sound of the front door opening. "Yoo hoo!"

Cherish walked out of the kitchen, drying her hands on an old towel, her brows scrunched up over the bridge of her nose. "What are you doing here?"

"Babysitting," Glen said as he walked through the doorway to the hallway.

He stopped by earlier saying he needed some more clothes. Cherish hadn't realized he intended on changing right then and there, however, which only added to her confusion when she glanced at him. He was dressed up...well, dressed up for him. He wore a pair of dark jeans and a gray pullover. He even wore socks with his sneakers. "Why is she babysitting?"

"Hey, Aubrey!" Jordie ran out of the hallway and hugged their neighbor. "Daddy said you were going to hang out with me tonight. Can we have pizza?"

Aubrey gave Cherish a smile as she walked past her to tousle Jordie's hair. Cherish watched for a moment and then turned her attention back to Glen. She popped an eyebrow at him, one hand on her hip, as she waited for him to explain.

He gave her a sheepish smile, suddenly appearing nervous. He gave her a weak shrug. "I thought we could go out and get a drink. You said you wanted to get out more, right? Have an adventure? It is Friday night after all. Isn't this the night people go out?"

She stared at him, debating within herself whether going out with him was actually a good idea or not. *But I promised to try. I need to try. For Jordie.* She nodded, biting her bottom lip as she walked past him. "I'll go get dressed."

His smile brightened, and the sight warmed her. She had missed his smile, she realized. She stopped in the hallway for a moment, smiling at the fact she had indeed missed his smile. That was a far cry from where her mind had been over the past few months while she chased Edwin, but it was also a revelation that maybe, just maybe, she wasn't too far gone in her marriage. At least, she hoped that's what it meant. She never really fell out of love with Glen, she just became disillusioned with her life. She neared thirty and already she missed her twenties. She didn't want to grow old, didn't want to sit around every night glued to game shows on television. Life should be more than laundry and going to work and cleaning house and picking up after a child. There had to be more. She wanted more.

When she walked into the bedroom, she stopped and stared, her mouth slightly open, at the bed. Glen had laid out her clothes for the evening. He never did that before, taken an interest in what she wore. Walking over to where the pile of clothes was, she picked each piece up one at a time, glancing over his choice for the evening. She couldn't help but smile at his daring. She forgot she even owned the outfit. He had started with a matching bra and thong, purple in color with lace on the bra, and then followed it up with a short blue jean skirt that hit just above mid-thigh and a violet spaghetti-string top that would show off her cleavage. *Not that there's much there to show off*, she thought as she held it out in front of her. She hadn't worn the outfit since she gave birth to Jordie, always thinking it wasn't conservative enough for a mother.

She glanced back at the doorway as if she could see Glen in the other room, smiling at his attempt. *Maybe he meant what he said the other night.* There was only one way to find out how far he could take her or how much he could take. Dropping the top on the bed, she started to strip out of her clothes.

Thirty minutes later, they said goodbye to Jordie and Aubrey and headed out.

"So, what did you have in mind for tonight?" Cherish asked as Glen weaved through the Melbourne streets. Pulling at her shirt lightly, she said, "And interesting choice of outfits, by the way. It's been a while since I've worn this. I forgot I even had it."

Glen shot her a smile as he gave her a one-shoulder shrug. "You said you missed the way things were, so I thought maybe to recapture that we'd start over, go back to the time you were missing. That outfit reminds me of those times, when you were dancing, flirting, having fun."

"And wherever we're going..?" She drawled out the words, hoping to get more clues to their destination.

His grin grew. "Crocket's, to see if perhaps the place would stir some of those old feelings in you."

"In me? What about you? Have you not missed any of that? The pool nights, the parties, late nights without caring about getting home to send the babysitter home?"

"Of course I do. I think everyone misses those days at some point. But," he shrugged again, "I wouldn't trade it for what I have now." She was about to say something, some snarky comment about how he wasn't forgiving her and moving on, but he stopped her with an upheld hand. "I'm not accusing you of doing that or making some smartass rebuke. I'm merely answering your question." He reached over and took her hand, giving it a light squeeze. "I made the decision to give all that up and become a husband and a father. I wanted the home life, watching Jordie grow up, seeing you succeed at your career and being a mother. I like bedtime stories and Saturdays at the park. I like waking up to you next to me and going to bed with you at night. I even like going grocery shopping with you. Weird, huh?"

She squeezed his hand. "Anyone who enjoys grocery shopping is weird." She took a deep breath and then said, "No, it's not weird. Makes me look like a bitch, though." She started to pull her hand away, but he held it firm. She gave him a weak smile before turning her gaze back to where they headed. Perhaps this was a bad idea. "It's okay. I feel like a bitch."

"I never called you a bitch." He gave her a smirk. "Well, not out loud anyway." He squeezed her hand again as he gave her a soft chuckle before continuing. "You were just missing some things, going through some…blahs. They proved stronger than you could handle. It happens. It's not a free pass, but… Well, I get it. It was a sudden change and, as you said, not the way you saw your life going." He pulled into the North Wickham Plaza and found a parking spot under a small maple tree toward the back of the parking lot. He shifted the car into park and turned to face her. "We settled into a normal routine. You never were one for normal. Or routines. I knew that even in high school. So, we need to recapture that *unnatural* adventure you seem to be missing without tossing everything else out. You ready?"

She took a deep breath, wondering how weird this would get. "I'm ready."

Crocket's was a small bar in the corner of North Wickham Plaza, owned, or at least it used to be owned, by Jerry Keller who had an obsession with anything *Miami Vice*, thus the name Crocket's. Scenes from the TV series as well as signed autographs from the actors hung on the walls while Phil Collins and Don Henley filled the speakers most of the time. It was definitely a step back into the 80s, but it was friendly and fun and the bar tabs were always low.

Glen opened the glass door for her, and it was like stepping back into time. Nothing had changed, not even the owner.

"Oh my god, Glen! Cherish!" Jerry stood by one of the three pool tables, a beer in his hand as he watched them step through the doorway. "Now, aren't you two a sight for sore eyes. Where the hell have you been the past few years? I just assumed you moved away."

Cherish just smiled at the tall man, the overhead lights glinting off his bald head, and only brightening his smile. "Raising a son," she said, just as the man threw his arms around her and squeezed her to him tightly.

~ ~ ~ ~ ~

Glen couldn't help but smile as Jerry embraced Cherish. It was like stepping back in time, back into a period when his life was uncertain and Cherish's was chaotic. Yet, she was happy back then, and he wanted her happy again. He wasn't sure what that would take, but he knew he would do whatever was necessary. So far, the only way he knew to get that started was to take her back to where it all began, where *they* began.

Once Jerry finished hugging Cherish, he turned and grabbed Glen, hugging him as well. "Man, the place has not been the same without you two around here. How's that baby boy?"

"He's doing great," Cherish said, a smile on her face that Glen had not seen in days. "About to turn five."

"Wow," Jerry said, shaking his head. "Has it really been that long? You two have stayed away way too long. First round's on me." He turned to the waitress walking by, a small girl with breasts that oozed out of her skimpy top, and blond hair she had pulled back into a tight ponytail. "Erin, how about two beers, Florida Lagers, for the prodigal customers here?"

She offered Cherish and Glen a smile. "Sure thing. Be right back."

Jerry led them over to a small bistro table near the pool tables, gesturing for them to sit down. "So, tell me what two of my favorite customers have been doing these past few years, besides not visiting my bar."

While they told Jerry all about their past five years as new parents, Erin brought their beers, including a whiskey neat for Jerry. Cherish pulled a cigarette out of her purse and lit it, taking a long pull as Glen told a story about Jordie learning how to walk. He glanced at his wife, her hand on the stem of her beer bottle as the cigarette rested between her index and middle finger, the only bad habit he could not get her to give up. Cherish took over telling the stories as Glen thought about everything she gave up in order to be a mother. He had made her make those changes, slowing her down, cutting out the nights out. It was what married people did; it was what parents did. It was how you behaved when you tried to be responsible. Yet, he had pushed her too far, and that led to her affair with Edwin. While she had made the decision to sleep with her boss, Glen knew he played a part in it as well. Now, he had to make it right and get his wife back.

A bartender called out to Jerry, waving him over. "Ah well, business calls." He patted the table as he stood. "Well, it's good to have you back. Make sure you don't stay away too long this time. Family needs to visit more often." He gave Cherish a wink and then headed back to the bar.

Glen watched as Cherish took a long pull of her beer. "How about a game of pool?" he asked before she could take another hit of her cigarette. "Could make it fun. A little…wager?" He made sure he said that last part with enough of a suggestive tone that he saw her eyes widen and a slight blush color her cheeks. "If I remember correctly, we had quite a bit of fun doing that."

She grinned, took another swig of her beer before smashing out her cigarette. "Sounds like fun, especially if you lose." She waggled her eyebrows at him and slid out of her chair. "If memory serves, you sucked at pool. You sure you want to do this?"

"Oh yeah. Whether I win or lose, I win. I get to have sex with you. One just requires I do the work, instead of laying back and relaxing."

"Maybe we should change the bet."

"No way. Just like old times," he said as he grabbed a pool stick from the rack, twisting it in his hands to make sure he liked the feel. He turned and smiled at her. "I'll even let you break."

"Oh, feeling cocky, are you?" she asked with a slight giggle.

He shrugged. "Like I said, I win either way."

He won. Cherish even convinced him to go two out of three games, and he won all three, taunting her the entire time. Cherish downed several more beers, but Glen slowed down his drinking as the night progressed, knowing one of them had to drive home. This was, after all, supposed to be her night out, a test, of sorts, to see where they went from here. Glen did his best to shrug his conservative tendencies as well. As she would bend over the pool table, lining up her shot, he would step behind her, running his hand up her leg, stopping just below the hem of her skirt. It was probably those distractions that helped him win the night, but it was also fun watching her blush a little at the public displays. Once, when he positioned his hand at the base of her skirt, he leaned over and whispered, "This is mine," in her ear. Her blush deepened.

After the third game, Cherish admitted she was tired and ready to go home. Glen didn't comment about the party girl wanting to call it a night at only eleven o'clock, but rather simply paid their tab and wished Jerry a goodnight. Besides, the night wasn't over yet, Glen thought, as he escorted her out to the car. Cherish still had to pay off her bet, and he was determined to take her all the way back to the time period she seemed to miss.

After opening her door for her and allowing her to get settled, he slipped behind the driver's wheel and turned to face her. "You ready?"

She gave him a puzzled look. "For?"

"To pay off your bet. You did lose remember. Three times, but I'll count all as one."

Her eyes widened. "Glen... Here? Now?"

He unbuttoned his pants, reaching in and pulling his cock out for her. Then, leaning back in his seat, his right arm on the back of her seat, he said, "You lost, remember? Isn't this how you paid me last time you lost? Right here?" He glanced around the parking lot. "I think it was even in this spot if memory serves me right."

"You can't be serious. The parking lot is still busy. What if someone sees us?" She had that deer caught in the headlights look, and Glen had to force himself not to laugh.

"Tinted windows. Besides, what if they do? It's all part of the adventure, isn't it? Isn't that what you want? An adventure like before? Well," he pointed with his chin at his cock, "here it is. Now, pay up." He grinned as he gave her a wink and waited to see what she would do.

She just stared at him, mouth parted and eyes wide in disbelief. She then glanced around the parking lot, looking to see if anyone was close by before turning her gaze to his semi-hard cock. He could hear her breathing grow heavier as he saw the struggle on her face. He was about to tuck his cock back into his pants and call her bluff when she smiled at him, reaching her hand out to stroke his growing member. She raised her eyebrows a little and then, without saying a word, leaned her head down in his lap as she stretched over the center console and ran her tongue across the head of his cock, bringing a groan from his lips as well as a panicked glance around the parking lot. Then, he felt her take him all the way into her mouth, her head bobbing up and down as her tongue swirled around the shaft of his cock. He forgot where they were, the panic replaced by passion as he slid his hand along her back and surrendered himself to her mouth.

Cherish massaged his balls with one hand while she gripped the base of his cock with the other, still sucking his manhood with an eagerness he hadn't seen in…well, forever. It didn't take long. The place. The car. The chance of getting caught. Even the fact of why she even did it. It all combined and brought him to an orgasm faster than he wanted. His whole body tensed, and before he was ready, Cherish swallowed his passion, her hand still working his shaft as the noises of her mouth on his cock filled the car.

When his cock finished twitching, she ran her tongue once more over the tip before raising her head, her tongue gliding over her lips as she grinned at him. "Can't have it said I don't pay off my bets."

He just grinned back at her, his breathing still heavy. "No. No, we can't." Okay, maybe this was the perfect idea after all.

Fifteen

Cherish stretched, sleep fighting her to ignore the morning and just stay in bed. As she reached out, her arm touched… She jerked to the side of the bed, eyes wide, wondering… Glen slept soundly beside her, his arm tucked under his head, his dark hair mussed up from a hard night's sleep. Confusion added to the fog of her waking brain as she stared at him. *Why...? How..?* She closed her eyes as last night's adventures broke through the cloudiness of her mind, the games of pool, the beers, the… the blowjob she gave Glen in his car. She felt the blush warm her cheeks and neck, waking her up even more. She couldn't believe she went through with it. Hell, she couldn't believe he even suggested it.

She leaned back down on the bed, propped up by her elbow, hand on her head as she smiled over at him. His breathing was calm, restful. It had always given her a peaceful feeling at night whenever she would wake up and hear him beside her, like everything was right in her world. She felt safe. Well, up until the past few months, when she felt like everything closed in on her.

Glen shifted beside her, his eyes opening a little. He smiled as he noticed her watching him. "Morning," he said, his voice groggy, still full of sleep.

"Good morning. I didn't realize our date would lead to a sleepover." She arched an eyebrow at him, her lips turned up into a smirk.

"What can I say? I tried to go home, but you begged me to stay. Something about two more games to pay off." He grinned at her as he said it, reaching a hand out to pull her close. "I think you've paid your debt in full. Of course, if you don't remember..."

She swatted at his arm playfully, allowing her to be pulled to him. "You. Are. Bad."

"That's not what you moaned last night." He grinned as he pulled her in tighter, kissing her shoulder and neck.

"Stop." She rolled her eyes, but inwardly she blushed at what she remembered as some of the hottest sex she had in a long time, right in her own bedroom. She had begged him. Pleaded with him actually. Their little fun in the car only stirred her wetness, bringing a longing to her sex she did not want to go to bed without fulfilling. And it had been worth it. Oh, god, it had been so worth it. "You know this will confuse Jordie when he sees you here this morning."

Glen nodded, never lifting his head from the pillow. "We'll figure it out. We can bribe him with pancakes at Betsy's. He's always a sucker for that place."

Cherish giggled as she matched Glen's position, their faces inches apart. "That's because Tina spoils him like he's one of her own grandkids."

"Well, I've been going there for years, so she probably sees him as one of her own. I don't care. She usually gives him extra food for free and me right along with him. It's a win-win."

"Just what he needs," she said with a laugh. Then she took a deep breath. "Glen, what will we tell him? If he sees you here this morning, and then you leave again tonight, it'll confuse the hell out of him. I don't want that."

"You want me to sneak out the window?" Glen asked her, grinning. "I've snuck into your place before, so I could just do it backward."

She swatted at him again. "You know damn well what I mean, brat."

Lying there, snuggled under the sheets like they were, Cherish thought it almost felt like it did in the beginning of their relationship, when things were normal and life was good. When she hadn't screwed up her family. Yet, she knew as soon as she left that bed, the longings would return, and she'd be right back where she was with her emotions. "I wish we could stay here, like this, forever," she said, her voice soft, hopeful.

He smiled at her. "It would be nice," Glen whispered back. She felt him place a hand on her waist and squeeze. "We got this. Relax."

"Mommy!" A little knock came at the door just before she heard it opening. "I'm hungry." Little feet padded into the bedroom, and then, "Daddy!" Jordie ran, all pretense of being quiet gone, and leaped up on the bed. "You're here! Mommy, Daddy's here."

"Oh? Where?" Cherish pretended to search the room. "I don't see anyone."

Jordie just giggled as he straddled Glen's waist, attempting to pull the covers off his father, who did his best to keep the covers right where they were. "He's right here. Beside you." Glen laughed along with his little boy, doing his best to stay decent.

Cherish, tucking the covers around her naked body, just feigned shock when Jordie pointed to his father. "How did he get there?"

Jordie laid down on his father's side. "I like him here."

A hollowness filled Cherish's chest at her son's words, knowing that when Glen went back to his parents' house, Jordie's little heart would hurt all over again. They would have to be more careful going forward. Jordie didn't need any more heartache. "Well, Daddy was thinking about taking us to Betsy's for breakfast. I think it's a bad idea. What do you think?"

"Yay!" Jordie bounced on Glen's side. "Betsy's is great. Let's go. Let's go." He pulled harder on the covers, making Glen grip them tighter while laughing.

Cherish reached out and tried to get Jordie to calm down. "Slow down. You need to get out of those pajamas and into clothes. You go get dressed, and Mommy and Daddy will do the same."

"Yes!" Jordie yelled as he slid off Glen's side and onto the floor. "Hurry up and get ready." He still yelled at them to hurry up as he ran out of the room.

Glen just laughed as he rolled over onto his back. Cherish smiled. She missed these types of mornings. The best part, she didn't even have a hangover. "You know he'll be right back in here, right?" she asked. "If we don't get out of this bed, it could get embarrassing. I mean, I know I'm not wearing clothes..." She raised an eyebrow as she glanced down to where she knew his cock rested against his thigh.

"But it feels so good right here." He smiled over at her, his dark eyes sparkling.

"It does," she admitted with a sigh. Why had she screwed this up?

Then she watched his face turn serious and knew their peaceful morning was about to be ruined. "We still need to talk. Figure things out." His frown shifted into a smile. "But it feels good to be in my own bed again."

She nodded. "Well, get out of it and get your pants on before that little monster comes in expecting us to be up already."

He sighed dramatically. "Oh well, reality soon swallows the morning peacefulness." He turned to her and grinned. "Race you to the shower." He jerked the covers off himself and dumped them onto her as he sprinted from the bed and headed to the master bath.

She could only laugh as she became twisted in the blanket and sheets, only making it worse as she tried to extricate herself. "You cheat!"

He turned at the doorway and grinned at her. "I don't cheat," he said, and then by the look on his face he realized how what he just said sounded. She watched his shoulders rise and fall as he took a deep breath, forcing the smile back on his face. "But I do win." And then he shut the door.

~ ~ ~ ~ ~

Tina did as expected, and Jordie had extra bananas on his pancakes as well as double chocolate milk. She said nothing about not having seen Glen in a while or Cherish eating there by herself earlier in the week. Glen and Cherish sat across from each other with Jordie kneeling in the booth beside his mother as he leaned on the table. Tina gave him some coloring pages and crayons to keep him occupied, which left Cherish and Glen time to sit and chitchat without the little boy interrupting them too much. Not that they could talk about too much with tiny ears right there, but they still managed to appear like a normal couple and not one in the throes of upheaval. They appeared normal, and for the first time in a couple of weeks, Glen felt normal, a feeling he didn't want to lose anytime soon. He even reached out, taking Cherish's hand in his as they waited for their food, and Cherish didn't pull away, but rather smiled, holding his hand in return.

Glen made a fuss over the food and service and earned extra bacon for his kindness. He kept the karma going by adding extra to the tip before they walked out, waving at Tina as they left, part of the heaviness he felt over the past few days lifted.

While he had to admit he enjoyed himself this morning, everything feeling back to normal, he still knew they had to talk, get things out in the air, so they could move forward. Yet, it wasn't a conversation for little ears. Nor did Glen have the stomach for it right then, not on Tina's biscuits and gravy.

"Do we have to go home now?" Jordie asked when they reached the car.

"Why? What would you like to do?" Glen asked, opening the door so Jordie could scoot inside. Glen saw Cherish's look and wasn't sure whether it was a panicked expression or a welcome possibility.

Jordie shrugged his little shoulders as Glen strapped him into place. "I don't know. Anywhere but home."

Glen felt the tug on his heart as he stared down into his son's eyes. He could understand the feeling Jordie struggled with right now. If they went home, then he knew his father wasn't going to stay. Yet, as much as Glen didn't want to see his son hurting, he also knew it wasn't time to go home yet. Cherish hadn't come out and said she was ready to make a go of it again, and he wouldn't move out again in front of his son. He also knew that if he returned home right now, all they would do was fall back into bad habits, the same habits that led to her affair in the first place. No. When he returned home, they had to do it right and at the right time. This wasn't it.

"Okay, Slugger," he said, tousling Jordie's hair. "We'll find something else to do." He shut the door and started walking around to his side of the car, Cherish having already slid into the passenger seat. Once he settled behind the wheel, pulling his seatbelt into place, he asked Cherish, "Did you have any plans for today?"

"Nope. I'm free. What did you have in mind?" She glanced over at him, a soft smile on her lips as she waited for his decision. She allowed him to decide for them, which meant she wasn't ready to go home either. That was a plus in his favor.

He shrugged. "Well, we haven't been to the zoo in a while."

"Yay!" Jordie screamed from his seat in the back. "Let's do it. Let's go to the zoo. I want to see the otters."

Glen glanced over his shoulder at his son wiggling in his car seat. Glen couldn't stop the smile that pushed up his cheeks at the pure joy that was in that little boy and the way it made his own heart swell. Glancing over at Cherish, Glen asked, "What do you think?"

She glanced back at Jordie, a smile also on her face, before nodding. "Well, it seems someone is already excited about it. I guess we really shouldn't disappoint him."

Glen started the car. "To the zoo then." It was really the safest place for them to continue their day. Animals had a way of taking the awkwardness away from a situation and giving you something to smile about, and right now, they could all use something to make them smile.

Jordie sat in the back seat, two of his toy cars racing back and forth in the air, as Glen and Cherish rode in silence, lost in their own thoughts of the twists of life. Glen wasn't sure where they would wind up, although he knew where he would love to see them go. He took Selby and Brent's words to heart and decided somehow to give Cherish the adventures she wanted. It had been a while since either of them did anything except the homebody family life, but he was willing to step out and see where life took them. He had put his feelings on hold before, when he watched Cherish chase after others who would only hurt her and knew he could do it again if he must. It was obvious it was a must. He could do it. He *would* do it. Nothing would make him lose his family.

Traffic was light for a Saturday, it seemed, and they pulled into a parking spot at the zoo before they knew it. Cherish helped Jordie out of his seat and, after locking the car, the three of them headed to the ticket booth for over-priced tickets to see the animals. Jordie walked between them, holding each of their hands and swinging their arms. The little boy's excitement was contagious, and he had both of his parents smiling. The mood was like the afternoon, bright and sunny. Perfect.

As they walked, Jordie still between them, they would pause at each cage and exhibit, watching the monkeys swing from branches, the tigers prowl the ground of their cage, and the alligators drift in the water under a bridge they had to cross to reach the rhinoceros exhibit. Cherish started out a little tense, her arms over her chest when Jordie wasn't clutching to her, dragging her from one animal to the next, her back rigid. However, by the time they reached the glass case of the otters, she had loosened up, laughing at Jordie's enthusiasm and Glen's corny jokes. As they stood there, Jordie pressing his face against the glass as the otters dove into the water, diving and doing flips below the surface, Cherish even scooted close enough to Glen that he could slip an arm around her waist and pull her closer. She didn't resist, but instead, turned to face him, a soft smile on her lips as she bounced her gaze between his eyes and his lips.

Glen pressed her tighter to him as he leaned down, kissing her lips softly, savoring the feeling of her mouth against his. He breathed her in through his nose as they kissed, realizing how much he missed her against him. Last night was not enough to satisfy his hunger for her, for his wife.

When they broke the kiss, Cherish stared into his eyes, her own holding a tear as she pressed her lips together. Glen could only smile at her, his heart fluttering in his chest. "I love you," he whispered, his voice almost catching in his throat.

She nodded, sucking in a breath. "I love you, too."

"I want this," he told her, unable to stop himself. "I want us. Whatever it takes. I want you in my life."

She reached out, clutching his arm. "I want us as well." She took a deep breath. "I'm sorry, Glen. I'm so, so truly sorry. I never meant to hurt you. I never meant to go down this path, to cheat on you. I was selfish. I know that. I want to…"

He placed a finger on her lips, silencing her. "We'll figure it out," he assured her. "Together. We'll figure it out together." He squeezed her to him, running a hand down her back to the top of her ass. Out of the corner of his eye, he saw Jordie watching him, bouncing up and down slightly with a little smile on his lips.

Sixteen

It had been two hours, and Cherish already wanted to scream. The woman she replaced, Kim Rosa, was a disorganized mess. None of the files had any semblance of order, and some even had information in it that belonged in someone else's file. The records were a shambles, the record books riddled with coffee rings, and the computer files a spider web of chaos. How the woman managed to function or answer any of Bernie's questions was beyond Cherish's capacity for comprehension. She blew out a burst of frustrated breath, her bangs flipping up at the gesture. It would be a nightmare just getting everything organized.

"You settling in okay?" Bernie leaned in her doorway. Her office was next to his, and she usually saw him as he went in and out, getting a cup of coffee, following his wife around, or talking to the installers out in the warehouse. Whether he left his office or returned, he always stuck his head in her doorway to check on her and see how she was doing. So far, in the mere two hours she had been there, he checked on her twelve times. It was more than distracting; it was annoying as hell.

"I am," she said with a forced smile. "Just sorting through Kim's files and notes, trying to get a handle on things."

He nodded, his lips pressed into a thin line, his glasses propped up on his forehead. "I wish she gave me time to get the two of you together, so she could show you the ropes. She pretty much had a unique way of doing things."

Cherish glanced down at the files in her hands as she nodded her head. "That would be an understatement." Turning her gaze back to Bernie, she worried she might have said something wrong and quickly apologized. "Sorry. I'm sure for her it worked great. I'll figure it all out, and soon, I'll have things the way I like to work. No worries." She forced a smile on her face, hoping he would take the hint and leave. "Everyone has a different way of doing things."

"Well, if you ever need to get a hold of her, her number's in her file. Give her a ring; I'm sure she wouldn't mind."

"Thanks, but I'm sure I'll figure it out." There was no way she would reach out to Kim. If the woman couldn't physically organize her file, then her verbal instructions would be all over the place. Cherish was better off figuring it out herself.

"Okay, just keep it in mind. I'll let you get back to it." He tapped the doorframe as he pushed off and turned toward his office, leaving her in peace.

She stared at the empty doorway for a moment, dreading the task of returning to the files. She missed Rutherford Construction already.

She sighed, lowering her gaze back to the inevitable. Harbor

City Carpet didn't have many employees, so that part was easy. The financial books, however, were a mess, as were the current jobs. Cherish dumped the files in one stack on her desk when she first began and started sorting them into three piles: employees, customers, and other. The employee files went quick, and Cherish made a list of things missing in the files, so she could get the employees to fill in the missing pieces. She skipped the *others* pile for now, putting that nightmare aside for when she had more coffee—or alcohol. Instead, she focused on the customers, putting Harbor City Carpet's jobs in some semblance of working order by where they appeared on the schedule.

Thumbing through the folders, she jotted down notes, made her own order of importance on things, and sipped cup after cup of coffee. And then she opened one folder and stopped, staring at the name as if someone just slapped her. It was all right there in front of her, all his personal information, like phone numbers, address, email, even where he worked and the best time to reach him by phone. Everything she needed to know to get in touch with Nick Pepper.

Their brief encounter flashed in her mind as well as his arrogance and churlish behavior. It was obvious from those few moments at the coffee shop that the boy—the man—hadn't changed all that much. She rushed off when she ran into him at the coffee shop, but now, staring at his name, at all his personal information, she didn't remember the bad times, the times he failed her. All she could remember was that… He was Jordie's father. She lived with him for a year, thought he was her world, only to have him leave her in a bar as he ran off with another bimbo who fell for his charm just as she had. But what if… What if he had stayed and not ran off? What if he stepped up as a father and a husband? What if he knew Jordie was his? Would he have stayed and finally grown up? Or would he have still run off with the next pretty skirt? Nothing about Nick shouted a growth in him, so why did she even wonder about him? Glen had been the one to protect her, the one to grow up and become a father and husband. Then again, Glen was always the grownup, even in high school, even amid their wild days. He kept one foot in both worlds, allowing her to go off the rails as much as she wanted without allowing her to go too far. He kept her safe in her dangerous living.

She couldn't keep the smile that seeped over her face, pulling the corners of her mouth up as the shaggy-haired image of Glen Lansky entered her mind as he sat in Mr. Walker's science class, three rows behind her, staring at her when he didn't think she saw him. Yet, she always saw him. She knew he was there, on the fringes of her friends. She just hadn't cared.

"He's doing it again," Amy whispered, giggling as she leaned over toward Cherish.

"Stay in your row, Miss Wynn," Mr. Walker said, looking at her from over the top of his glasses.

Amy leaned back in her seat, still giggling, as she raised her eyebrows at Cherish, pointing at Glen with her eyes suggestively.

Cherish just rolled her eyes as she turned her attention to the front of the room. She didn't need to turn around to see Glen staring at her. Mr. Walker had a glass cabinet in the front corner of the room beside the chalkboard; she could see Glen's reflection in the glass. He was too busy staring at her to notice she stared back at him.

Once class was over, Amy and she headed to the cafeteria for lunch. Glen left as well, but soon disappeared in the crowded corridors of Eau Gallie High. He wouldn't be out of sight long, however, Cherish knew. They shared the same lunch period, and Glen always found a spot with his friends near whatever table Cherish and her friends ate. It wasn't like he would sit there, gawking at her, but he always seemed to be around, just within range of whatever she did.

"How long before stalker boy shows up, do you think?" Amy asked in a teasing tone as they took their seats, sliding their trays onto the table in front of them. "I would say he'll be here in...one....two...thre... Oh, there he is, and I didn't even get to finish saying three." *She giggled again as she opened her chocolate milk.*

Cherish just shook her head. "Why doesn't he just come up and say hello? I mean, Captain Obvious over there has made it quite apparent he's interested in me, so what's his deal?"

"Well, girl, you are kinda intimidating."

"I am not. That's just rude."

"Hey, Cherish," Timothy Daiss said as he slid into one of the empty chairs around the table. "Going to the party this weekend at Nick's house?"

"Of course," Cherish said, as Amy echoed her reply. "Bonfire, music, alcohol, why wouldn't I go?" She glanced over at Glen as he sat laughing with his buddies, probably over something geeky, like Star Wars or some silly comic book hero. She wondered if he would be at the party. Nick and Glen were friends, of sorts, and Cherish saw Glen at some of the parties she attended, so she knew he ventured on the wild side once in a while. Yet, it seemed so unlike the version of him she witnessed at school, all studious, all honors class. It was like he was afraid to live. She glanced over at him and, at the same time, he glanced at her. And smiled. An enigma. Glen Lansky was an enigma.

He was still an enigma. Even after she cheated on him, he was still willing to stay and be her husband and Jordie's father. He would do whatever was necessary to keep their family together.

So why was she sitting there still staring at Nick's phone number? She took a deep breath. The difference between Nick and Glen, even between Glen and Edwin, was assertiveness. Glen was a lot like Cherish's mother, allowing Cherish to get away with everything with no real repercussions. Nick took what he wanted, even if it hurt others, simply because he wanted it. In the beginning, Cherish found that intoxicating, the whole alpha, bad boy image. That is, she did until he turned on her and wanted someone else, leaving her in the dust, crying her eyes out. Then, the dominance wasn't so attractive.

It had been the same with Edwin. His rough, playboy image drew her in, until he dumped her just like Nick did for another woman, this time, her sister. She closed her eyes as she took in a deep breath. She liked the bad boys, the men who took what they wanted, but she needed the safety and security of Glen. How sick was she? Glen had strength; he proved that when he stood up to her mother and took the blame for knocking Cherish up. He proved it by sticking around and being a father. He proved it by sticking by Cherish's side even when she stepped out on him, just like Edwin and Nick did to her. Glen probably had more strength than any of them. So, why was she attracted to the others?

God, I'm a warped bitch.

~ ~ ~ ~ ~

"Finally went for it, huh?" Brent shut the driver's door to their work truck and moved to the bed of the truck and his tools. "I know what I said before and all, but are you sure this is what you really want? After what she did?" He shook his head as he pulled his tool bucket from the back of the truck. "Glen, what makes you think she won't do it again when she gets bored?"

"I don't know that she won't." Glen grabbed his own tool bucket from the back of the truck and followed Brent to the back of a house along the Indian River. "I can only hope she doesn't. Hell, I'm hoping we can figure out what made her do it in the first place and fix it. Jordie deserves a whole family."

"But you deserve a wife who won't cheat on you. What happens if she does it again?"

"Then we deal with it." The truth was, Glen didn't have an answer for his friend. He could only hope Cherish and he could work through their issues and salvage their marriage. He could only hope she wanted it as much as he did and was willing to work for it. He could only hope... He sighed. He could only hope; it was all he had, and he clung to it as if it was his only lifeline.

He took a deep breath, giving himself a mental shake. He would not allow himself to continue down this line of thought. He needed to be positive, focus on the rebuilding of their trust and not the what-ifs. It could happen again. Cherish had been honest about missing her wild side. She was tired of being cooped up in the house all the time playing the doleful wife and mother. The question was whether they could figure out a way to make that change in their lives she seemed to need. That was what Glen needed to discover before he lost her altogether. How did he make her feel alive again?

"When did I become such a fuddy duddy?" he asked as they reached the dock in the back. The breeze caressed the Indian River, bringing the tang of the river to their nostrils as it tugged at their hair. Glen set his bucket of tools on the wooden decking and then stood straight, hands on his hips as he stared out at the water. "Everything became so routine. I get up, go to work, go home, eat dinner, play with Jordie, and then go to bed, only to wake up and repeat it all over again. No wonder our life bores Cherish. It really is boring."

"You're kidding, right?" Glen heard the clang of tools behind him as Brent tossed hammers and chisels onto the dock. "You've been a fuddy duddy ever since I met you," Brent said, laughing. Then he stopped and stared at Glen, his hands on his hips. "Your entire life has been about taking care of Cherish and Jordie. You told me you quit college, so you could take care of them, provide for them once you found out she was pregnant. Your life isn't boring. It's just...life."

Glen turned around and stared at his friend a moment. "Life doesn't have to be boring."

"You're right. It doesn't. But it also can't be excitement and adventure all the time, either. At some point, you have to pay the bills, go grocery shopping, bring home the bacon. None of that's exciting." He dropped to the deck and slid over the side and into the water. "That's what living is all about, my friend." He leaned on the side of the deck and stared up at Glen. "The trick is not to get lost in the mundane while you're living that life."

Glen squatted down, his right arm resting on his knee as he glanced down at his friend. "That's just it. Cherish and I *did* get lost in the mundane. That's the problem. What I need is a way to get out of the rut."

"Then you need to know what she wants. What is it that she thinks she's missing? Dancing? Vacations? Drunken orgies?" He said the last with a wink and a grin. "Maybe she just needs some adventure in her life."

Glen shook his head as a chuckle slipped past his lips. "Why is it your adventures always involve sex?"

Brent laughed out loud, slapping the wooden deck as he did and pushing off into the water. "Because that, my dear friend, is what adventure is all about. Now, get me my tape measure, and we'll see what's going on down here."

Glen shook his head some more as he stood and moved to the buckets of tools. Leave it to Brent to always be thinking from between his legs. Yet, as Glen grabbed the tape measure and headed back to Brent, he couldn't help but wonder if perhaps his friend was right. Their adventure at Crocket's seemed to have put a spark in Cherish. The heavy flirting, the public displays of affection to the point of him groping her ass at the pool table, even Cherish sucking him off in the parking lot ignited something in her that changed her mood for the better. He had to admit; it worked wonders for him as well.

Was that it, then? Was it that Cherish just needed to sow some more of her wild oats? Be a little reckless once in a while? He sat on the edge of the deck and watched as Brent measured the planks that would need repairing. Cherish partied pretty hard when Glen first met her. She was out every night, drinking herself silly and... And dating Nick Pepper. Nick and Glen never saw things the same way. Nick lived for the moment, for any experience he could discover without worrying about the consequences. And there were always consequences. While Cherish was with Nick, she experimented with different drugs, uninhibited sex, and risky behavior that would make a stripper blush. Now, she was a simple wife and mother, working a normal, boring job while taking care of her family. Glen sighed. No wonder she was bored. That she lasted six years before venturing out beyond the bonds of her vows surprised him.

Yet, that brought up another struggle for Glen. Was Cherish's affair based strictly on her boredom with her life or did she truly not love him anymore? The answer to that was the difference between being able to save their marriage or not. They could find a way to keep her from being bored; he couldn't make her fall back in love with him, however. Of course, she told him she loved him at the zoo Saturday, but was that because of the moment, or did she truly mean it?

Glen sighed as he glanced out at a sailboat skirting across the Indian River. What made her fall in love with him in the first place? He wasn't like any of the other men she dated before him. He was just the one to step up when everyone else stepped away.

And that hadn't been enough for Cherish, not in the long run. He somehow needed to become like the others. He needed to be more like Nick and Edwin, become them so Cherish felt what she needed to feel. He needed to be less caring and sweet, and more bad boy. He chuckled to himself as he shook his head. *Glen Lansky—bad boy. Oh, god, there's no way.*

Seventeen

She shouldn't have done it, she knew. It was an impulse. A knee-jerk reaction to the changes that became her life recently, a lifeline to a past she longed for even though it had changed the course of her life. However, Cherish couldn't stop herself from writing Nick's cell phone number down, not sure if she threw his business card away or not. She knew she wouldn't use it, so she wasn't sure why she even bothered. She tried to justify it, at first. What if Jordie grew seriously ill, and she needed Nick's medical history? It was a precaution against future possibilities. She would never need to use it. All right, she doubted she would use it. No. She *would not* use it. She picked up the piece of paper, ready to rip it into shreds and throw it away. However, she stopped herself just before she tore the paper, the numbers staring at her, reminding her of the experiences, the adventures, the carefree nature Nick Pepper brought with him to her life. They had fun. They didn't care about society's rules or taboos. If they felt like doing something, they just did it, to hell with the consequences.

Lowering her arms to the table, she kept staring at the numbers, remembering the laughter, the drunken parties, the car sex they would have. God, Nick was as rough and dominating with the way he had sex as he lived his life. He took it, not caring if he hurt her in the process. Her pussy ached for days afterward, as did other parts of her body. He was rough with every part of her. So was Edwin. Spanking her. Bondage. Nipple clamps. God, they did it all to her. Glen couldn't even talk dirty to her while they fucked. She missed the roughness.

Cherish folded the piece of paper in half, about to stuff it in her purse, when out of the corner of her eye, she saw Jordie's picture on her desk, his hands wrapped around a small ball as he sat there, legs folded in front of him in his dark shorts and beige sweater, smiling as if he had no cares in the world. A twisting wrapped itself around her heart as shame once again filled her. Jordie was one of those consequences, the only one she really didn't regret. As she stared at Jordie's photo, the other memories flashed through her mind: the fights over Nick's laziness, the way he cheated on her, the way her parents bailed them out time and time again. Cherish sighed as she reached out and touched Jordie's picture. She remembered the way Nick made her feel when he abandoned her in a bar while he vanished with some blond he just met. Or, at least, Cherish assumed he just met the other woman. The one time she confronted him, he made it all seem like his infidelity was her fault when all she wanted was to love him and for him to love her.

Just like I did with Glen.

Taking a deep breath, she ripped the piece of paper in half, ripped it in half again, and then threw it away. While she wasn't sure what she wanted, or even with whom she wanted it, she knew Nick Pepper was a step backward, a step she didn't need to take.

So, what do I want? God, she wished she knew.

She stared back down at the stack of files on her desk. She knew what she didn't want, though. She didn't want to deal with someone else's mess. Falling back into her chair, she shook her head, trying to figure out how this place functioned under someone so disorganized.

"They've stuck you in a hole."

The sound of her mother's voice snapped Cherish out of her self-pity as she turned her gaze to where Valerie Driscoll stood in the doorway of the tiny office. "Mom, what are you doing here?"

Her mother glanced around the office, her lips twisted into a grimace and her nose turned up in her snobbery. "I wanted to see what you chose as your new career." Valerie turned her attention back to Cherish, her distaste for the office clear in her expression. "Are you sure this is the new beginning you wanted? Wouldn't it be better to return to Rutherford and get your old job back?"

"Faith has my old job, remember? Besides, I'm not sure Glen would be happy with me returning there after everything."

"You think he'd rather you be in this hole?"

"Mother!" Cherish rushed out of her chair, walking over to her mother, and closing the door behind her. "Mr. Overton walks back and forth like a million times a day. He'll hear you. Are you trying to get me fired on my first day?"

"Getting fired might be a step in the right direction," Valerie said, her voice full of contempt for the place.

Cherish stopped halfway back to her desk, turned, and just stared at her mother. This was not like the woman. Valerie Driscoll doted on Cherish constantly, giving in to her antics and never blaming her for anything. For Valerie to stand there and criticize Cherish's workplace was totally out of character. "What's going on with you?"

Valerie straightened her shoulders, reaching one hand up to grab her purse strap. "I don't like you here and don't see any reason for you to have to start over. You should never have left your job at Rutherford."

Cherish pointed to a chair in front of her desk as she walked around to take her own seat. She understood her mother's feelings, because Cherish also wished she hadn't left Rutherford, but at the time, she had no choice. Glen wanted her away from Edwin. Too bad she hadn't known they would transfer the ass to a new office in a different state. She would never have quit if she knew that nugget of information ahead of time. "I had to quit. Glen wanted me to quit."

"Well, you should talk to him and tell him you want your old job back," Valerie said as she sat in the leather-upholstered chair, her legs pressed together, purse perched in her lap as she gripped the top of it.

Tilting her head to the side, Cherish stared at her mother through narrowed eyes. "What's this all about? You've never cared about my jobs before."

Valerie took a deep breath. "Your father has a new career, or at least, that's what he's calling it. You've got a new job. Faith is doing all kinds of different things I cannot even attempt to figure out. It's all just too much. Too much change at one time. I don't like it. I like things I can predict, that I can count on. I can't count on anything anymore." She kept her gaze downcast, refusing to look at her daughter as she made her confession, shifting uncomfortably in her seat, her hands gripping the strap to her purse with white knuckles.

Cherish just stared at her mother, unsure what to say or even to think. Valerie Driscoll was never one to admit any failing of her own, much preferring to criticize others who were not like her or held her own beliefs. Her agitation now, however, at everything going on in her life had her body jittery to the point Cherish could actually see her mother's shoulders trembling. Valerie Driscoll was afraid and witnessing her so unnerved made Cherish nervous. The woman before her had always been so stalwart in her rudeness and condescension. Her behavior now was…unsettling.

Cherish leaned forward in her chair, her hands clasped in front of her as she stared at her mother. "Mom, Dad will do great with this new venture, and him being at home will give you more time together to enjoy each other. Faith is living her own life, and doing it quite well actually, as much as I hate to admit it. I made my own mistakes, and I'm paying for them, but I'll be fine. I promise. You can get through this. We need to make these changes to keep the people in our lives happy. We can't begrudge them that." Each word she said sounded like a contradiction to all her previous behavior, twisting in her stomach at the realization of what a bitch she had been to the people she claimed to love. Why on earth had Glen stayed with her so long? She had been a miserable person to everyone in her life, and only now could she see how far she fell into her own self-pity and misery. Was there even a chance she could make it right to the ones she loved?

"So it seems," her mother said stiffly. She shifted in her seat again, her back straight as she faced Cherish. "We still need to discuss Jordie's birthday."

Cherish bit down on a groan. She had yet to tell her mother Glen wanted Jordie's birthday party at their house and not Valerie's, a conversation Cherish refused to have with her mother at work, knowing how her mother would react. "Mom, I have a lot to do today. Why don't we do lunch one day this week, and we'll discuss it?"

"What's wrong with today?" her mother asked with a slight shrug of her shoulders. "We're running out of time."

"Because it's my first day here, and I might not even take a lunch. There's a lot to do and much I'm still figuring out."

Her mother gave another snort of derision. "Another reason you should still be at Rutherford."

Cherish took a deep breath, ignoring her mother's comment. "We'll go to lunch Wednesday. Will that work?"

"It's cutting it close, but if that's what we have to do, then I guess we have little choice."

"It is," Cherish assured her mother. "It'll be fine. I promise." *Oh, it's so not going to be fine.*

~ ~ ~ ~ ~

Glen tossed his tool bucket into the back of Brent's truck, his shoulders sore from the day's labor. He could feel the sting of the sun where he stayed exposed to it too long without protection. He should know better, but sometimes, he just became too engrossed in the project at hand and tuned out everything else. Of course, he compounded the situation by how distracted he was with his marriage. He sighed as he leaned on the truck's side. He was tired of being distracted.

"So, what's the plan for tonight?" Brent asked as he dumped his own bucket into the back of the truck. "Feel like grabbing a beer or something?"

"What? Need a wingman?" Glen said with a chuckle. "Actually, I'm thinking of swinging by the house and seeing Jordie. I also need to see what we're doing for his birthday coming up. You know, that parenting-type stuff."

Brent acted like he shuddered, shaking his shoulders. "Please, don't say those words out loud."

Glen laughed harder. "Sooner or later, some poor woman will

regret getting her hooks into you, and you'll be doing the whole daddy thing as well. Can't wait to see it."

"Why would you curse me like that? That's just mean." Brent tapped the top of the truck as he turned toward the driver's door. "Rude."

Glen just laughed as he moved to get into the truck. "I'm just saying; it'll be a funny day when it happens."

"I swear, I think you hate me. I thought we were friends." Brent slid behind the wheel and started the truck, shifting it into gear as soon as the engine roared to life. "Just plain mean, that's what you are."

Glen fastened his seatbelt, still chuckling. "People have called me worse."

"You probably deserved it." Brent pulled out onto the street and headed back toward the office.

Glen just shook his head as he glanced out the passenger window at the houses they passed. "I probably did."

Once they were back at the office, Glen made quick his escape before he had to endure Brent's begging him to hit a bar with him. Glen's focus was his family, not helping his partner get laid.

The traffic was light as he weaved through Melbourne's streets, the late-afternoon sun still blaring above him, making the air sticky and thick. He held the steering wheel with a gentle hand as he rested his other arm on the door, his thoughts lazy for once. The day at the zoo was nice. They almost felt like a family once more with Cherish relaxed and not snapping at every little thing he said. Jordie bounced all over the place, wanting to see every animal he could and then never wanting to leave the otter exhibit as the animals dove into the water and did flips, seemingly for the little tyke's personal enjoyment. Glen would give anything to return to those types of days, instead of the constant walking on eggshells he seemed to endure now.

To Be Cherished

He pulled into his drive, Cherish's car already there. He braced for whatever he would endure once he walked through the door, determined to keep his temper in check no matter what she threw at him. With a deep breath, he opened his door, stepping into the heat once again.

On the other side of the front door, he could hear Jordie giggling, a good sign as to what Glen might find inside. He turned the doorknob and stepped into his house, the air-conditioning a welcome relief to the Florida heat. Jordie saw him as soon as he entered, screaming out, "Daddy!" as he raced across the living room and leaped into Glen's arms, bringing a sharp pain to Glen's shoulders again. "I didn't know you were coming home today."

Glen set his son back on the floor, tousling his dark hair once the little boy's feet hit the floor. He rubbed at the pain in his shoulders as he straightened back up, stretching his back as he did to try and loosen his muscles. "Well, I wanted to see you and hear all about your mom's first day of work." Looking up, he noticed Cherish coming out of the kitchen, wiping her hands with a towel. "So, how was it?"

Cherish noticed the pain on Glen's face, apparently, by the way her right eyebrow popped up. "What happened to you?"

Glen shrugged. "Just a long day and a lot of lifting and hammering. I think I pulled some muscles in my shoulders."

She shook her head, tossing the towel onto the kitchen counter through the doorway. Turning, she reached out and took his hand, leading him to the couch. "Come on, let me try rubbing your soreness out."

Glen allowed her to pull him to the couch, confusion at Cherish's behavior pinching his nose. Out of everything he expected from her, this was not it.

"Sit down and let's get this shirt off," Cherish said. "Jordie, why don't you get your father some water." She sat beside Glen as she helped him pull the shirt up over his head, plopping it down on the couch beside them. Turning him so that his back was toward her, she placed her hands, cool to the touch, on his shoulders and started to massage, working the muscles in gentle motions, making him wince a bit. "How is that?"

He gave a short laugh. "Hurts but feels good at the same time. Thanks."

"No problem. I know you work hard," she said, and he could hear the genuineness in her voice.

"So, how was your first day on the job?" He winced again as she squeezed a little harder. Jordie brought Glen a bottle of water and then hung on his legs, grinning that his father was home. Glen glanced back down at his son, grinning as well. It felt good to be there, with them, in his home. He missed it.

"It sucked," Cherish replied, and he could hear the laughter in her voice. "That place is so disorganized, I spent most of my day just trying to find things, so I would know what was missing, and there is a lot missing. Then my mom stopped by to criticize the place."

He listened as she told him about her mother's breakdown in her office and how Valerie felt lost among the changes in her family's lives. Cherish continued talking as she worked the muscles on his shoulders and back, her fingers digging into him, her warm breath on his neck, stirring more thoughts into his mind than he needed right then. When he felt her hands start to loosen their grip, he turned to face her, and stared. She was right there, her face just inches from his as he stared into her eyes, both of their lips parted slightly. Cherish stopped talking, her gaze fixed to his.

Glen started to say something, but nothing came out. Everything seemed...frozen.

He leaned forward. She leaned toward him. He touched her

arm, holding her still, and then their lips pressed against each other, gently at first, and then with more hunger. Jordie plopped down on the floor, screaming, "More kissing!" as Glen and Cherish embraced, their arms sliding up each other's backs, their kiss becoming even more passionate. Nothing else entered Glen's mind except the woman in his arms right then and how much he missed her kisses.

Eighteen

Cherish tucked the covers up under Jordie's arms, leaning down to kiss his forehead as she did. "You get a good night's sleep, young man," she said, smiling down at him. "No getting out of bed and wandering around. You've had your water—both glasses. You're all set."

He nodded, his dark hair sliding up and down on his pillow. "Is Daddy still here?" he asked. "Is he staying here tonight?"

The question tugged at her heart, and she fought to keep the tears at bay. "Your mommy and daddy still have a lot to work out, but none of it is about you. Always know both of us love you very much, no matter what happens between us."

He nodded, his dark hair swishing against the pillow. "Does that mean he won't be here in the morning when I wake up?"

His face was so innocent, even though the question was so

earnest. She leaned down, kissing his forehead. "We'll have to see what the morning brings, all right? For now, you just focus on getting a good night's sleep."

"Yes, ma'am," Jordie said with a sigh, still lost in what was happening to his family.

Cherish finished tucking Jordie into bed, pausing at the door before she slid out of his room and turned back to him. "I love you, Squirt," she said, the pain of hurting her son clutching at her heart.

"I love you, too," Jordie simply said as he shifted in his bed to get comfortable.

Cherish nodded and then joined Glen back in the living room.

Glen glanced up at her, and by his expression, she could tell her melancholy still showed on her face. "Jordie asked if you would be here in the morning," she said with a weak shrug. "I hate seeing him hurting so much because of me." She sat down on the couch, her arms over her chest as she held herself together.

Glen reached out, running his fingers through her strawberry-blond hair. "He doesn't think you're hurting him. He just knows something has changed and can't figure out what that something is. He's a tough kid. He'll be all right." She then felt Glen's fingers bending into a fist as he gripped her hair, pulling her toward him. He gazed into her eyes, and the hunger she saw there brought an instant heat between her legs. "If you want, I can stay the night, so he sees me in the morning. Might calm him down some." He gripped her hair tighter, bringing a moan from her lips she didn't mean to make. "Do you want me to spend the night, Cherish?"

She swallowed the tightness in her throat, her thoughts going to the kiss just before she tucked Jordie into bed. She wasn't sure whether or not she wanted Glen to spend the night, but she damn well knew what she wanted right then. She wanted him. "Kiss me," she whispered.

Glen grinned at her. "Not until you answer my question. Do you want me to spend the night?"

She groaned inwardly. "What I want is..."

"Oh, I know what you want," he smirked, cutting her off, and just the way he said it sent burning embers to her pussy. "But I want an answer to my question first. Do you want me to spend the night? Or are you wanting me to just pound you, get you off, and walk back out that door?"

Glen had never been one to talk so crudely. This side of him, however, while shocking, made her pussy drip, her breathing a deep, huskiness in her voice. "I want you," she said. "Glen, I need you. Please." She forgot her concern for Jordie for the moment, replaced by her need to feel Glen inside of her.

He grinned, his lips twisted into a hungry, wolfish smirk as he leaned down and kissed her, shoving his tongue inside her mouth, claiming her for the moment. She groaned as she fell into his kiss, sliding a hand to his chest and downward until she felt his hardness in his jeans, which made her moan even louder.

When he broke the kiss, Glen pulled her away from him by her hair, his grin turning into a leer. "Stand up," he commanded, causing another shiver to race through her body, settling between her legs.

Cherish did as he asked—ordered, really—not sure what he had in mind. Still, she stood in front of him, nervous but tremendously aroused as well, her arms at her sides as she waited for whatever he wanted.

Glen just sat there a moment, raking her with his gaze, a hungry look in his eyes. When he looked back into her eyes, he merely said, "Take off your shirt."

Biting her lower lip, Cherish reached down to the hem of her top, pulling it up and over her head. She tossed it to the ground, dropping her arms to her sides once more.

Glen cocked his head to the side, grinning. "Now, the bra."

This was torture. She had been naked in front of him a million times, and yet, right then, with the way he commanded her to take one piece off at a time, she never felt more vulnerable or exposed. It was like a stranger forced to strip in front of him. She reached behind her, unclasped her bra, and then slid the straps over her shoulders and down her arms, exposing her breasts to him. She tossed the bra down with the shirt.

Glen sat there, soaking in her bare breasts, his grin revealing how pleased he was with what he saw. "I've always loved your tits," he said with an uplift of his brows. "I love how hard and long your nipples get."

She felt the blush warm her cheeks. "Thank you," she whispered, struggling with words right then. "I've always loved the way you've played with them."

He motioned to her pants with a lift of his chin. "Take them off but turn around first. Keep your gaze forward."

She swallowed again, her nerves tight as she did as he ordered, turning so that her back was to him. Where his assertiveness came from suddenly, she had no clue, but each order he gave her sent heat to pool between her legs. With a deep breath, she focused on the window in front of her as she unbuttoned her pants, pulling the zipper down slowly. Reaching to the sides of her waistband, she eased the jeans down over her hips and ass, bending to give him a perfect view of her backside as she slid the pants down her legs and off. With her right foot, she kicked them over to join the shirt and bra as she stood straight once more, remaining facing away from him. She left her panties on since he had not told her to take those off yet, choosing to obey the letter of his words.

Her body trembled at the exposure, vulnerable to the man behind her, unable to see his face, his expression as to whether or not he approved of what he saw. She knew she allowed herself to get a little overweight the past couple of years, still holding Jordie's baby fat, but Glen had never commented on her appearance unless it was to tell her how sexy she looked. However, didn't all men say that right before they got their rocks off?

"God, you have such a gorgeous ass," he said, making her blush with his words. "You really need to show it off more often."

She felt her chest puff out with his praise as well as the notion of him showing her body off. He never suggested such a thing before, and the idea sent more heat between her legs.

"Now, the panties. Take them off." His voice broke no argument. He expected Cherish to obey him, and his tone sounded as if there would be consequences if she didn't.

With as much seduction as she could put into it, she slid her panties down her legs and off, pushing her ass back to him for his pleasure. Once she piled them with the rest of her clothes, she stood back up, waiting. She could feel the wetness between her legs and knew it coated the top of her inner thighs. His orders drove her wild, making her hungry for his cock to the point she fought not to turn around and jump him right then.

"Without turning around, I want you to back up until I tell you to stop," he ordered her.

Taking a deep breath, Cherish eased backward, one step at a time until he seemed satisfied. Her nipples were tight buds of need, her pussy dripping with hungry want. God, this felt so...hot.

"Bend over, but no peeking behind you," Glen commanded. As she did, her hands going to her knees for support, he added, "Spread your legs. I want to see that pussy of yours."

She obeyed instantly, spreading her legs for whatever he desired. She could hear his heavy breathing behind her and then felt his hands on the sides of her ass. "So beautiful," he said as he glided his hands over her round cheeks, massaging in places, spreading them to open her up even more. She sucked in a breath, waiting, her body trembling with the electrical charges of his touch. Then, she felt a finger slide down her ass crack to the entrance of her sex, gliding between her folds as Glen explored her wetness.

When he spoke, she could hear the grin in his voice. "Seems someone likes to be on display." She then felt him plunge two fingers into her soaked pussy until she felt his knuckles hit her folds. She groaned loudly, unable to stop herself. "Is that true, Cherish? Do you like yourself displayed like this?"

"Yes," she moaned, pushing back on his fingers. "God, yes."

"Maybe we should do more of this in different places, then." He didn't wait for an answer as he began to finger-fuck her pussy, driving his fingers in and out of her wetness. The sounds of her moans filled the living room as he fingered her, driving her crazy with need.

"Please," she begged. "Please, Glen. Fuck me. I need it. Please!"

He just chuckled as he ignored her pleas, continuing his assault on her pussy with his fingers.

Cherish could only stand there, groaning as he toyed with her.

~ ~ ~ ~ ~

Glen watched her body tremble as he fingered her. He held onto her ass with his other hand, squeezing her delicious cheek as he pummeled into her pussy. "I think we'll do that," he taunted. "Take you out, put you on display for others." She said she missed the excitement, the rush of the adventures she experienced before they were married and started a family. Brent suggested giving her what she craved. Even Glen's sister had suggested the same thing. Perhaps they were right.

Glen yanked his fingers out of Cherish's pussy, her moans at the sudden emptiness between her legs filling the room once more.

"Turn around and kneel," he ordered, and she obeyed without hesitation, kneeling in front of him, her face a mask of hungry want. God, he missed that look. Maybe she wasn't the only one who missed the old days.

As soon as Cherish knelt in front of him, Glen stood and stripped out of his clothes. Once he was naked, he sat back down, motioning for her to move closer. "You know what to do."

She licked her lips, and the sight of her tongue gliding across her lips made his cock twitch. He watched as she slid closer, taking his throbbing cock in her hand as she leaned forward, running her tongue over the tip of his cock, lapping up the pool of pre-cum that rested at the top of his shaft. Now, he moaned at the sensation of her mouth on him. She ran her tongue around the head of his cock, licking her way around his thick shaft before she devoured him. He slid a hand to the top of her head, gripping her hair in a fist as he guided her back and forth on his manhood, leaning back, and enjoying her mouth on him.

He glanced down, watching as her head bobbed up and down on him, her tongue twirling around his hardness as she knelt between his legs. He had to admit, he missed feeling her mouth on him. However, he could only take so much, afraid to shoot his load too soon, and pulled her head from his cock.

She glanced up at him, her tongue once more gliding over her lips, now coated from where she sucked him off.

Glen just grinned, ready to push her buttons a little bit more. "See that window over there," he asked, pointing to a large window on the side of the house that looked out at Aubrey's house. "I want you to go stand there, facing out."

Cherish's eyes went wide. "Glen, Aubrey could see us. I

can't..."

"But you will," he said with a grin. "You like to be displayed, remember? Besides, Aubrey has seen you naked before. Now, go."

He watched Cherish swallow another protest as she stood to her feet, her gaze never leaving his. She turned, slowly making her way over to the window, her firm ass swaying slightly as she walked, her back straight even though he could see her trembling slightly. Once she reached the window, she just stood there, staring out at the yard between their house and Aubrey's next door.

He chuckled slightly at her nervousness. Cherish was never the timid one, so seeing her vulnerable was different and intoxicating. "Place your hands on each side of the window and spread your legs," he ordered as he pushed himself off the couch.

Cherish obeyed, slowly placing a shaking hand on each side of the window, exposing herself completely as she spread her legs. Her pussy glistened with her wetness, and Glen felt his cock twitch as he slid up behind her, running a hand up her back and into her hair. He gripped a fistful of her strawberry-blond locks, pulling her head backward so her ear was right beside his lips. "So, do you still want my cock?" he asked, one hand sliding down her back, over her ass toward her sex.

"God, yes, please," she begged, pushing back against his hand. "Please, Glen. I need to feel you."

He grinned as he ran his tongue over the edge of her ear. "And do you need it bad enough to let me fuck you right here in front of this window?"

Her body shivered in his hands, and at first, he thought she would refuse, but desire won out over the risk of being caught. Or perhaps that risk spurred it on. "Yes," she groaned. "God, yes. Fuck me. Please. Right here. Right now. Take it."

He shoved two fingers into her wetness. "If I take you, you're mine. No other cock goes into this pussy unless I say so. Are you ready to be mine again? Only mine." He desperately wanted to bury his cock balls deep inside of her, but he wasn't ready to just be a one-night-stand to relieve her horniness or his. "Are you ready for that?"

She started fucking herself with his fingers, sliding her pussy back and forth, her wetness coating him, dripping down her legs. "Yes," she moaned. "I'm yours, Glen. Only yours. No one else unless you say so. Please. Take your pussy. Please!"

The lights in Aubrey's windows came on, but Glen wasn't sure if Cherish noticed or not as she hung her head down, her hair covering her face. He yanked his fingers out of her passion, gripped her hips, and thrust deep inside of her, his fingers digging into her flesh.

Cherish cried out, her hands clutching the frame of the window as she shoved her ass back to meet his thrusts. He pounded into her, driving his hardness back and forth as he gripped her hip with one hand. With his other hand, he reached around, pinching at her swollen nipple, making her jump slightly as she groaned even louder. He continued to hold her, pummeling her pussy with his cock, taking back his wife.

"Oh, god, Glen!" she cried out, and he felt her body tightening in his grip. "Glen, I'm going to.... Oh, god!" she shoved back on him, her head dropping to her chest as her body shook in his grip. "Coming!"

Glen held her tightly against him as her whole body trembled with her orgasm. He felt his cock twitch, felt it explode into her, filling her with his cum as he just pressed into her. As he finished filling her, he noticed the curtains in Aubrey's house move slightly, and then, he saw the other woman peek out, her brows raised, eyes wide. He just winked at her as he slid a hand up into

Cherish's hair, pulling her head back. "Open your eyes," he ordered.

"Oh, my god," she exclaimed, trying desperately to move out of the window. "I told you she could see us."

Glen held her there a moment, and then pulled her up, spinning her to face him. "And I told you I don't care. Consider yourself displayed." He grinned at her as he leaned down and kissed her, running his tongue over her teeth and lips, tasting her. "You're mine, remember? I'll show you off to whoever I want."

He watched her swallow as she just nodded, not even bothering to argue with him. *So her adventures were all about control. Interesting.* Glen gripped her hair, pulling her face closer to him. "I'm spending the night." No question, no room for argument. A statement. A fact.

"Yes, sir," Cherish whispered. "Whatever you want."

He grinned down at her. "Sir. I like that. You may have to use that more often."

Cherish smiled, her heart beating hard enough in her chest that he felt it against his. "Yes, sir."

Nineteen

Jordie jumped on Glen first thing in the morning, shouting his enthusiasm that his father was there. That wake-up call made Glen's day.

Cherish rolled over, smiling at both of them as she snuggled into her pillow. "Do we really have to go to work?" she asked. "Let's just call out. Take a day to ourselves."

Glen chuckled as he leaned over, kissing her nose. "You just started yesterday," he reminded her. "Do you really think you should call out already?"

"You are no fun," Cherish sighed as she rolled back over onto her back, arms out at her sides as she stared up at the ceiling.

He snuggled closer to her. "That's not what you said last night."

Her eyes popped open, wide, as she glanced down at Jordie.

"Glen!" She took a deep breath, shaking her head. "Jordie, go get dressed for preschool while I fix you some breakfast."

Glen chuckled as he moved to slide out of bed, watching Jordie race off to his room. When he stood, Glen turned back to Cherish, his expression turning serious. "Last night was fun—hot, really—but we still need to talk."

Cherish slid out of bed, her naked body making Glen's cock rethink the whole calling out of work thing. She nodded. "I know, but I meant what I said last night. I'm all yours if you'll still have me. I'll make this work any way you want it to."

He nodded. "Good to know," he said. There were still things he needed to know, things he needed to get off his chest, but right then was not the time. "We'll plan some time to just talk it all out."

She agreed and then went to get breakfast started after slipping on her robe.

Glen watched her leave before hopping in the shower, feeling happier than he had in a few weeks even if still unsure where they went from there. Last night showed him a glimpse into what Cherish seemed to want, and as he thought back to her relationship with Nick, she had been more the submissive type to his needs than the boss. Glen wondered if it had been the same with Edwin. He wished there was a way for him to find out without talking to either Cherish or Edwin about it. Then he thought of Faith. The whole reason Edwin broke it off with Cherish was because of her sister. If anyone would have some of the answers to Glen's questions, it would be her.

As soon as breakfast was over, he kissed Cherish goodbye, hugged Jordie, and sent them on their way. He slid into his vehicle, pulling out his phone as he turned on the ignition.

"You picking up donuts?" Brent asked as he answered the phone. "I want the Boston Creme. Two of them."

Glen shook his head, chuckling. "Sorry, dude, no donuts today, but I may owe you lunch. I'm calling to say you're on your own for the morning. I need to run a quick errand. Can you cover for me?"

"Of course," Brent assured him. "Finally hook up with Rachel? Need a little morning time to recover?"

"Who's Rachel? Never mind. No, I need to see someone really quick. You sure you can cover for me?" He didn't need Brent knowing he went to his sister-in-law for sex advice. He'd never hear the end of it.

"Yeah, yeah, I got ya covered," Brent said. "But, of course, Rachel's going to be hurt you forgot all about her. See ya when I see ya." And then, he hung up.

Glen just chuckled as he tossed his phone into his seat beside him as he pulled out of his driveway and headed for Rutherford Construction, the one place he never thought he would step foot in again. Neal Rutherford wanted the Brevard offices of his construction company close to the interstate since their jobs were located in so many locations. The interstate provided quick access in all directions. Of course, some of the bigger projects where the construction company would require a presence for a longer period of time had a trailer on site for immediate needs. However, Neal housed the bulk of the operation on this small four acres of land practically in the middle of nowhere. It housed two buildings, the offices, and a warehouse, and had plenty of room for trucks and materials, which Neal had been adamant they keep stocked so they didn't waste time waiting for trucks to deliver or lost on backlogged items. Eau Gallie Boulevard dead ended into the St. Johns River and air boats and lovers in parked cars always crowded the road. However, the area was otherwise pretty quiet, something else Neal required. The surrounding area contained an animal shelter, a giant flea market, a Park & Ride parking lot that always seemed to be empty, and the new Fire and Rescue Training School. Otherwise, it was a gravel road surrounded by palm fronds and alligators, isolated, but not alone.

Glen pulled into the parking lot in front of the main building, staring up at the front door. This is where Cherish cheated on him. For how long it went on, he didn't know, but it happened. Glen wondered how many inside the building knew what Cherish did. He took a deep breath. He really didn't want to go inside, but what choice did he have if he wanted to talk to Faith? *God, this sucks.*

He shoved his car door open and made his way out into the early morning sun, already rethinking his idea. Once inside, he walked up to the receptionist desk, a small woman with tits that were far from natural glanced up at him, her smile syrupy and very fake. "May I help you?"

"Yes. Is Faith here today? I'm her brother-in-law and hoped to have a word with her." He leaned on the wall in front of the woman's desk as he gazed down at her, doing his best not to glance at her breasts, but he found it hard since they were like right there, really right there.

She smiled up at him. "Faith actually just got here," the blond said as she reached out and picked up her phone. "Hold on and let me buzz her." She hit a couple of buttons and placed the phone up to her ear. If the woman figured out who he was, she was great at covering it up and not gawking at him like the pathetic husband. "Hey, Faith, you have a visitor." She paused, listening. "I'll tell him, thanks." She hung up the phone as she glanced up at Glen, her artificial smile firmly in place. "She'll be right out."

Glen nodded as he tapped the wall in front of the receptionist and then backed up a few paces. "Thank you."

A few moments later, Faith came out of the back, smiling even though she had a puzzled look on her face. "Well, this is a surprise. What brings you by? Everyone all right?"

"Yeah, everyone's fine," he assured her. "I was just hoping you could answer a couple of questions for me." He glanced over at the receptionist, who didn't seem to pay much attention to them, but Glen knew she probably was. Turning back to Faith, he added. "Somewhere a little more private, perhaps?"

Faith glanced over at the woman behind the desk and nodded. Gesturing to the front door, Faith led Glen back outside and off to the side. Turning, she asked, "So, what's up? What's with all the secrecy?"

Glen took a deep breath, bracing himself for the awkwardness of the conversation he felt he needed to have. "I need to ask you a question, and it's a rather personal one. I'll understand if you don't want to tell me, but I'm hoping it can help me with my relationship with Cherish."

Faith slid her arms over her chest as she nodded. "Sounds mysterious," she said with a giggle. Then, she tilted her head to the side, slowly shaking it. "However, I'm not sure what I can say that would help your relationship with my sister."

Well, here it goes. "I need to know about both of your relationships with Edwin," he said. "I need to know about the attraction, what drew both of you to him." He shrugged. "I'm hoping it'll help me give Cherish what she feels she's missing."

He watched as Faith raised her eyebrows, ducking her gaze to the ground as she gave a slow shake of her head. "You weren't kidding about it being personal." She shook her head again. "Edwin has a little bit of a controlling nature. He takes charge in the bedroom. That's actually what I enjoyed, what I looked for at the time, someone who would make me do things, not giving me a choice, someone I trusted with that power where I could lose myself. He knew what I wanted, and by doing what he told me to do, I could experience those thrills without feeling guilty." She shrugged. "I surrendered to him. At least, I did until he fucked me over. Trust broken."

Glen nodded, knowing the broken trust Faith referred to included Cherish. "What if he told you to do something you didn't want to do?"

"Well, that's where that trust comes in," Faith replied. "He wouldn't tell me to do something he knew I was against or didn't want to do. Still, that leaves a lot of room for unknowns, so in that case, we had a safeword in place. If he pushed a boundary, or I felt uncomfortable, I used my safeword, and everything came to a quick halt."

"Did you ever use it?" Glen asked. "Your safeword, that is."

"Not out loud," Faith said, "However, I did it with my actions, but you know that already." She cocked her head, her brows pinching together. "What's all this about, anyway? You still searching for closure with what Cherish did?"

Glen shook his head. "No" He shrugged. "Not really, anyway." He took a deep breath. "I'm trying to figure out what Cherish thinks she's missing. What did Edwin give her that I didn't? What did she have back with Nick Pepper that she gave up when she married me? It has to be the same thing, right? I mean, she already said she hated giving up things from back then. So, what did she give up besides the way her and Nick fucked? What did Edwin give her that I didn't besides the way he fucked her?" He took another deep breath. "Sorry," he said. "I'm just trying to make sense of it, so I can give her what she needs. I know it's strange..."

"Very," Faith cut him off. "Look, Glen, I'm sorry about what happened between you and my sister. Really, I am. You deserve better than to be done that way. But, I truly think asking me, someone Cherish has been happy to make miserable her whole life, to help you know how to have sex with her is a little more than bizarre. It's..." She took a deep breath, closing her eyes. "Look, I don't remember anything about Nick and Cherish. I was already out of the house and with Selby at that time, pissing my mother off in a whole new set of ways. However, if Cherish and Edwin explored the way he and I did, then he probably did boss her around sexually, testing her boundaries and making her do things she missed or wanted to do but didn't have the guts on her own. My advice, just test her like that. Discover the things that turn you both on. Explore."

Glen stared at her, unsure what to say. Faith was the last person he should have come to for help after everything Cherish did to her. He nodded. "You're right," he said. "I should have thought of all that before now." He took a step back, preparing to turn and walk away. "Thanks for talking to me. I'm sorry to have pulled you from work."

Faith reached out, touching Glen's arm. He glanced into her eyes, full of sympathy for what he was going through. "Look, I meant it; I am sorry. I hope you figure out whatever it is that's going on with Cherish. You deserve it. Cherish on the other hand..." She smiled at him as she squeezed his arm. "Good luck."

Glen watched his sister-in-law go back inside Rutherford Construction. She had helped him all she could, all he really deserved considering how bad his wife tried to fuck Faith over. It was up to him, now, to make out of it what he could.

He turned to return to his car, wishing somehow he knew what to do next.

~ ~ ~ ~ ~

Cherish walked into work already dreading her day ahead. She could see the mountain of files stacked on her desk she still had to sort through, a chaotic system left over from a woman who couldn't organize a cabinet with only two cups in it. Cherish sighed, regretting for the hundredth time quitting Rutherford

Construction.

As she walked through the showroom, Bernie waved hello and his wife, Mary, just glared at Cherish. Cherish walked by, rolling her eyes as she moved behind the main counter to the back room, shoving her way through the swinging door into the back of the building toward her office. She wasn't sure how she would get Mary to lighten up, considering what the woman possibly heard from the gossip system that was the construction world. Of course, Cherish wasn't sure she wanted to deal with it, either.

"Cherish?" a voice called out to her from the loading dock opposite the offices.

Turning, she noticed Jed Jorrell from the Rutherford offices standing on the dock, hands on his hips as he stared at her. "Jed? Hey, there, how's it going?" She diverted her course, moving to walk over and say hello. "How are things at Rutherford?"

He smiled, crossing the floor to meet her. "I thought I heard you worked here now. Things at the office are going well. Business is picking up again, which is always good and frustrating at the same time." He chuckled. "How are things here? Getting settled in all right?"

She shrugged as she glanced over her shoulder, making sure no one was nearby to overhear her. "It's only my second day, but I'm already hoping it was my last." She shook her head. "Seems word travels fast in this town."

He pressed his lips into a thin line, nodding. Cherish was sure he didn't know how to respond to her statement, which is why he ignored it more than likely. "Don't let it get to you. Their memories are as long as the next bit of gossip."

"Well, if you ever need someone at Rutherford, please call me," she said.

He cocked an eyebrow at her. "You would come back there even after everything that happened? Wouldn't that be uncomfortable?"

A couple of the warehouse guys moved by the bay door, more than likely moving Jed's order to one of Rutherford's big bay trucks. She thought about what he asked, but only for a moment. "I'm sure working there would be awkward at first, but I'll take awkward over boring every time." She sighed. "Anyway, I'd appreciate it if you'd just keep me in mind. I promise to be…" She sighed. "Well….not me, if you know what I mean."

Jed just chuckled, nodding. "I'll keep you in mind, but I'll be honest, I'd have to make sure Faith was all right with you coming back."

Cherish nodded. She expected as much. "I doubt she'd want me anywhere near her. We haven't talked since Edwin Coldwell blew up in our faces. I'm not sure she's too eager to do anything but ring my neck." She shrugged. "I can't say I really blame her. I was a bitch to her for a long time."

Jed nodded. "Family is always tough, but I'll bring it up to her. We haven't replaced you yet, but if you came back, you wouldn't be in your same spot. I've already moved Faith there, and Nessa into her spot. Still, if Faith's okay with it, I'll see what I can do about finding you a place."

"Do you think Neal would approve?" she asked, feeling hopeful of escaping a place she just started.

Jed shrugged. "He kept Edwin on the payroll. I don't see why he'd say no to giving you a second chance."

Neal Rutherford was never quick to toss people away, and he hired his fair share of rascals, considering Morgan Brewer and Edwin Coldwell were two of his prizes. She thanked Jed, told him it was good to see him again, and left him to see that the warehouse workers loaded his order onto the truck properly. Probably smart on his part, considering how the rest of Harbor City Carpet was organized.

She entered her office, set her purse on the floor beside her desk, and dropped into her chair. *Another day, oh goodie.* She sighed, and then reached down into her purse and pulled out a picture frame holding a photo of her, Jordie, and Glen sitting out on the beach, setting it on the corner of her desk where she could see it throughout the day. Running her finger over the edge of the frame, she thought about how her night ended last night, snuggled into the crook of Glen's shoulder, her pussy still throbbing from where he took her, her mind still ringing of how he ordered her about, the shock of how she actually obeyed him. She smiled as she glanced at the picture. She obeyed him. She shook her head, laughing softly. She wasn't even sure what gave him the idea to go the route he took, but she was so caught off guard she only had one choice, which was to do what he said. She grinned, shaking her head, remembering the way he put her in front of that window. God, she thought she'd die of embarrassment. But she did it, and the results were amazing.

He still needed to talk, to work through her betrayal, see where they went from here, and she didn't blame him. She owed him that. Owed him so much more. She realized she needed to be honest with him this time, give him everything she felt and what she needed, but did she even know what that was? She missed the wild days, the freedom before family life became her way of life, missed the control of not being in control. Did she really want all that again, though?

She reached for the top file on her desk, now smiling at Jordie bouncing into their room that morning, jumping on the bed all excited to see his father right there in bed beside her. Her son's laughter still filled her ears. She had missed seeing her little boy happy, but could she return to the way things were and do without the things that made her feel alive?

She dropped the folder on her desk and leaned back in her

chair, gazing out the door. Could Glen give her what she needed? Was last night a one-off? She closed her eyes, remembering his hands on her body. Last night felt so good she didn't want it to end. She bit her lower lip as she opened her eyes and scooted up in her chair, her panties already soaked at the possibilities.

She stared down at the stack of manila folders. Work was the last thing on her mind right then, especially with the bullshit she faced in the aftermath of the lady she replaced.

"I hope you won't be having visitors every day," Mary Overton said as she stood in Cherish's office doorway, her arms over her stiff chest.

Cherish just glanced at her, eyebrows furrowed in confusion. "I'm sorry? Visitors? My mom was only here for a few minutes yesterday."

Mary's face twisted into a knot of disgust. "I referred to your visitor this morning. Jed Jorrell, from Rutherford Construction. He was here to see you. He never comes to the warehouse to pick up inventory. Usually, we deliver it. I can only assume then he was here to see you. I will not have our business turned into your new play place."

Cherish glanced at her office wall toward the bay doors as she heard Jed still talking to the men in the warehouse. Did he really come here to see her? Interesting. She turned back to Mary, forcing a smile on her face as she stared at the other woman. "Well, I didn't know he was here or that he would be here. I merely said hello to him. If you have a problem with him being here, then I suggest you call Rutherford and sever your ties with them. Or, at least take up your issue with Jed. You will not blame me for what others do." She leaned forward a little, clasping her hands in front of her. "Or accused."

She watched as Mary stiffened, one eyebrow raised. "I would think a new employee should watch how they talked to their boss."

Cherish grinned. "I'm always pleasant to Mr. Overton." She turned her attention to the folders in front of her, opening up the top one. "Now, unless you have something relevant you need..." She didn't even look up at the cold woman.

Silence followed for a moment, and then Cherish heard Mary turn and walk away, leaving her alone. Cherish sighed and fell back into her chair. *God, I hope Jed can bring me back to Rutherford.*

Twenty

Cherish walked through the front door of her home, glad the day was over. Jordie darted away from her as soon as the door was open, racing to his room and his tiny action figures. As she turned to close the door, she noticed Aubrey crossing the yard. Cherish felt her face flush, knowing the other woman witnessed Glen and her having sex in the window last night. *God, what will Aubrey think of me?*

"Well, well, well," Aubrey said in a sing-song voice. Cherish felt the blush heat her cheeks. "I'm guessing you and Glen have worked things out. Or, did what I witness last night just mean you two were horny, and no one else was around?" The woman gave Cherish a cocky grin as she reached her, walking past her and into the Lansky home.

Cherish shook her head. "Please, come on in." She shut the

door, dropping her purse on the bench, and moved toward the kitchen. "And Jordie is here, so please tone down your questions."

Aubrey grinned as she followed Cherish into the kitchen, leaning back on the counter, arms over her chest. "I'm glad you know you're about to be bombarded with questions," the redhead giggled. "Or, you could just save me the time and tell me what you know I need to know."

Cherish laughed. "Need to know? And just why do you *need* to know anything?" Cherish started emptying her lunchbox, dumping what she didn't eat into the trash as she put the dishes in the sink.

"Cherish!" Aubrey hissed at her, her eyes wide with shock. "How can you even think of keeping something like last night from your bestie? I'm hurt you would even joke that way." She did a fake sniff as she gave a harrumph, her shoulders rising and falling with her deep sigh of dramatics. "Wounded, I tell you. Mortally wounded."

Cherish rolled her eyes as she laughed. "I know better. You just want to hear the gritty details." She reached into the fridge, pulling out two beers. Popping the tops off both bottles, she handed one to Aubrey and then leaned back on the counter herself, taking a long swallow to wash away her day. Mary avoided her for the rest of the day, but by the way Bernie spoke to Cherish, she knew his wife had filled him in on the rude, insubordinate secretary in the back office. Cherish didn't care. She would not allow Mary to treat her like some worthless bitch. She didn't have to explain her life to Mary Overton or apologize for her choices. The only one she owed anything to was Glen.

"So, there are gritty details," Aubrey said, a lecherous grin pushing up her cheeks.

Cherish just looked over at her friend, memories of last night flashing through Cherish's mind. She arched her eyebrows. "Yeah, I'd say gritty is a good word for it." She giggled as she shook her head. "God, it was incredible."

Aubrey nodded, still grinning. "From my angle, it looked like it. Now, spill the tea as the kids say these days."

Cherish looked over at her friend. "How do you know what the kids say these days?"

Aubrey shrugged. "Stop avoiding the question. I want the dish. Spill."

Cherish laughed. "You're just full of the modern slang, aren't you?"

Aubrey just let out another dramatic sigh as she glared at Cherish.

"Fine, fine," Cherish said, laughing. She told Aubrey about her evening after Jordie went to bed last night, doing her best to ignore her friend's facial expressions and giggles. As Cherish recited the tale, she felt the wetness between her legs grow, the passion of last night once again filling her, making her squirm where she stood.

When she finished, she wasn't the only one squirming. "Wow," Aubrey whispered. "Who would have thought our Glen had it in him? I'm impressed." She nodded her head as she said that last sentence. "Do you think there's more to come? And yes, I used that word on purpose." She bounced her eyebrows at Cherish.

Cherish shook her head, laughing. "You're a mess," she said. "And, I don't know. I'm not sure what he has in mind or where this will lead. I think he has this idea in his head of what I need and is doing his best to give it to me."

"And that's a bad thing?" Aubrey asked, giving her friend a quizzical look. "Isn't that part and parcel of a relationship? Each of you doing what you can to meet the other one's needs? You cheated on him for a reason. He just wants to know what that is and fix it."

Cherish stared down at the beer bottle in her hand. "Isn't that selfish of me at this point? What about his needs? What am I supposed to be doing in return?"

Aubrey shrugged. "That's up to you to discover. Of course, if you want, I'm more than happy to step in and pinch-hit for you. Glen's a hottie." She wiggled her eyebrows at her friend again.

Cherish shook her head. "That's my sister's lifestyle. I'm not sure I'm the sharing type of partner."

"You're no fun. Still, if he's making the effort, so should you. That is, if you're wanting this marriage to work." She tilted her head slightly. "Do you want it to work?"

"Yes," Cherish replied without hesitation, and she meant it. She wanted her family back. She just wasn't sure how to fix the parts already broken. "Jordie deserves a healthy family."

"Wrong answer," Aubrey said with a shake of her head. "You have to do this for you, not your son. Jordie will survive no matter which direction you choose, but if you stay and you're miserable, or if you cheat again, then you're only delaying the inevitable. This has to be something you want. Do you want it?"

Cherish nodded. "Yes, I want it."

Aubrey shrugged. "Then, it's up to you to make it work. Seems Glen is willing to do what's needed. Now, you have to show him you are as well."

Cherish nodded some more as she took another sip of her beer. "I know," she said, lowering the bottle. "I just wish I knew where to start."

"That's easy. You start by talking. Just ask him."

"Such practical advice," Cherish deadpanned. "Tell me again how you became so wise."

Aubrey shrugged. "Just a natural gift."

After taking another swallow of her beer, Cherish told Aubrey about the conversation with Jed that morning. "He actually seemed like he wanted me back, and Mary said he never shows up at their warehouse, just has the supplies delivered, so maybe he does want me back."

Aubrey cocked an eyebrow at her. "Are you sure that's a good idea? Would Glen be all right with you going back to the place where you cheated on him? What about facing Faith every day again, knowing what happened?" She shook her head. "Seems like a bad idea to me."

"More Aubrey MacDonald wisdom?" Still, the other woman's words made sense. Cherish had the same thoughts earlier today. It would be tough facing everyone again, knowing by now they all knew she fucked their boss, but it would sure beat the hell out of dealing with Mary Overton on a daily basis. "I could handle it. Hell, I'm sort of handling it now with the way that bitch treats me at Harbor City Carpet. Glen, I'm not so sure about, though."

"Another thing to talk to him about," Aubrey told her with a shrug. "I hope you're keeping a list." She grinned over at Cherish.

Cherish just laughed.

Aubrey only remained a little while longer, making sure to give Jordie hugs before she left. When she did, Cherish turned her thoughts to dinner, still replaying her conversation with her friend in her mind. What did Glen want from her? How could she make sure she met his needs the way he seemed to try to meet hers? She owed him that and so much more. She just worried she couldn't do it. He was happy being the homebody, cuddling on the couch in front of the television, hanging with friends or family. He never said he wanted anything else. So, how did she get him to open up to her? And what would he think of her returning to Rutherford? She couldn't stay at Harbor City Carpet, not and deal with the witch married to the owner. Cherish knew she deserved the looks and scrutiny. She never cared what people thought before, but now, now she cared very much, because how people thought of her reflected on Glen and Jordie. She hurt the two of them enough. She didn't want to hurt them anymore.

She sighed as she pulled chicken out of the freezer, tossing it into the microwave to thaw. Her men deserved so much better than her. She had to make this up to them, especially to Glen. She just needed to figure out how. *What is it you need Glen?*

~ ~ ~ ~ ~

Glen helped Cherish clear the table as he sent Jordie to watch TV. Cherish had been smiling, but unusually quiet throughout dinner. She promised him nothing was wrong, but that she just had a lot on her mind. He worried that last night had not been enough for her, and she had second thoughts about the direction they traveled.

As they washed dishes together, though, she grinned over at him. "I had a visitor when I came home today," she said as she handed him a plate to dry. "Aubrey stopped over to make sure I knew she saw us."

Glen laughed, the redness warming his cheeks. "I figured she would pop by sooner or later after I saw her in the window." He glanced up at Cherish, a sheepish look on his face. "Did she razz you too much?"

"Oh, she made me give her every little gritty detail of our evening," Cherish said with a laugh. "The woman is a perv of the highest degree."

He walked over to Cherish and kissed her on the cheek. "So are you. No wonder the two of you get along so well."

Cherish opened her mouth to protest, her eyes wide, but then she just giggled as she shut her mouth and reached for another plate. "Okay, I guess I need to own that." She shrugged. "Pervs have fun; what can I say?"

As he dried the next plate, he noticed Cherish staring at him. "What did you think of last night?" she asked. "Really."

Glen grinned over at her, a lecherous glint in his eyes. "Are you kidding? Last night was hot as hell." His grin grew. "Just ask Aubrey."

Cherish shook her head with a soft laugh. "Aubrey has already said as much, but I meant with how you," she shrugged, "how you kind of took charge, me obeying you, even to the point of being fucked in front of the window so our kinky neighbor could watch."

"Oh, that was some of the best parts," he said with a chuckle, even though part of him wondered if he could maintain his air of control. He took a deep breath. "Is that what you want? Me in control like that? Is that what you were missing when you…" He took another deep breath, forcing the next words out without malice. "When you cheated on me? Is that what Edwin gave you?"

Cherish didn't answer right away, keeping her focus on the plate in her hands that Glen knew had to have been clean two minutes ago. After about the fiftieth swipe of the rag on the plate, Glen was about to just give up and change the subject. However, Cherish set the plate back in the sink and turned to face him. "Would you believe me if I said, I don't really know?" She shrugged as she picked up the plate again and washed it. "At the time, it was something new, something I hadn't had in a long time. Part of it was nostalgic, part of it was the rush of doing something I shouldn't again." She closed her eyes, taking a deep breath. "Selfish, I know. Hearing it just now, it sounds even worse, but at the time, I just got in over my head, caught up in the rush of adrenaline that Edwin offered."

Pain ripped at his heart with each word she uttered, but he bore it, forcing the pain down so he could focus on their marriage, their relationship. If this is what Cherish needed, then he had to figure out a way to give it to her. Somehow, he had to give her what she was missing. "Why didn't you just tell me what you needed?" he asked, doing his best to keep the judgment from his voice. "Why turn to Edwin before giving me the chance to at least try to give it to you?"

She handed him the plate, a sad smile twisting her lips. "To be honest, I didn't know I missed it until he gave it to me." She took a deep breath. "Glen, you've always been there for me, even at my worst. You've been the soft, caring, gentle soul who coaxed me back from the brink of my self-destruction, holding me together with your strong, tender arms until I could face myself in the mirror again, until I could stand on my own two feet without feeling as if I were about to collapse in on myself." She shook her head as she reached for a pan, shoved it into the water, and started to scour it with a vigor that Glen thought would tear the coating off the inside. She stopped, shoving the pan back into the water as she glanced over at him. "You gave up college, defended me to your mother, who I know hates my guts, and took a job working with your hands when you had dreams of so much more. You gave up everything you wanted for me."

Glen glanced over at her, his head cocked to the side a little as he smiled at her. "I wanted you," he said. His smile grew bigger. "I got what I wanted. You. Jordie. I happen to love our life."

She gave a sad chuckle as she shook her head, gripping the edge of the sink. "That's just it. You love this life. You're content to go to work, come home, watch TV, and for a while, so was I, but Glen, I miss what we were before, the fun, the parties." She took a deep breath. "The crazy ass sex." She glanced back up at him, grinning. "God, we had some awesome sex back then."

Glen walked over, placing the dry plate in the cabinet. "I happen to think we have great sex now, but I get what you mean."

He walked back over to the counter, leaning back on it, arms over his chest. "For the record, I didn't give up anything, and I gained everything. I love being cuddled up with you on the couch watching Land Before Time while Jordie sits on the floor playing with his dinosaurs. I love family picnics and trips to the zoo. I love lying in bed watching you blow dry your hair as you get ready for work and helping you with the dishes. You're right. I'm content. However, that doesn't mean I don't miss some of the things we did back then." He shrugged. "I just grew so happy being a family that I forgot about being a couple." He glanced over at her, a soft smile turning up his lips. "And yes, we had great sex back then."

"I'm a selfish bitch, aren't I?" Cherish asked, hanging her head. "Are you sure you want me back?"

Her broken demeanor tore his heart, and he reached out, taking her arm, and pulling her over to him. Sliding his arms around her waist, he pressed her to him as he gazed into her bright green eyes. "You were selfish; I'll give you that, but then, I obviously missed something along the way as well." He grinned as he kissed her nose. "And I've got you back. Now, we just have to figure out how to make us work again, set that spark back into a flame, and recapture some of what we lost." He kissed her again, releasing her as he leaned back on the counter. "But, I need to know everything. I need to know what you want, how we can make this work. I need to know if you want to continue what we started last night or if that was just something for that night alone. Are you wanting that type of control? Is it an open marriage you're wanting to explore?"

He watched as she stood there, arms over her chest, as she contemplated his question. He was glad she didn't just rush into an answer, worried she would jump at anything as a quick fix, thinking short-term, instead of playing the long game. Now was not the time for Band Aids. They needed to focus on a long-term healing, so they didn't find themselves right back where they were.

After a couple of brief moments, Cherish glanced over at him. "Do you think you could do it? Would you even want to?"

He reached out, running the back of his hand along her cheek. "Sweetheart, I'm willing to do whatever I can to make this work and see you're satisfied in all areas of our lives. Besides, like I said, last night was hot as hell. It was fun watching you walk over to that window, all nervous like, and still horny as hell, knowing I was the one who made you do it. I definitely could handle more of that." He winked at her. "We'll need to talk more, set up some rules and boundaries, see what we both want or don't want, but I think it's definitely something worth exploring."

She nodded as she smiled over at him. "Me, too."

He held a finger up, his brows arched. "But total honesty at all times. No more secrets. If we do this, we have to do it right. Deal?"

She moved over, wrapping her hands around his waist as she kissed his chin. "Yes, sir. Promise."

He took a deep breath, his hands sliding down her back to cup her ass. "Yeah, I can definitely get used to that."

Twenty-One

Cherish slid onto the bench around the concrete table at The Burger Inn, a drive-up burger joint that has been around since her parents were teenagers. Luckily, the April weather was still cool enough to make eating outdoors bearable or Cherish would have insisted on someplace else to meet her mother for a midweek lunch. Of course, with the sour look on Valerie Driscoll's face, Cherish wished she had picked a better lunch companion as well. "If you weren't in the mood to go to lunch, why didn't you call and tell me?" Cherish asked as she stabbed her Diet Coke with a straw. "It's not like I don't have a ton of crap to do."

Her mother stiffened at the rebuke as she dumped another two sugars on top of her already sweetened iced tea. "Well, pardon me for wanting to discuss the rest of the preparations for my grandson's birthday. I thought you would want everything finalized before his birthday arrives, so we were on the same page."

Cherish fought the urge to roll her eyes. "I always enjoy discussing things with you, Mother, but the plans for Jordie's birthday are already finalized," she told her mother, bracing for the argument that was about to start. "We're going to..."

"That can't be right," Valerie said with a shake of her head as she wrapped her hands around the Styrofoam cup. "I would know if the plans were finalized, because we would have discussed things. Since we haven't discussed things, then things cannot be finalized."

Cherish sighed. She knew this wouldn't go over well. Still, it was what Glen wanted, and he called the shots now. With a deep breath, she forged ahead. "Glen wanted to keep things simple this year," she said, not looking her mother in the face. "We're just going to have a small get-together at the house, family, a few friends, maybe even rent one of those bounce house things for Jordie and his friends. Nothing elaborate. Maybe grill some hot dogs and hamburgers, a couple of side dishes." She bounced her shoulders, doing her best to make light of the whole thing. "See, simple. Jordie should have fun."

However, Cherish knew it would not be simple. Nothing with her mother ever was.

Valerie stiffened even more, her lips pressed into a thin line. "At your house? Why would you have my grandson's party at your house? You always have it at my house. I see no reason to change things. Why would you change things?" She glanced down at her burger and fries as if expecting it to crawl away. She glanced back up at her daughter, her eyes scathing. "It makes no sense."

"Glen wanted to have it at our house," Cherish said, forcing her tone to remain pleasant in the face of her mother's irritation. "He just feels since Jordie is his and most of the people who come to the party are our friends, that it just makes sense to have the party at our house." She shrugged. "It's less to carry home and gives us more time to get things ready if it's at the house. It makes sense if you think about it."

"I have thought about it," Valerie snapped. "And it's never been a problem before. I don't see why it would be a problem this year. Jordie expects his birthday party at our house. Why would we disappoint him?"

This time, Cherish did roll her eyes. "He's about to be five, Mom. He doesn't care where we hold his party as long as he gets cake and plenty of presents. Hell, by the time he's ten, he won't even remember we had his party at our house. Trust me, he won't be disappointed."

"This is all Glen's doing, isn't it?" Valerie asked, fire in her eyes. "He doesn't want us to be a part of Jordie's birthday party. He's never been happy with how involved I am in your life and the life of my grandson."

"Oh, god, Mother," Cherish sighed. "That is not true. Glen just wants to do things for his son. What's wrong with that?" She snatched up a fry and shoved it into her mouth before she said anything else.

"Oh, *now* he wants to do things for his son?" Valerie sniffed in disgust. "Why didn't he ever have Jordie's party at your house before? Why is this year so different?"

Cherish sighed, placing her forehead in her palm as she hung her head. "This year isn't different, Mother. Glen always does things for Jordie. He wanted to do parties for Jordie at our house before, but I always allowed you to have your way." Cherish glanced up and stared at her mother. "Well, this year, I'm letting Glen do what he wants for *his* son. I'm sorry if that doesn't fit into your perfect plan, but that's what needs to happen. I'm sorry."

"First, he walks out on his family, and now, he wants to take Jordie away from his grandparents," Valerie said, disgust in her voice. "What have we ever done to him? How can you give him what he wants after he walked out on you like he did, leaving you and Jordie alone to fend for yourselves?"

"Please, Mother, stop," Cherish said, doing her best to control her temper. Usually, she did great putting up with her mother's dramatics, but today, Cherish had just been through too much to tolerate any more disruptions to her life. She needed to give Glen the control he wanted to take care of…. She froze, staring at the basket of food in front of her. That was it. That's why Glen never took control. Cherish never allowed it. She surrendered that control to her mother. He gave up everything to help Cherish raise Jordie, to keep her from appearing the harlot to those around them, and how did she repay him? By giving her mother control of their family. Cherish closed her eyes, feeling the weight of her failure once again to take care of her family. She did everything her mother wanted, even if Glen was against it, and he always went along with it. *God, how could I have been so blind and stupid?*

She opened her eyes again, staring at her mother. "Glen is the man of the house, and this is what he wants to do for his son, so that's what we're doing. End of story."

Valerie shook her head. "He walked out on the two of you. He doesn't deserve to…"

"Stop!" Cherish snapped. "Glen gave up everything for us. He quit school, got a job building decks and docks. Everything he's done, he's done for Jordie and me. He never had to do any of that."

"What do you mean, he never had to do any of that?" Valerie

asked, giving a short shake of her head. "He got you pregnant. It's his job to take care of you. If he didn't want to take care of you and your son, then he should have kept his pants zipped."

Cherish closed her eyes, anger coursing through her as she clenched her fists. "Mother, leave Glen alone. He is doing more than you know."

"Please," Valerie said, giving Cherish a sad shake of her head. "He left you. He is not doing…"

"Damn it, Mother!" Cherish hissed. "Glen married me, claiming Jordie was his, so people wouldn't look at me like I was some loser. He's not Jordie's biological father. He gave me a home, a family. He protected me, and in doing that, he sacrificed everything he worked toward, his own goals and dreams. You will not talk shit about him again." She threw her napkin down on her burger, no longer hungry. "I've got to go." She shot from her seat, disgust filling her at her mother's rudeness and the revelation of what she did to Glen herself.

"Wait," her mother reached out, trying to stop Cherish from leaving. "What do you mean Jordie isn't his son? Who's Jordie's father? You were only with…" Then her eyes widened as realization dawned her. "That vile creature, Nick Pepper. Isn't it?"

Cherish clenched her eyes shut, regretting saying anything to her mother. Glen spent the past five years protecting her secret, and here she goes and tells the one person she never should have told. *I'm a fucking idiot.* She shook her head. "We're having Jordie's party this Saturday at our house at one. Be there or don't. It's up to you. Now, I have to go." Exhaling her frustration, she turned, leaving her mother sitting there gawking after her, mouth open, eyes wide. *This day just can't get any worse.*

~ ~ ~ ~ ~

Glen slid into the booth at Royal Chef, his back sore from where he spent the last two hours pounding in two-by-sixes to construct a longer pier for some cranky old man who stood at the edge of his property, criticizing everything Brent and Glen did. Glen ordered a Coke, but he really wanted a stiff drink. "That man was a total asshat," he said as he shoved his straw into his drink. "I swear, by the time we finished, I was ready to toss his ass into the river myself."

Brent chuckled, nodding. "Yeah, he was pretty full of himself. He had an opinion for everything, including telling us we used the wrong type of hammer."

Glen fell back into the booth, sighing. "I was ready to hammer him."

Rachel stepped up to the side of their booth, reaching into her apron for her notepad. "You two look more beaten than usual," she said as she poised her pen over her pad, ready to take their order. "Too much sun out there?"

Brent shook his head. "Too much wind in the form of a crotchety old man. Some people just like to bitch."

Rachel grinned, winking at Glen. "Says the man sitting there bitching."

Glen laughed and then placed his order—bacon cheeseburger with fries. Brent matched him as he craned his neck, searching for Bonnie.

Rachel grinned at Glen's partner. "Relax," she said. "She's here, just in the back checking on someone's order."

Brent shrugged, grinning, not at all bashful at being called out. "If she needs help in the back..." He bounced his eyebrows at Rachel.

The server just shook her head. "And make the customers' food cold. Just keep it in your pants. She'll be by to tease and torture you, I'm sure."

Glen watched the dark-haired woman walk away, her ass

swaying back and forth teasingly. He just chuckled, shaking his head. "She definitely has your number."

Brent grinned as he leaned back in his seat, his drink in his hand. "She could have yours if you'd just give it to her. Rachel's panted after you for a while."

Glen rolled his eyes. "I told you, I'm not looking for anything extra. As of right now, I think Cherish and I are heading back to a good place. I'm not risking that with a casual fling."

Brent shook his head. "You know I'm happy for you, but I still think you're missing out with Rachel."

Glen just grinned. "I'll just have to miss out then. Now, are you coming to Jordie's party this Saturday? One o'clock at the house. You can help me grill the burgers and hot dogs. Bring Bonnie if she'll be seen in public with you."

Brent cocked an eyebrow at him. "At your house? Not the Wicked Witch of the West's? How did you manage that?"

Glen chuckled at Brent's description of Valerie Driscoll. Shrugging, Glen said, "By putting my foot down finally. If we're going to give this another shot, I'm taking full control of my family. Valerie's rein is over."

"And Cherish is okay with that?" Brent stared over at Glen with disbelief, and Glen couldn't blame his friend. Ever since he had known Glen, Valerie Driscoll ran roughshod over the Lansky family, controlling everything Cherish did, and Glen in the aftermath. He had been content to give Cherish—and Valerie as a byproduct—her way, but not anymore. He sacrificed enough for Cherish's happiness. The time had come for him to take control, and that meant doing things his way, not Valerie's.

"She'll have to be," he told Brent. "There's no reason I have to lug Jordie's presents from their house to ours just because Valerie wants to show off in front of my family and our friends." He shook his head as he lifted his glass to take a sip. "Things can't go back to the way they were, not if I'm going to save my marriage."

Brent nodded, wrapping his hands around his own drink. "And just how is that going? I'll admit, you've seemed more on the chipper side lately. If I didn't know better, I'd swear you'd already hooked up with Rachel and just weren't telling me."

Glen chuckled as he shook his head. "Not likely."

"Come on," Brent pleaded. "There has to be some gritty details you can give a single guy to live vicariously through."

Glen leaned forward, his arms on the table, hands wrapped around his glass. "To be honest, I'm still sort of figuring it out. Between Cherish's past and her affair with Edwin, I think she missed something with me she enjoyed back then. I think I figured out what it is, but now, I have to figure out how to give it to her."

Brent cocked an eyebrow. "Sounds complicated. You saying her affair wasn't about just getting another man's dick?"

Glen shot his friend a dirty look. "No, it wasn't, jackass."

Brent shrugged, unapologetic. "Hey, what do I know? I thought affairs were all about sex."

Glen shook his head. "Most are about feeling or experiencing something the person thinks they're missing."

"Okay, so what was Cherish missing?"

Glen took a deep breath. "Well, if I'm right, she missed being controlled. She prefers the guy to tell her what to do; at least, during sex." He cocked his head to the side. "I'm not sure how she'd handle being controlled in every aspect. Interesting idea, though."

"And you think you can do this? Glen, you've permitted that woman to walk all over you since the two of you hooked up. You really think she's just going to hand the reins over to you without a fight?"

He shrugged. "I honestly don't know. Maybe fighting it is part of the rush? I don't know. I've done some research online, and there's a ton of books and articles out there. Seems this isn't as taboo as it sounds."

Brent chuckled. "It sounds more old-fashioned than taboo, like you're stepping back into the fifties. You're going to have the fems all up in your shit once you start bossing Cherish around."

"Not if it's something she wants," Glen said. Of course, he still wasn't sure it *was* what his wife wanted. Still, between the sex they had the other night and what she told him about her affair with Edwin, this was the only thing Glen could come up with; it was the only thing he had left to try.

Rachel brought their food, making sure to smile extra big for Glen, and then left them to devour their lunch in peace. At one point, Bonnie came out of the back, sliding into the booth with Brent, her hand on his thigh as she leaned forward, talking to him. The way she sat, the other customers couldn't see just where her hand rested, but by the look on Brent's face, Glen knew exactly the spot Bonnie stroked.

Leaving the others to their heavy petting and flirting, Glen became lost in his burger and thoughts. According to the books he read, the couple exploring this sort of power play had rules that the dominant gave to the submissive, which she obeyed or faced consequences for not obeying. He gave an inward chuckle at his Cherish being punished for anything. Her own parents didn't even punish her. But was that what she wanted? He popped a fry into his mouth as he thought about it. Her lack of control had left her floundering in her early years. Could that be why she craved it with Edwin? Nick gave it to her while they dated, another reason Valerie didn't care for the man. She saw him as her competition for her daughter, not in the heart, but rather in who controlled Cherish's life. Now that Glen thought about it, it was the reason

Valerie didn't really care for Selby. He never allowed Faith's mother to dictate the rules of their marriage, keeping the control for Faith and himself. Faith thrived in that environment while Valerie stewed, so much so she never did anything nice for Faith.

So, what rules do I give Cherish? Glen honestly didn't know. The books he read suggested bedtimes, clothing, ways to do things, even sitting on the floor and kneeling at certain times. Basically, they said the rules were founded based on what turned the dominant on the most and what he preferred, but Glen had no idea what he preferred. He had been content with the way things were before he discovered his wife was unfaithful. How did he move forward now? How did he give her what she wanted if it was based on what he ultimately wanted? *This just gets more and more confusing.*

He took a bite of his burger as he mulled over what he wanted, and he kept circling back to the same answer. He wanted Cherish. That's it.

Then he thought of Selby again. Faith's husband wasn't the dominant type even though he controlled their marriage. He was more the soft romantic type, so he allowed his wife to venture out with someone else to experience that part of her sexuality. He heard the stories afterward, relived them with her, enjoying her excitement, but hadn't taken part in most of it.

Glen sighed as he popped another fry into his mouth. There was no way he could do that, especially now that Cherish had broken his trust. Perhaps, if she went about things differently, he would have been able to see her needs met that way, but she didn't. She chose her path, and it was the wrong one. Now, they could only try to recover what they had lost due to her infidelity, which meant, Glen had to be the one who gave her what she thought she was missing. Now, he just had to figure out how to do that.

Twenty-Two

Over the next two days, things simmered down, and Glen and Cherish slid back into a normal routine, a familiar routine, a routine that scared Glen, actually. He pulled into his driveway Friday evening after work, knowing he couldn't permit more time to pass before he talked to Cherish about how to proceed. If they just allowed things to return to the way they were, they would wind up back in the same situation, with Cherish becoming frustrated and cheating on him again. As much as it was Cherish's responsibility to keep her legs closed, it was his to make sure she remained satisfied. Tonight, he had to figure out how to do that.

When he walked into the house, Cherish had already changed into what she called lounging pants, standing in the middle of the kitchen with a beer in her hand. He cocked an eyebrow at her as he scanned her choice of attire. A pair of his old pajama pants, a baggy T-shirt, and a gray pair of socks. She looked...comfortable.

Walking over to the fridge, he pulled out a beer for himself, closed the fridge, and leaned back on the counter. He could hear Jordie playing in his bedroom. "We all set for the party tomorrow?" he asked as he lifted the bottle to his lips.

Cherish leaned on the counter across from him, one arm over her waist, the other bent as she held her beer. She shrugged. "As much as we can be, I suppose. I still need to get the cake tomorrow. We need to wrap his presents as well. They're dropping the bounce house off at ten and picking it back up at seven, so Jordie and his friends will have plenty of time to enjoy themselves."

Glen nodded. "We can wrap the presents when he goes to bed, and I can run and get the cake tomorrow morning while you set things up here for the party. I'm sure Aubrey will be around to help until I get back, and we both know your mother will have to insinuate herself into the preparations." As he spoke, he watched her shoulders stiffen, her whole body turning into a tight cord that appeared ready to snap. "Are you all right?"

She took a deep breath as she shook her head. "Not really," she said. She glanced up into his eyes, her expression pinched with worry. "I think I fucked up again, and I'm not sure how bad it is."

Glen cocked an eyebrow at her, wondering if she had cheated on him again. Then he gave himself a mental shake. It could be anything. He did not need to jump to infidelity right off the bat. He wondered how long it would take for that thought not to be an automatic response. "What do you mean?"

"I had lunch with my mother Wednesday," Cherish said, her tone low, troubled. "It was the first chance I had to tell her we were having the party here."

"I bet that went over well," he said, his lips twisted in a lopsided grin. He could imagine the mighty Valerie throwing a fit because someone dethroned her from the pedestal of their family. It was something he should have done a long time ago.

"Yeah, not so much," Cherish said with a sigh. "She became mean and nasty, criticizing you, accusing you of trying to take her grandson away from her. The morning had already been a terrible one thanks to Mary Overton and her bias against me. The more Mom fussed and criticized, the angrier I became." She shook her head, then glanced at the open doorway before turning back to Glen. "I'm afraid I got so fed up with her telling me how you walked out on us, not even blaming me for you leaving, that I kind of blew up and said something I shouldn't have."

Glen cocked an eyebrow at her but said nothing. What could Cherish possibly have said that had her so upset?

"I told Mom about Jordie and how you married me anyway," Cherish said, her voice a bare whisper, her body already flinching at the outburst she expected. She wrapped her arms around her chest, her beer clutched tightly in one hand. "I'm sorry. I know you didn't want anyone to know, and here I go and tell the worst possible person to tell.

Glen just smiled over at her, his head tilted to the side slightly. "I'll just spank you later."

"Glen, this is serious," she hissed. "I betrayed you again by telling her. I allowed my anger to get the better of me."

Setting his beer on the counter beside him, Glen crossed the floor, taking Cherish in his arms even though she didn't move her arms, and held her tightly, kissing her forehead. "Sweetheart, you didn't betray me," he assured her. "This is your secret to tell or not tell. I said for us to keep it quiet to protect you, remember? You were worried what others thought of you back then, so we decided I'd bear the brunt of it, saving you from your mother's accusations." He shrugged, still holding her, his head resting on her forehead. "It would have been great if you gave me a heads up first, but really, I'm not upset about it." He slid his hands to her upper arms, holding her away from him a little as he gazed into her light blue eyes. "How could I be mad? You stood up to your mother for me. You standing up to your mother about anything is a win in my book." He pulled Cherish closer, kissing her forehead again. "Of course," he said as he pulled back, "I'm still going to spank you just for fun."

Cherish giggled in his arms as she dropped her head to his chest. "I deserve it," she said. "For that, and so much more."

He nodded. "That I *will* agree with," he said. "Perhaps, we'll have one night of just punishing you." He winked at her, making light of his statement, but inwardly, he thought it might just be a good way to start the next chapter of their lives. He held her out at arms' length again, raking her with his narrowed eyes. "However, for tonight, I think I want you in something besides baggy pants and a shirt too big for you. Go find a sundress, a short sundress with a low-cut neckline." He bounced his eyebrows at her, grinning. "Yeah, definitely low-cut."

Cherish's eyes went wide as she stared back at him. "Glen, what about...?"

"Jordie?" Glen said, cutting off her protest. "He'll see you in a sundress." He shrugged. "No big deal. Your sexy attributes will remain covered, but I'll still be able to see you in something I find sexier than what you have on now." He stared at her through narrowed eyes as he tilted his head to the side a little. "You did say I was in control, correct? Are you changing your mind?"

Cherish gave a quick shake of her head, smiling up at him. "No, sir, I'm not changing my mind. I'll go change and then start dinner."

"Good girl," he said and then swatted her ass as she passed

him on her way out of the kitchen.

Cherish yelped, giving a little hop with his swat. Turning back, she grinned at him, her eyes sparkling. "I'll be right back, sir."

"Good girl," Glen said again, grinning back at her. He watched her leave, her ass swaying slightly as she did. Yeah, the baggy clothes had to go for a while. He gave a shake of his head as he reached over for his beer and took a long swig. He stood there a moment, looking at the open doorway. Cherish actually stood up to her mother for him, defended him in the face of one of Valerie's tirades. That showed change right there, growth even. He gave another shake of his head. He should have done this when they were first married, like Selby did. Then perhaps, Cherish never would have strayed.

Tomorrow would be interesting with Valerie, and more than likely Arni, in the know of who Jordie's true father was, something Glen never even told his parents. There was no way he would give his mother another reason to hate Cherish. Hopefully, Valerie would worry about her daughter's reputation enough to keep the secret, but Glen knew he couldn't count on anything with that woman.

Taking another swig of his beer, he went to find his son.

~ ~ ~ ~ ~

Cherish sat in the middle of their bed, wrapping a Toy Story figure for Jordie, Glen sitting across from her, wrapping a race car set. She tucked her sundress tight around her upper legs, giving her space to work in front of her. As soon as Jordie went to bed, Glen made her take her bra and panties off and constantly reached under her dress to grope her, making her giggle, trying her best not to make too much noise and wake up their son. She still couldn't believe how easily Glen took her news earlier. He hadn't been mad at all, not even appearing disappointed in her.

Glen never ceased to amaze her with how laid back and accepting he was with things, giving even. Her cheating on him was the only real time she saw him truly upset. She truly didn't deserve him, and he deserved better than her.

Once they finished wrapping the presents, he helped her clean up the wrapping supplies, clearing the bed. It was only ten o'clock, too early to hit the sheets yet. She glanced over at him. She grinned. "Would you like a drink, sir?"

He glanced over at her, his head tilted to the side as he stared at her. "Did you ever call him that?"

The knot tightened in her stomach at his question. There would probably always be questions. She gave a slow shake of her head. "No, sir, I didn't. Only you. Promise."

Glen just nodded, then slid off the bed, holding his hand out to her.

Confused as to whether or not his question put him in a funk, worried even, she took his hand and allowed him to pull her from the bed. When she stood to her feet, he spun her so she faced the bed and bent her over, her ass facing him. She felt him slide her sundress up her legs to her waist, exposing her backside.

"I'm not mad," he assured her. "I'll probably have questions now and again, even get depressed at what happened on occasion, but I am not mad. That's over. Understood?"

She nodded as she took a calming breath. "Yes."

Then she felt his hand smack her ass, making her yelp. "Yes, sir," he told her.

She bit her bottom lip a moment, grinning. "Yes, sir."

He caressed her bare ass, sliding his palms over each cheek, massaging once in a while as he did. "If we do this, me in control, I want it all," he told her. "Do you agree to that?"

She pushed her ass back into his hand. "Yes, sir. All of it. You're in control."

He slid a finger between her ass crack, toying with her dark hole a moment before slipping his finger further down to her wet slit. "I'm now the master, and you're my submissive. I make all the rules, and you *will* obey them without hesitation. I trump everyone else, even your mother, especially your mother. Agreed?"

She nodded, moaning slightly as she felt his finger toying at her entrance. "Yes, sir. I'll obey only you in everything."

"I will punish you however I see fit if you disobey," he told her, and she felt a tremor go through her at the thought of him spanking her. "Do you agree to this?"

She nodded, wiggling her wetness on his hand. "Yes, sir."

Her mouth popped open as she felt him shove two fingers into her pussy until she felt his bottom knuckles hit her folds. "You will dress as I see fit from now on, nothing baggy. I deserve to see your body displayed for my pleasure, and I don't care who is around. Sundress, low-cut tops, tight shorts, skimpy bathing suits. No more baggy pants and shirts. When it's just us, you won't wear a bra or panties, either. Is this understood?" He continued to finger-fuck her as he spoke, soft mewling noises of pleasure escaping her lips as she pressed her forehead onto the bed.

"Oh, god, yes sir," she said as she gripped the bedspread. "Whatever you want, sir." She felt her honey drip even more at the thought of what he wanted. She hid her body since giving birth to Jordie, and now he wanted her to show it off for him. For him. God, the mere thought sent heat to the valley between her legs.

As he fingered her wetness, she felt his other hand on her ass, squeezing her cheeks, his fingers digging in a little. Then, his hand left her flesh, but only for a second before he smacked her ass hard, the sting spreading over her skin. She cried out again, her body jerking slightly with his smack. His hand left her again, followed by another swat in the same place, making her cry out louder.

"You will also call me sir at all times," he said, and she could hear the grin in his voice. "Even in front of your mother."

She groaned. "Yes, sir." Her pussy ached for him to fill her, hungry for his cock. Her entire body felt like it was on fire with need.

He yanked his fingers from her pussy, and Cherish moaned at the sudden void as he stepped away from her. "There will be more rules, but for now, those will do."

She heard him remove his pants and gripped the bedspread tighter.

"Spread your legs," he ordered, and Cherish obeyed instantly, opening herself to him, her pussy a soaked slit begging for his cock.

She felt him grip her hips, his fingers digging into her flesh with his own need just before the head of his cock rubbed against her entrance. "You are mine, Cherish. Never forget that." And then he thrust deep inside of her, his balls slapping between her legs as he buried himself inside of her.

Cherish cried out as she clutched the bedspread, shoving herself back onto his hard shaft as he plunged into her. "Yes!" she screamed just as he pulled back out only to thrust inside of her again.

Over and over he drove into her. "I'll fuck you where I want, how I want, and when I want from now on," he grunted as he rammed his manhood in and out of her wet pussy.

She whimpered as he pounded into her, shoving her body back onto his cock, wanting him deeper. "Yes! Oh, god, yes."

"I may even fuck you in front of others," he told her, and she felt her pussy get even wetter.

She could only groan in response. Would he really do it? God, she didn't know, but just the thought of it turned her on so much that she hoped he would.

She felt one of his hands leave her hips just seconds before he spanked her ass again, making her yell out once more before her cry turned into another groan. She had never been spanked before, and Glen doing it right then sent her into a lust-filled tizzy. She wanted more. "Again, please, sir," she begged.

"What?" Glen asked, and she heard the smirk in his voice. "Tell me what you want, Cher."

"Spank me," she pleaded. "Please. Spank my ass."

He smacked her ass again, the sting spreading throughout her body. "Whose ass?"

She wiggled on his cock. "Your ass, sir," she corrected. "Please, spank your ass."

And he did, over and over again. She felt his hand smack her ass in several places, her entire backside stinging as her pussy throbbed. Then, it hit her, her orgasm welling up inside of her as she felt her body tighten into a cresting wave. He spanked her one more time as he thrust deep inside of her, and she cried out, the hardest orgasm she remembered ever having breaking through her, her entire body shuddering as she shoved herself back onto him, clutching the bedspread with white knuckles. "Yes! Oh, god, yes!" Her body shook, her mouth open, eyes wide as Glen shoved himself into her over and over.

As soon as her orgasm subsided, her breathing loud in her ears, she felt his cock twitch inside of her dripping cavern. He grunted as he yanked her back onto his shaft one more time, pinning her into place as he emptied himself into her, filling her with his hot cum.

Cherish moaned as she felt his passion hit her inner walls, mixing with her own juices to run down her inner thighs. When he finished, he shoved her forward off his cock to lie flat on her stomach in front of him. She then heard him climb into bed beside her, the bed shifting with his movement as he slid a hand up her stinging ass and onto her back. He kissed the side of her head, both of them breathing hard.

She turned her head, so she faced him, smiling, her eyes glassy with leftover passion and complete satisfaction. "That was...was...Wow," she said. "Just wow. Where did you learn that?"

He grinned over at her as he caressed her back. "I've done some reading since the other night," he admitted. "You approve?"

God, did she ever. "Yes, sir," she said, grinning. "Very much so."

"Good, because there's more to come. I just thought that would be a good starting point. I meant what I said. You're mine, and I expect those rules to be followed."

Cherish couldn't stop grinning. "Yes, sir. It will be my pleasure." She could only imagine what else lay in store for them. Whatever it was, she was more than ready to explore it with Glen.

Her master.

Twenty-Three

They were up early the next morning, Cherish already in the kitchen cooking breakfast, getting things ready for Jordie's birthday party. Glen hopped into the shower, a sense of peace overcoming him after his scene with Cherish last night. She agreed to his terms without arguing, even enjoying his spanking of her ass. She even begged for more. He couldn't believe it. She told him Edwin didn't spank her, and while part of him struggled to believe her, he had to force himself to take her words at face-value. It was hard, considering she lied to him for so long, but if they were to make it, he had to give her the benefit of the doubt. Of course, he still possessed a slew of other questions. While he knew Nick just ordered her about, making her wait on him hand and foot like a servant, Glen wondered if Edwin gave her rules to follow. Glen didn't remember her ever changing the way she dressed, so he doubted the rules had to do with clothing, but did she serve him at work?

He forced the question out of his mind. Today was not the day for those type of thoughts. Today was his son's birthday, and Glen would allow nothing to spoil it.

By the time they finished breakfast, Aubrey knocked on the door, a giant package in her hands as she entered the house. "I'm here to be put to work," the redhead said as she placed the gift on the dining room table. "Where do you...?" She stopped as she eyed Cherish, her brows pinched in confusion. "You're wearing a dress? Are you okay?"

Cherish rolled her eyes while Glen chuckled. Walking over to his wife, he kissed the side of her head. "I think she looks awesome," he said.

"I didn't say she didn't," Aubrey quickly said. "She just looks...different."

"I'm fine," Cherish assured their friend. "Glen happens to like these dresses."

Aubrey looked around for Jordie who, luckily, was in his room playing, and then walked over to Cherish, running her hand over Cherish's ass. "A thong, huh? I bet I know why Glen likes these dresses." She turned to Glen and winked. "Nice."

"I think so," he said with a grin and a bounce of his eyebrows.

As he poured himself another cup of coffee, Cherish fussed at him. "That's my job, sir," she scolded, taking the cup from his hands and finishing the job.

"Sir? Your job?" Aubrey repeated the words. "Have I entered some alternate universe? Where the hell is Cherish?" She glanced over at Glen. "You killed her and created a robot who serves you, right? Tell me this is some Sci-Fi drama unfolding."

Cherish just rolled her eyes at her friend again. "Why don't you get started cutting up the vegetables for the party, brat?"

Glen just shook his head at both of them as he snatched his keys from the hook on the wall in the kitchen. He walked over to Cherish and kissed her on the side of the head. "I'll go grab the cake and a couple of bags of ice," he told her. "I'm taking your car since we need to move it anyway for the guy to get the bounce house into place."

"Sounds good," she told him. "Although, I'm not really sure where it's at with gas." She gave him a sheepish look as she ducked her head a little.

Glen just laughed as he kissed her nose. "No worries. I'll gas it up while I'm out."

"Thank you," Cherish said as she kissed him back.

Swatting her ass, he told them he'd be back shortly and headed out the door.

The day was gorgeous, perfect for an outdoor birthday party, and Glen looked forward to the celebration. Cherish and he seemed to have things under control for now, a direction to travel to make their marriage work. He had to admit, the path they now explored seemed hotter than hell, and last night had just been the beginning. He spent a little time each day studying websites and online books, trying to get a grasp of what was involved in this lifestyle, and the more he read, the hotter the whole thing excited him. This was the path they should have taken when they were first married. Then they might have avoided the whole catastrophe they went through over the past couple of weeks.

Glen purchased the birthday cake, two bags of ice, and even picked up a small bouquet for Cherish, something he realized he hadn't done in a couple of years. It was time to bring back the romance as well as begin the dominance. Cherish would have both; he'd make sure of it.

On his way home, he stopped at the gas station, remembering he needed to fill her tank up to keep her from worrying about it. If she was to serve him, then he needed to make sure he took care of her just as well, and part of that would include making sure he filled her gas tank for her, so she didn't have to do it.

As he stuck the nozzle in the gas tank, clicking the lock into place, he decided he would be extra sweet and clean out the trash from inside the car. Starting in the back seat, he snatched up the candy wrappers and trash left behind by Jordie, and then moved to the front. He started in the passenger side, making sure to check on the sides of the seat before moving to the driver's side, and then to the center console, picking up straw wrappers, candy wrappers, and scratch paper. He found a couple of business cards and made sure they were unimportant before tossing them.

The second one he glanced at brought him to a cold halt. Nick Pepper. *Why the hell is his business card in Cherish's car?* Anger churned Glen's stomach as he bent over the front seat, staring at the business card with Nick's phone number. *How long has she had this in here? Did she call him? How did she even get it?* Glen couldn't silence the flood of questions that washed over him as nausea threatened to undo him right there at the gas pump. Cherish promised no more secrets, no more lies, and yet here another one stared him straight in the face.

The nozzle clicked off in the gas tank, but Glen couldn't force himself to move. He stood there, frozen in his bent over position, staring at Nick's business card. How could Cherish do this to them? Glen thought things were on the right track, that he had discovered where he had failed his wife to make her cheat on him, but now, it seemed she kept even more secrets, more affairs. How could he look at this business card and *not* think Cherish slept with Nick? She lied to him before; what was there to say she hadn't lied about Nick, only confessing the affair with Edwin that had busted her?

Glen closed his eyes, clamping down on the tears that

threatened to undo him. With a deep breath, he stood, sliding the business card into his back pocket, and moving over to remove the gas nozzle from the car. Today was Jordie's birthday. Glen would do nothing to ruin his son's special day. However, as soon as the party was over, he would leave his lying, cheating wife. If she couldn't be honest with him, he couldn't remain with her. He had only asked for one thing ever, that she was always completely honest with him. She had failed, taking from him the one thing he thought they had above everything else.

He closed the lid to the gas tank and slid behind the steering wheel. With another deep breath, he started the car, shifting it into drive, and headed toward the last birthday party of his son's he would share with his wife.

~ ~ ~ ~ ~

"No, seriously, what's with all the sirs and this is my job talk?" Aubrey asked as soon as Glen was out the door. "This is totally *not* Cherish Lansky. Where's the grumpy woman I know and have come to love?"

Cherish laughed as she shook her head, pulling out the punch bowl from the bottom cabinet. "We're exploring something new," she told her friend. "And, I have to say, so far, it's hot as hell." She turned to face the redhead. "I can't believe how hot Glen is when he's being all dominant and stuff, giving orders," she sucked in a breath, "spanking me." She giggled, actually giggled. "God, Aubrey, I've never been so wet in my life as I was last night."

"Dominant, huh?" Aubrey said. "So that makes you, what, his little submissive? That'll be hard to get used to. Is this a bedroom thing, or are you submitting to him all the time? I noticed you said it was your job to get his coffee."

As Aubrey cut carrots and celery, Cherish continued to gather the rest of the things she needed for the party: paper plates, plastic cups and utensils, paper towels and napkins. "It'll be all the time," she told Aubrey while she stacked her supplies on the counter. "He even made up some rules I have to follow or he'll punish me."

Aubrey stared at her, eyes wide. "Punish you? Like spanking you? Oh. My. God. Is Cherish going to get her little bottom tanned?"

Cherish shook her head. "Why do I think you're enjoying this too much?" She then giggled again. "And Cherish has already been spanked, thank you very much. Glen spanked me last night just before he fucked me doggy style."

"God, I really need to talk to Glen," Aubrey said with a giggle. "I want in on this."

Cherish laughed as she moved over to the fridge. "You would, you perv."

"You bet your sweet red ass, I would." Aubrey dumped the carrots into a bowl. "Who would have thought our Glen had it in him. I'm impressed."

Cherish paused as she turned to her friend. "I am as well to be honest. He thinks this is what I need, and after obeying him, I kind of agree with him. He's different, I'm different, and together we're different. It's hot. I'm not sure how long it'll last or where he'll take it from here, but I'm enjoying it so far, and it seems to be bringing us back together. He told me he has more rules, and he's even been reading up on the lifestyle."

Aubrey started in on the celery. "So, what are some of your rules?"

Cherish noticed her friend didn't even hesitate to ask. They had shared so much since they met, even nudity, that there were no real lines between them. Cherish shrugged as she moved to the fridge and started pulling out the condiments. "Things like how I dress, not wearing a bra or panties when it's just him and I, calling him sir." She slid the mustard and mayonnaise on to the counter. "He even said he'd fuck me when he wanted, where he wanted, and how he wanted, even if other people were there."

Aubrey turned to her, grinning. "I'll suggest he let me watch." She winked at Cherish and chopped down on the celery.

"You've already seen him fuck me thanks to that window display the other night," Cherish reminded her friend, the memory sending heat to pool between her legs. Being watched had turned her on, even if she didn't know about it until afterward. She wondered how it would feel to know from the start that someone watched Glen fuck her. They had sex within group settings back before they were married and Jordie was born, not side-by-side so much as within the same vicinity. Would Glen actually do it? Her pussy throbbed at the thought. She hoped he would.

"Hello," Cherish's mother's voice could be heard just after the sound of the front door opening. "Cherish, where's everyone at? There's a guy in a truck out front wanting to know where to put the bounce house. Your father's with him now." As Valerie finished that last part, she entered the kitchen, her arms loaded with bags of party paraphernalia. She stopped cold when she saw her daughter. "What in the world are you wearing?"

Cherish rolled her eyes. "It's a sundress. Chill." She turned to Aubrey. "I'll be right back. I'm going to go show the guy where to put the bounce house."

"But you don't wear dresses," Valerie said as Cherish slid around her and out of the kitchen. "Since when did you start wearing a dress? This is a party. Shouldn't you be in shorts?"

"I'm fine in a dress, Mom," Cherish said as she moved through the living room to the front door. "Just put whatever you brought on the table, and I'll sort it out when I get back."

"But you don't even know..."

Cherish opened the door and slid out of her mother's range, closing the door behind her. She took a deep breath before moving over to where her father stood talking to a heavyset man with dark hair. Out of the corner of her eye, she noticed Glen pulling up along the curb. *Good, he'll know more about this than I do.* "Hi," she greeted the man. "I think we want it in the backyard. Is that possible?"

"I can put it anywhere you want as long as there's power nearby for my cords," the man told her.

Cherish's father said he'd show the man to the back and help while Cherish turned to make her way over to Glen to help him carry the cake and ice into the house. She smiled as she watched him slide out of her car, her pussy throbbing as she thought back to last night and how he took her in their bedroom. She suddenly wanted to skip Jordie's party just to have Glen to herself.

"Welcome back, sir," she said as she came to a stop in front of him, a slight bounce in her step as she stood there, hands clasped behind her back. "I missed you."

He turned an icy gaze to her as he handed her the cake. "I'll get the ice and dump it in the coolers," he said as he reached back into the car for the ice.

Cherish stared at him, her brows pinched over her nose in confusion. "Something happen at the store? You seem agitated all of a sudden." He had left in such a good mood and hadn't even had to deal with her mother yet, so why the icy demeanor?

Glen slammed the car door with his foot, a bag of ice in each hand. "Nothing happened. Everything went smooth. Are we all set?"

He started to walk away, leaving Cherish a clear view into the front seat of the car and the bouquet sitting there. "Who did you buy flowers for?" she asked, still staring at the bouquet. She turned to face him, a knot in her stomach. There's no way he would have bought flowers for someone else. Was there?

He turned, glancing at the car door instead of at her. "I bought them for you," he told her, his voice dripping ice.

She stared at him, the cake held in front of her like a shield she felt she needed right then. "Something happened," she said. "What aren't you telling me?"

He glanced up at her. "Nothing happened. The same shit happened. Everything happened." She watched as he took a deep breath and then glared at her. "I cleaned out your car while I filled the tank."

She gazed at him with pinched eyes, still not comprehending. "And you're upset because my car was a little dirty?" She shook her head. "I'm sorry. With everything happening, I just didn't think about it. I can make sure it doesn't happen again if you want." Was he really this upset over a few candy wrappers and a little trash? She never even cleaned the house as well as she kept her car.

"It's your car," he told her as he turned and stormed away. "You can keep it any way you want. Now, I need to get this ice in the cooler before it melts. What else needs to be done before people start arriving?"

She stood there, watching as he walked away as if she watched a tornado twirling its destruction across her front yard. Something happened while he was out, and he refused to talk about it. Why? He was all laughter and smiles when he left. He wasn't even gone an hour. What the hell could have gone wrong in such a short span of time?

She sighed as she shook her head. In her world lately, it could be anything.

With a deep breath, she shoved Glen's mood to the side and started for the house. She just needed to get through the party. Hopefully, Glen's mood would lighten up during the get-together.

Maybe he just struggled with what had already gone before, dealing with emotions from what she did that he struggled to bring under control. She would help him work past them, taking the anger she knew she deserved while he worked through them. That had to be it. She just couldn't think of anything else that would have set him off.

As soon as she entered the house, Aubrey was at her side. "What happened to Mr. Sexy Pants?" she asked, her voice low as she leaned in to whisper. "He just came in here, about bit your mother's head off, and stormed back outside mumbling something about the bounce house being in the wrong damn place."

Cherish handed her friend the birthday cake with a sigh. "I wish I knew. He was like that with me outside. Whatever it is, I hope he shakes it quick."

"Did you do something to deserve a spanking?" Aubrey asked with a bounce of her eyebrows.

"If I did, I wish he'd just spank me and get it over with," Cherish said with a shrug. "If he stays this way during the whole party, it's not going to be much of a party."

Aubrey looked out the window as Glen helped the bounce house man move the giant inflatable to the other side of the backyard. "Perhaps you should go out there and find out before anyone else gets here or before Glen kills your mother."

Cherish smirked. "And that would be a bad thing?"

"Only if it happens at her grandson's birthday party." Aubrey glanced over at Cherish, her expression grim.

Cherish just nodded. Her friend was right. Cherish needed to talk to Glen, find out what happened while he was out. There was no way this was over a dirty car.

Twenty-Four

Cherish walked outside, the paper plates and plastic cups in her hands. Aubrey was right, Cherish needed to discover what Glen was so upset about, but she couldn't allow his mood to affect Jordie's party. She forced a smile onto her face as she moved over to the table set up for the supplies, watching as Glen talked to the guy who brought the bounce house as they finished up. She placed the plates and cups on the table and then turned to wait until the two finished talking. Her father had already returned inside, probably a smart move considering how Glen talked to the bounce house guy. Cherish made sure she smiled while she waited, doing her best not to set Glen off any more than he already was.

The man started to fill the bounce house with air, the compressor ruining the quietness of the late morning. As he went about his business, Glen moved off to the side, his entire posture shouting anger and frustration. Why?

As he neared her, he glanced up, noticing her outside for the first time. She watched him approach, his face expressing he wanted to do anything right then but talk to her. Too bad for him. "Hey, can we…?"

Glen kept walking, not even bothering to look at her.

What the fuck? Cherish pushed away from the table and followed her husband. "Okay, stop," she called after him.

He showed no signs of stopping.

Cherish picked up her pace until she walked beside him, and then she stepped in front of him, forcing him to stop. "Glen, please, talk to me," she urged him as she placed both hands on his chest, bringing him to a halt. "What has you so pissed off?"

He stopped, looking up into the sky as he took a deep breath. He still said nothing. With a deep breath, he reached into his back pocket and pulled out what appeared to be a business card.

Cherish stared at it as he handed it over to her, her brows pinched in confusion at first until she recognized the dark green color on the front. Nick Pepper. Her eyes widened as she stared at it. She thought she threw that thing away. Then she jerked her gaze back to Glen. He thinks I cheated on him with Nick. *That has to be it. That's why he's so angry right now.* She closed her eyes, taking a deep breath. When she opened them again, she stared into his accusing gaze. She shook her head, her stomach a twisting mass of nausea threatening to make her hurl all over the ground. Tears pooled in the corner of her eyes as her body trembled. He doubted her. For the first time in their marriage, Glen doubted her, and it was all her fault. She made him doubt everything about her.

She took another breath, shaking her head. "It's not what you think," she said. "I swear."

Glen cocked an eyebrow at her but said nothing.

"After I did the interview at Harbor City Carpet, I went to Starbucks for some alone time to regroup," she told him, standing there, her fingers twisting around each other. She heard car doors from the road, and knew others were arriving for the party, friends, family, Jordie's friends from preschool; people she didn't want to see her having a fight with her husband. She pushed them out of her mind as she focused on convincing Glen to believe her. "As I was leaving, he was there, in the doorway. He said hello, asked how things were, just small talk. Before I left him standing there, he handed me his business card. I tossed it in the center console of my car, shoving him out of my mind. I swear, Glen. It's the only time I've seen him since he walked out on me, and I haven't reached out to him. I meant to throw the card away. I promise. I didn't do what you're thinking I did." She pleaded with him with her words, her tone, her eyes. He had to believe her. They were working their way back to a good place, traveling a new path, one they were doing together and enjoying. They just started; this couldn't derail them now. "You have to believe me."

He glared at her for a moment and then gave a sad shake of his head. "No, I don't," he said, his words full of venom as he gave a sad shake of his head. "You made it so I couldn't believe you."

"Hey, Arnie," Selby's voice called out from the road.

They glanced in that direction as Selby waved at Cherish's father, Faith and Tracey beside him, each carrying a gift. Cherish just rolled her eyes. *Oh, great, Faith's new adventure is here to see my life fall apart. Again.*

Glen turned back to Cherish, his lips pressed into a thin line.

"I know," she said, a tear escaping to snail down her cheek. "I know I did, and I will forever pay for that, but I promise you, nothing happened, ever. I don't want him. Hell, I didn't even want Edwin, really. I want you. I need you. I need us. Please, you just have to believe me."

"No, I don't," Glen hissed as he leaned in, glaring at her again. He leaned back, sighing as he slid his hands into his pockets. "Cherish, I don't know if I can believe you. I want to, trust me, but my first instinct is to think you're only telling me now because I busted you. You didn't want to tell me about Edwin until I pressed the issue. How do I know you didn't do the same thing now? You didn't tell me about Nick, because you didn't think you needed to tell me." He shook his head, and she could see the battle he waged etched in his features. He didn't believe her, and she had no idea how to make him. He blew out an exasperated breath. "After today, I'm moving out. I can't do this." He turned and walked away, leaving her staring after him.

And that's all she could do, stare at him with her mouth open as he stormed off, his back and shoulders a tight knot of rage. He thought she betrayed him again, but she didn't. She didn't want Nick. She wanted Glen. Yet, how would she convince him how she felt if he thought she still lied to him?

"You know, it won't be easy, right?" Aubrey said from behind her.

Cherish turned and faced her friend, not sure how the redhead managed to sneak up behind her or when she even left the house. "He doesn't believe me, and I don't know how to make him. I've broken his trust, and I can't get it back if he's always going to think I'm lying to him." She turned back and watched as Glen shoved his way into the house, feeling lost and desperate.

"Then go make him believe," Aubrey said. "He's worth fighting for, Cherish, but you have to fight. You two are trying this whole dominant-submissive thing, right?" She shrugged. "Then go in there and show him how submissive you can be; beg his forgiveness, kneel at his feet and prove you're serious."

Cherish turned and stared at Aubrey, one eyebrow cocked.

"You seem to know a lot about this lifestyle."

Aubrey shrugged. "I watch a lot of television." She pointed to the house. "Go get your man. I'll finish the prep out here and keep Jordie busy."

Cherish just stood there, staring around her as more people arrived. Children, including Jordie, already piled into the bounce house. Glen's partner, Brent, arrived, a blond on his arm, and joined Cherish's father and Selby by the grill where they seemed deep in a discussion about the best grilling practices while Faith and Tracey sat in camp chairs talking to Cherish's brother and his wife. Another car pulled up, and Cherish watched as Glen's parents and sister slid out of the car. Cherish couldn't go to Glen now. There were too many people there for her to risk causing a scene, but she also couldn't risk waiting and Glen continuing to stew over something that just wasn't true.

"Would you just go," Aubrey said, pushing at Cherish's shoulder toward the house. "I've got this out here."

Cherish faced her friend again, nodding. Aubrey was right. Cherish needed to convince Glen, and she needed to do it now. She took a deep breath and headed inside. "Keep an eye on Jordie." This would work or not.

~ ~ ~ ~ ~

Glen just needed a few minutes to calm his temper. He knew he had acted rude since returning home, and he didn't mean to snap at everyone, taking out his frustration with Cherish on everyone but her. He shoved his way inside the house and headed for the bedroom at the back of the house. Just a few minutes, that's all he needed.

However, what he needed and what he received were two different things. As soon as he plopped down on the bed, his hands clasped together as he rested his elbows on his knees, doing his best to take deep breaths, Cherish walked into the room, shutting the door behind her. He didn't even turn to look at her. He couldn't right then. She had lied. Again. That's all she ever did lately.

Cherish walked in front of him and dropped to her knees, sitting back on her heels, her hands on her thighs as she stared up at him. She said nothing. Just knelt there, waiting.

Glen closed his eyes, taking another fortifying breath. Before opening them again and staring at his wife. His stomach twisted into a knot of anxiety as he stared at her. "I can't do this."

"Then, why did you start it?" she asked, her voice low as she stared back at him.

He felt his brows pinch over his nose. "What?"

"Why did you start this path if you couldn't do it?" she asked. "You wanted control, and I gave it to you. I'm yours. You can't run at the first sign of a bump. I even agreed to accept whatever punishment you felt I deserved, but you didn't punish me; you ran, instead." She shook her head. "I didn't cheat on you with Nick. I saw him at the coffee shop and forgot to tell you about it. If you want to punish me for that, then punish me, but don't run off because this is hard." She slid forward, reaching out and placing her hands on his. "I fucked up and made it hard for you to trust me. I get it. I deserve that. However, I don't deserve you telling me you want to do this and then running from it." She nodded. "You want to leave, then I won't stop you, but you're not giving us a chance."

He stared at her, his insides churning as he listened to each word she said. What she said made sense, and he hated it. He closed his eyes again, fighting to rein in his turmoil. Could he trust her again? He was willing to give it a shot an hour ago, and Cherish was right, the first sign of doubt caused him to run. What kind of master could he be if he couldn't even control himself?

When he opened his eyes again, Cherish just sat there, smiling up at him. "I've never knelt in front of someone before," she said. "However, I'll kneel in front of you every day from now on if you want, and only you. I meant what I said about giving you full control. Now, you have to decide if you want it or not."

Glen stared at her, her strawberry-blond hair framing her face, the slight dusting of freckles along her cheeks and neck, leading to the shoulders that carried his mood swing at present. Outside the window, he could hear the children screaming and laughing as they bounced in the giant inflatable. He had almost ruined his son's birthday by allowing his own doubts to get the better of him. Glen knew he should have asked Cherish first, given her a chance to explain before he assumed the worst, but with everything that happened over the past few weeks, he struggled to think of the positive.

Cherish just watched him for a couple of minutes, then he saw her nod as she stood. He thought she gave up and was about to walk out, but instead, she moved to his side, pushing him back slightly before she bent over his lap, hiking her sundress up to her waist as she did. She glanced over her shoulder at him, her face a serious mask. "Punish me," she said. "I should have told you about running into him, and I didn't. I deserve it."

He stared at her a moment, then glanced down to her bare ass over his lap. He couldn't stop the smile that spread across his face as he reached out and caressed her warm flesh. "The books I read would call this topping from the bottom," he said, still focused on her ass as he slid his hand across her offered backside.

Cherish shrugged. "Then punish me for that, too. Seems I have a lot to learn. Now, will you be here to teach me?"

He squeezed her ass, spreading her cheeks slightly as he did. If he were to do this right, he would need to control his own emotions before he could ever expect to control her. He lifted his hand and swatted her ass once, hard, making her yelp as she squirmed in his lap. He then reached over and pulled her into a sitting position in his lap as he wrapped his arms around her waist. Gazing into her eyes, he said, "I'll be here. I'm sorry. I know I handled this all wrong."

"So did I," she admitted. "But, Glen, I meant everything I said. I know I have a long way to go before you trust me again, but I'm here, committed to us, to our family, and to this path we're taking. I won't screw it up again."

He nodded, pulling her closer as he held her. Kissing her shoulder, he said, "I know, and I know I'll struggle once in a while, but I'll do my best to trust you. I want this, too."

"Good," Cherish said as she laid her head on his shoulder. "I love you."

He squeezed her tightly. "I love you, too."

They stayed that way for a few moments, lost in each other's embrace, until Cherish whispered, "As much as I'd love to stay like this, we really should make sure our mothers aren't killing each other."

Glen chuckled as he kissed her nose. "You're right, of course."

Cherish stood, sliding her dress back into place, but not before Glen spun her, swatting her ass one more time. "Get us both a beer, please. I'll be right out."

She turned, staring at him with narrowed eyes. "You all right?"

"I am," he assured her, nodding. "Promise."

She smiled at him, her expression revealing she still didn't believe him. However, she squeezed his hand once before turning and doing as he asked.

Glenn watched as she passed through the doorway, her posture straight as she left him with his thoughts. She had knelt in front of him. He couldn't believe it. And she had draped herself over his lap and asked him to spank her. That was definitely not typical Cherish Lansky behavior. He ran a hand through his dark hair, still feeling the doubts tug at his gut. However, if she was willing to go to such lengths to prove she was serious about the journey they wanted to take, he would force those doubts down and believe her. While it was too soon to believe her completely, he would at least begin to show a little faith in what she said.

He shoved himself off the bed and walked over to the bedroom window, looking out at those gathered in his backyard for his son. Valerie sat on one end of the gathering with her family gathered around her while Glen's mother sat on the other with her family and Brent, Bonnie, and Aubrey. Glen shook his head. It was like two separate camps waiting along the edges of the battlefield. Valerie would expect Cherish to sit with her while Glen's mother would expect him to sit with her. He took in a deep breath. Not today. Today was Jordie's birthday, and Glen decided to take a page from Selby's book. Today, Cherish and he would make their own camp and enjoy themselves, choosing not to give in to their mothers' bitterness. Control. Cherish gave him control, and he was determined to take it completely, starting right then.

He took another breath and left the safety of the window for the chaos of the party. Hopefully, no casualties would litter his yard when it was all said and done.

Twenty-Five

Glen stepped back out into the yard, two camp chairs in his hands. Valerie Driscoll was accustomed to calling all the shots, and he knew she set up her area far away from his mother to try to force a division in the party, drawing the crowd to her, so she could show off. That was one of the reasons he wanted the party at his house, so she wouldn't be able to pull a stunt like this. Yet, she still wrecked division wherever she went.

Glen moved to the middle of the yard, close to the bounce house, and set up the two chairs. He turned to find Cherish near her mother, two beers in her hand as she watched him, one eyebrow raised and a smirk turning up the corner of her lip.

"Excuse me," he heard her tell her mother. "I think I'll go join my husband." She then left her mother's side, Valerie's mouth ajar as she gawked at her daughter's retreating back. When

Cherish reached him, she handed him his beer as she slid into her chair. "Your beer, sir," she said, smiling at him.

He glanced over at her, taking his beer as he sat down himself. "To be honest, I wasn't sure you would come over here. You tend to stick close to your mother."

Cherish shrugged as she lifted the beer bottle to her mouth. "I much prefer to be by your side." She took a swig of her beer, then lowered the bottle to her lap as she glanced over at him. "Besides, I know what you're doing by sitting here instead of anywhere else. I think it's a great idea. No sides but ours."

He reached out, taking her free hand in his and squeezing it. "I'm sorry about earlier," he told her, his voice soft as he stared into her eyes.

She nodded, squeezing his hand in return. "It's all good. I understand how it must have looked after everything, but I promise; nothing happened."

He nodded, saying nothing.

A scream came from the bounce house, jerking his attention around. Jordie chased after a little girl Glen didn't recognize, the girl screaming almost as much as she laughed.

"Looks like the bounce house was a hit," a voice came from behind them.

Turning, Glen saw his father and Arni walking up, each with a beer in their hand. Glen nodded. "Best party entertainer ever," he said with a chuckle.

"And a beautiful day for it," Robert said as he stepped up to where Glen and Cherish sat. "Not too cold, not too hot. You've got to love April weather in Florida."

Arni nodded, chuckling. "Enjoy it before the heat index starts climbing in May."

"True story," Robert said, laughing.

"Let me get you both a chair," Cherish offered, standing

before any of the others could protest.

Glen watched her walk over to her mother's little camp and snag two camp chairs. Cherish was not the type to offer to help someone typically, and the fact she did it for both of their fathers right then made Glen smile.

"What are you doing?" Valerie asked as Cherish picked up one of the unoccupied chairs. "If they need to sit, they can come over here and sit down. Why are you dragging chairs over to them?"

Cherish shrugged. "Because they're over there, not here. Seems simple enough." She grabbed another chair with her free hand and turned to return to the others, smiling at her sister's raised eyebrow.

"You know, that seems like a great idea," Selby said as he stood. "Sitting closer to the kids so we can watch the birthday boy enjoy his day." He turned to Faith and Tracey. "Why don't we join them?"

Valerie glared at Selby, and Glen had to keep from laughing.

Faith and Tracey stood with him, each grabbing their chair and drink, and followed him over to where Glen and the others sat, leaving Valerie with her son, Dennis, and his wife, Debra. Their kids, Denise and Danny, were quite content in the bounce house. Of course, that didn't remain that way for long.

"I think that's a great idea," Debra said, looking over at Dennis. "Let's get closer, so we can watch the kids."

Dennis smiled at her, nodding his balding head. "Sounds good to me, love."

Glen watched as the two of them stood, picked up their chairs, and followed the others to where he sat, leaving Valerie Driscoll all by her lonesome.

"Seems like you guys have the best seats in the house," Brent said as he, Bonnie, and Aubrey plopped their chairs down beside them. "Of course, the screaming is a little loud, but hey, it's kids, right?"

Glen nodded, lifting his beer bottle to his lips. "As long as they're screaming from joy and not pain, all is right with the world."

Arni laughed as he slid into the chair Cherish brought him. "Oh, god, isn't that the truth. Hell, I remember one time when Cherish screamed like a banshee, jerking me off the couch, only to find out Dennis and Faith were tickling her into a fit in the back bedroom." He shook his head. "Scared the hell out of me until I saw what was happening."

Cherish sighed. "If I remember correctly, you didn't save me, either. Instead, you joined them in tickling me, making me scream louder."

"And then Mom came in, and we were all screaming for a different reason," Dennis added, laughing as he shook his head.

Robert took his seat, his beer resting on his knee as he held it. "Only having two kids, it was always a fair fight in our house," he said. "If they screamed, I'd just wait to see if anyone came out bleeding. If not, I ignored it and left Brenda to deal with it."

"And I was always on the losing end of those fights," Tanya said as she and her mother joined the growing cluster. Tanya then grinned over at her brother. "Until I wasn't, and then the fight was on."

Everyone laughed as they settled into their chairs. Everyone that is, except Valerie. She remained where she was, arms across her chest as she stared at the kids playing in the bounce house as if nothing was wrong. Glen just shook his head at the woman's stubbornness. She just couldn't bring herself to be nice to others unless she was the center of attention. Even Glen's mother could play nice, choosing to allow people to live their lives as they wanted whether or not she agreed with them. What happened in

Valerie's life to make her so miserable?

Cherish reached out, taking Glen's hand to get his attention.

When he turned to look at her, he could see the request in her eyes. He simply nodded, giving her silent permission to at least make an effort.

Cherish stood, leaving the small group to try to coax her mother to join them. He doubted it would work, of course, but if anyone could do it, it would be Cherish. Typical youngest child behavior. He watched his mother do the same with Tanya, spoiling his baby sister more than she ever did him. The two were joined at the hip most of the time, even more so than his mother and father were, it seemed. Of course, Tanya never tried to push those boundaries the way Cherish did growing up. At least, not that he knew, anyway. He had to admit, growing up, he was pretty self-absorbed and had paid little attention to what his sister did.

He glanced over at Tanya who stood clustered with Brent, Bonnie, and Aubrey. His sister was the quiet one growing up, always afraid to branch out too far from home. She was in her late-twenties and still lived at home. He doubted she would ever move out. He joked before that his parents would have to move in order to get a house to themselves, but he doubted that would even work.

"What's so funny?" Brent asked him.

Glen turned to his friend, a puzzled look on his face. "Excuse me? I didn't say anything."

"Nope, but that face of yours said it all," Faith said with a laugh. "You were thinking something you thought was funny. Gotta share."

Oh, he was so not sharing. He just chuckled as he shook his head. Better to deny. "To be honest, I don't even remember. Probably something Cherish said or something I heard." He shrugged. "Old age must be setting in."

His father rolled his eyes. "You're so full of shit," he said.

Arni chuckled. "Funny when the young ones think they're old, isn't it?"

"Well, Glen's always acted old," Tanya teased, and everyone laughed.

"Okay, I think that's my cue to start the grill," Glen said as he made a dramatic show of standing his ancient body to its feet. "If I can lift the spatula, that is."

"Come on, old man, I'll help you," Brent said. He leaned over and kissed Bonnie softly. "I'll be right back. He's not joking about being weak. I've seen him lift a hammer. Not a pretty sight."

Glen just rolled his eyes.

~ ~ ~ ~ ~

Cherish left the others and walked over to her mother, taking one of the remaining chairs beside the other woman. "Why don't you come join the rest of us? Has to be better than sitting over here all by yourself."

Her mother didn't even look at her, keeping her gaze on the children. "Why is she here?" she asked, her back stiff, hands clasped in her lap.

"There are a lot of shes here," Cherish said, even though she knew to whom her mother referred. "You'll have to be a little more specific."

"Your sister's new friend," her mother said, her lips pressed into a thin line. "Why did they have to bring her to a family event? It's rude."

Cherish glanced over and watched as Tracey Williams laughed at something Arni said, her feet barely touching the ground from where she sat in the chair. "She's close to Selby and Faith," Cherish said with a shrug. "We permitted Brent to bring

Bonnie; why wouldn't we allow Faith and Selby to bring Tracey? She seems to be getting along with everyone all right."

"It's not proper," her mother hissed. "I'm not exactly sure what's happening between them, but it's not right."

Cherish knew exactly what was happening between the trio, but she didn't volunteer that information to her mother. Glen told Cherish about seeing Tracey leave Selby's bookstore, kissing Selby goodbye. There was more than a little fling there, but Cherish had too much of her own drama unfolding to worry about her sister. "Something tells me you'll have to get used to it. I don't see Tracey going anywhere, anytime soon."

Valerie whipped around and stared at her daughter. "And just what does that mean?"

"It means it's none of my business. Now, why don't you grab your chair and come join everyone else. They're all having a great time."

Her mother stared over at the clump of people, all laughing and joking around. "Yes, yes, they are, aren't they?"

Cherish glanced at her mother, noticing the grim expression on the woman's face. Her mother was not used to someone else having control of things, and the fact the party was a success robbed her of her moment to tell Cherish that allowing Glen to have the party here was a disaster. Good thing, too. If the party flopped, Cherish's mother would never allow her to hear the end of it.

"Why did you never tell me?" her mother asked, still staring at Jordie as he slid back into the bounce house after Denise, both kids laughing as they tackled Danny.

This time, Cherish didn't play dumb. "Because I was ashamed," she said with a shrug, following her mother's gaze. "And scared. God, was I scared." She needed a drink but refused to get up and get one. This conversation was too long in coming.

"Nick had already pulled his shit, leaving me for that bimbo at the bar." She took a deep breath, sucking in her nervousness. "By then, I was already seeing Glen, and then I found out I was pregnant. I didn't know what to do." She gave a soft chuckle. "I was terrified of telling Dad. The way I lived my life back then..." She shook her head. "I knew he was already disgusted with a lot of things I did, and this would just be another way I would have disappointed him."

Her mother stared out at Jordie as the little boy leaped into the air, bouncing as high as he could. "Your father loves you. He would never turn his back on you." She sighed as she dropped her gaze down to her hands. "He always thought I was too easy on you. Perhaps, he was right."

Cherish nodded. "He was," she admitted. "You permitted me to get away with everything back then." She shrugged. "I took advantage of it. I don't know what I would have done if you had been a little tougher on me." She turned, glancing at her mother. "Why weren't you? Tougher on me, that is."

Her mother didn't answer right away, continuing to stare at her hands, her lips pressed into a thin line. "You've never been like your brother and sister." Cherish watched as the corner of her mother's lip twisted up into a lopsided grin. "Even younger, you were rambunctious, rebellious, always pushing every boundary. Dennis and Faith were always afraid of the consequences. You dared the consequences." For the first time, she glanced up at Cherish, and the anguish on her face twisted Cherish's insides. "After I punished you once for something you did—I don't even remember what it was—you screamed at me, telling me you didn't love me, that you hated me. You were six at the time. For a week after that, you refused to talk to me, wouldn't even look at me. Your father wanted to spank you. He kept telling me we needed to punish you again for your disrespectful behavior and hateful attitude." She shook her head. "I wouldn't let him. I was afraid it would only make you angrier, make the situation worse." Tears pooled at the bottom of her eyes as she stared over at her daughter. "I just wanted you to love me again. That's what I've always wanted. I was afraid if I didn't allow you to do what you wanted, you would have stopped loving me." She swiped at the tears, taking a deep breath as she did. "And in wanting that, I failed you. I'm sorry."

Cherish felt the tears streaming down her cheeks, felt the anguish clutching at her heart as she sat there, staring at her mother, the woman crying openly now as she stared back at Cherish. How could her mother ever doubt Cherish's love for her? Because I did a shitty job of showing it. I pushed her with everything I did. Cherish reached out, taking her mother's hand in her own, squeezing it tight. "I've always loved you, Mom. You did nothing wrong. It was all me; I was the selfish bitch who never seemed satisfied and happy. I'm so sorry I ever made you feel that way." She squeezed her mother's hand again. "I should never have treated you that way."

Her mother gave her a weak smile, squeezing her hand back before pulling it away. "I love you, too, and I'm sorry I ever made you feel as if you couldn't tell me you were pregnant." She shook her head. "Not a very good mother, huh?"

Cherish settled back in her chair. "I think we both made mistakes, but that was then. This is now. I need to take responsibility for my own actions. I am taking responsibility for my actions." She glanced over at the others clumped together, laughing, sharing stories, as Glen and Brent stood by the grill, sipping beers and flipping burgers. "And right now, my family is my responsibility, and I have to take it seriously." She turned back around, smiling over at her mother. "Why don't we join the others and have some fun? It's doing neither of us any good sitting here sulking."

At first, Cherish didn't think her mother would agree to join the others, but after a moment, she shook her head, her lips pressed into a thin line. "Yes, why don't we do that." She turned, her smile growing. "It'll be fun, I'm sure."

Cherish would take what she could. Smiling, she nodded, standing and grabbing the back of her chair. They walked back over to the others, Valerie moving to sit beside her husband, while Cherish placed her chair beside Glen's. The others laughed at something Faith just said, but the voices went weirdly quiet when Valerie sat down.

Arni must have noticed the awkwardness that swallowed the group, because he chuckled again as he shifted in his chair. "I don't see how you do it, Selby," Arni said as he glanced over as Glen walked back over, joining them. Turning back to Selby, Arni said, "Another week alone." He shook his head. "I'd go stir crazy in a totally silent house."

Cherish glanced over at Faith, her brows pinched over her nose. "Where are you going now?"

Faith shrugged, avoiding looking at their mother. "Morgan asked me to lend him a hand in Biloxi, training his new employees. I'm flying out Tuesday, coming back Friday." She turned to face her father. "So, it's not really a whole week. Selby's a big boy."

Tracey laughed as she shook her head. "He almost starved last time, forgetting to eat."

Faith nodded, laughing as well. "You'll have to make sure he eats while I'm gone."

Tracey tilted her head a bit as she stared at Selby. "Maybe. If he's a good boy."

Faith shook her head, her lips downturned in a frown as she looked at her husband. "Looks like you're going to starve."

Selby made a dramatic sigh. "I'm always mistreated."

The others just laughed at him.

Faith turned to Cherish. "Jed told me he talked to you about returning to Rutherford," she said. "He asked me if I'd be all right if you returned." She shrugged. "I told him it really doesn't matter to me. Maybe next week would be the perfect time, since I'll be gone. I'm sure Jed could use the help."

"Jed asked you to go back to Rutherford?" Glen asked, staring at Cherish, his face pinched with confusion. "You never mentioned that."

Cherish stared at Glen, the knot back in her stomach. She completely forgot about her conversation with Jed. Leave it to her sister to expose another one of her failures. "I'm sorry. I forgot all about it."

Glen nodded. "Are you thinking about going back?"

She wished she could read his face. "I hate working at Harbor City Carpet, but I'll find something else. I know you don't want me at Rutherford." She had no time to talk to him about it, and definitely couldn't do it in front of everyone gathered there.

Glen just smiled at her. "We'll discuss it."

Cherish nodded, trying to keep her nerves from making her throw up. "Yes, sir."

She ignored her mother's arched eyebrow.

Twenty-Six

Cherish placed the last of the glasses back in the cabinet, her back screaming at her due to the lengthy day she just endured. Jordie was already sound asleep in his bed, his tired little body crashing as soon as everyone left, and the constant energy faded away. She could relate as exhaustion tugged at her as well. She had to admit, however, Glen's idea of having the party at their house opposed to her parents' was definitely a winner, minus the cleanup part afterward. Jordie loved every gift he opened, and he and the other kids made full use of the bounce house. Even a few of the adults climbed inside to get their inner youth on while they made the little ones stand outside the giant inflatable while they took over. The children, of course, were far from happy about not being permitted inside, but they laughed like crazy as they watched their parents bouncing around, trying to do flips, and falling on their asses.

Valerie surprised Cherish with how she interacted with everyone else after their emotional conversation. She even got along with Glen's mother, which shocked everyone, including Brenda. The exchange between Cherish and her mother had been an eye-opener on both sides, and Cherish regretted how she treated her parents when she was younger, how she treated them even recently, if she was honest with herself. Cherish knew she had a lot to atone for but had no idea how to begin.

Glen walked into the kitchen, pulling two coffee mugs from the cabinet, and filling both to the rim. He set one beside Cherish as she dried her hands and took a tentative sip of his own. Rubbing his lips together when he finished, wiping away the excess, he took a deep breath as he slumped back on the counter. "Now, that was a party," he said with a slight chuckle. "I've never known that boy to go to bed without asking for several glasses of water or another story."

Cherish folded the towel, placing it on the edge of the sink as she laughed. Reaching for her coffee, she shook her head. "He was nonstop from the moment that man inflated the bounce house. I didn't think I would get him out of it long enough to blow out the candles on his cake."

Glen nodded. "Arni threatening to deflate the thing worked, though."

Cherish chuckled as she lifted her coffee cup to her lips. "That it did."

Glen tilted his head slightly as he studied her, and Cherish squirmed under his scrutiny, worried he was about to bring up Jed asking her to return to Rutherford again. "What was all that going on between you and your mother earlier?" he asked. "Seemed pretty intense from where I stood."

She nodded. "It was." She gave him a synopsis of the

conversation, her heart aching once more with the anguish she heard in her mother's voice as they spoke. Again, the tears threatened to undo her. Glen just stood there, sipping his coffee, as he listened to her. "I was such a bitch growing up. I'm surprised my family even talks to me."

Glen shrugged. "All families have their issues. The fact they still talk to you says something about how much they love you."

"I wonder how different my life would have been if Mom would have allowed my father to punish me more," Cherish said as she wrapped both hands around her coffee cup. "I mean, I was a kid, a teenager, pushing boundaries is part of the DNA. Once I discovered I could get away with things, I just naturally kept seeing how far I could go. I pushed myself right over the edge into the chaos that ruled my life back then, including putting up with Nick's bullshit for a year." She shook her head. "Mom never gave me a line and told me not to cross it." She glanced up into Glen's eyes. "I won't allow that to happen with Jordie."

"And if he screams he hates you and wants nothing to do with you?" Glen asked, reminding her how she had screamed at her mother, which made Valerie pull back the hard hand on Cherish.

"Then I'll punish him for being a little snit," Cherish said with a shrug. "He may hate me, but I won't allow him to grow up like I did."

Glen moved over to where she stood and kissed her forehead. "I don't think Jordie could ever hate you," he told her when he pulled away. She gazed up into his eyes, the love staring back at her sucking the breath out of her. "And if he ever spoke to you that way, he'd have to deal with me."

She smiled as she felt the blush warm her cheeks. "I don't doubt it." She shrugged again. "Of course, Jordie is a lot better kid than I was."

"We are lucky with him that way," Glen said, chuckling. "I

think that has a lot to do with how you raise him, though."

"And you," Cherish said. "You've been the best father he could have ever had."

Glen smiled, staring down into his coffee. "He's a good kid."

Cherish took a deep breath, deciding to tackle the topic of Rutherford even if Glen hadn't brought it up. "I'm sorry I didn't tell you about Jed. It's been a pretty emotional week all around, and I swear, it just slipped my mind."

Glen cocked an eyebrow at her. "A lot of things have slipped your mind lately. I should probably do something about that, eventually."

She bowed her head. "Yes, sir," was all she said, but she couldn't deny the tingle between her legs at the thought of Glen punishing her again. She would never have thought the idea of him spanking her would have such an effect on her.

He took a sip of his coffee as he studied her, and Cherish just stood there under his scrutiny. After a stretched-out moment, he said, "So, tell me about the conversation now. You said you weren't interested in returning. Is that the truth?"

She shrugged. "I don't know, to be honest. And, in the way of full disclosure, it was sort of a mixture of him asking if I would want to return and me asking if he'd take me back. At the moment, the bullshit at Harbor City Carpet had me over it all, especially with Mary driving me nuts with her snippy, judgmental attitude, and the chaos left behind with Kim's abrupt departure. The place is a madhouse, and I'm sure it's because I'm just not used to how they do things. I worked for Rutherford for eight years; I knew the ins and outs. I created most of them. I was comfortable there. Maybe I'm just struggling because it's something new and out of my comfort zone."

Glen nodded, his lips pressed into a thin line. "And could you handle returning to Rutherford, knowing everyone probably knows what happened, working with Faith again? You didn't really enjoy working with her before, even before you knew she slept with Edwin."

Cherish forced herself not to answer right away, knowing a flippant reply was not what Glen wanted or needed. Instead, she thought through his question. There was no doubt her affair with Edwin would be common knowledge among the others, and she'd probably get some snark from some of them. Then there was also Faith. She told Cherish earlier she didn't care if Cherish went back to Rutherford, but did she really mean it? Then, Cherish wondered where Jed would put her. Faith already had her old position, and Nessa had Faith's, so would Cherish just go back part time, like Nessa was previously? Could they even afford that? Finally, she could only shrug. "I honestly don't know. I'm sure I'd get the stare and even some snide remarks, but hell, I'm getting that now. As far as working with Faith, I already know there are things I need to work on there. This might just be the way I accomplish that."

She watched as he sipped his coffee some more, his brows pinched with thought. The question, she knew, really wasn't whether or not she could handle it, but rather, would Glen be able to trust her if she went back to work there. He already struggled, as was obvious with his reaction to Nick's business card, and he had a perfect right to doubt her. However, this would be more in the face of what she did on a regular basis as opposed to the one-offs that would pop up now and then. If Glen couldn't handle it, she didn't want to do it. It wouldn't be worth it.

Glen set his cup on the counter and moved to stand in front of her. Placing a hand on each of her cheeks, he pulled her forward slightly as he whispered a kiss along her forehead. When he pulled back, he smiled down at her. "If you think you can handle it, and it's what you want, then I say talk to Jed and see what he offers. I'll be honest; I'll struggle with trust wherever you work. You got away with cheating on me there, so you could probably get away with it anywhere. That's something I'll have to handle."

She nodded, unsure of what to say to that last part.

"It may only be part time," she told him, her face scrunched up in an apology. "Faith is in my old position, and Nessa is in hers. After what happened, I doubt they'd shuffle everyone back around."

He shrugged. "Then why not just work part time? I mean, the extra money would be nice, of course, but we don't really need it to survive. This would give you more time with Jordie, which you always said you wanted." He grinned at her as he bounced his eyebrows. "I might even be able to swing by on some lunches now and then, if you know what I mean."

"I love the way you think," she said with a giggle. "But are you sure we can swing it?" Cherish had worked since high school, never not having a full-time job. How would it be not to have to work every day?

"I'd make it work," he assured her. "Of course, there may be a no clothes policy when Jordie is out of the house. I love the idea of coming home and seeing you naked." He leered at her as he ducked his head to her neck and nibbled.

Cherish yelped, then giggled as she wrapped her arms around him, doing her best not to allow her coffee to slosh out of the cup. "I'll wear or not wear whatever you want, sir."

He wiggled his eyebrows at her again, grinning from ear to ear. "Now, *that* I like to hear. We should start right now, while Jordie is asleep."

Cherish placed her cup on the counter. "Yes, sir," she said as she reached for the hem of her sundress and slid it up her torso and over her head. She reached behind her, unclasping her bra, and then slid it down her shoulders and arms until she stood in front of Glen stark naked, hands behind her back, hands clasped. "As you wished, sir." Her pussy tingled as she felt her honey drip. This is what she wanted.

~ ~ ~ ~ ~

Glen soaked in her naked body, making no qualms about devouring her with his gaze. He had always thought Cherish was gorgeous and hated when she started to hide her body in baggy shirts and shorts. He wanted to see more of her flesh, more of her body tempting him under tight clothes or low-cut tops. He wanted her to be seductive, sultry, sexy. Hell, he even wanted her to dress slutty for him.

Reaching out, Glen ran a hand over her freckle-covered shoulder, up her neck, and into her strawberry-blond hair. Gazing into her eyes, he sucked in a breath as he stared at her. "You, Cherish Lansky, are beautiful."

He saw her cheeks redden with her blush, felt her squirm under his touch as his words embarrassed her, but he didn't care. While he thought the words often enough, he failed to say them out loud for her to hear. She needed to hear them. He needed to say them. They needed to get back to the spark that was them when they first ignited each other's passions. Looking at her right then, he admitted to himself, he missed part of who they were just as much as she did. He would make sure they never grew stagnant again.

Gripping her hair in his hand, he slid his other hand up her stomach, cupping her right breast as he flicked her swollen nipple with his thumb. He felt her body tighten as she sucked in a breath, her eyes never leaving his. He squeezed her nipple harder, making her moan as she pushed her chest into his hand. Yanking her head back, exposing her neck, Glen leaned in and ran his tongue over her heated flesh, making his wife groan louder. Then, he just grinned as he took a step back, unbuttoning his pants with one hand, and then pulled his stiff cock out into the open. He then yanked her head down so that her mouth was on his thick shaft, leaving her bent over, ass open for his hands.

Cherish didn't hesitate. She opened her mouth, and he felt her swallow his cock, her tongue swirling around the head before taking his full length inside of her mouth. Glen groaned as he slid his free hand down her back and over her ass. He slid his finger between her cheeks until he found her entrance, not surprised at how soaked he found her. He dipped his finger into her pussy up to his first knuckle while pressing his other fingers against her ass.

Cherish moaned around his cock, but never stopped sucking him off, her head sliding back and forth as he gripped her hair.

"Now, this would be a great lunchtime dish," he said as he slid his finger in deeper, fucking her with it as he clamped onto her head.

She slid off his cock long enough to groan, "Yes, sir," and then went right back to sucking him off.

Glen added another finger to the first and shoved them deep inside of her, her pussy sucking at his fingers as he pounded them into her. The kitchen filled with the sounds of her wetness and the slurping of her blowjob. He groaned as he stood there, thrusting into his wife's willing mouth, fucking her face with his cock and her sex with his fingers. Looking down at her, a devilish grin on his face, he pushed his thumb against her dark hole and pushed.

Cherish whimpered around his cock, her body tightening against this new intrusion. He pushed slowly, his thumb popping into her back door as he continued to finger-fuck her, the fingers not penetrating her, sliding back and forth against her sensitive clit. Soon, Cherish pushed back on his hand, her whimpers getting louder as she sucked his cock. He could hear her begging for more around his cock, and as he picked up the pace, he felt her body tighten and shudder, her moans growing louder as she shoved her body back onto his hand. He held her tight against him as her orgasm ripped through her, her body shaking and jerking as she wiggled her pussy on his fingers. He felt her juices gushing over his hand as he continued to pound her, her body thrashing in his grip as her climax controlled her.

His cock throbbed in her mouth, and he felt himself explode, filling her as she gulped each stream of his seed. He held onto her tightly, burying her face on his shaft as he emptied himself into her mouth. Once he finished, he took a deep breath and loosened his grip on her head, allowing her room to breathe. He kept his fingers in her ass and pussy, however, as he grinned down at her. "Now, this is a position I seem to like," he said as he wiggled his thumb in her ass.

Cherish ran her tongue around his cock as she slid her mouth off his manhood, taking the last drop of his cum with her as she leaned back to gaze up into his face. "Yes, sir," she said, her voice husky with her heavy breathing. "It definitely has its perks."

Glen shoved his thumb deeper into her ass, making her moan before he yanked his fingers out of her holes. "I'm going to bury my cock in that ass of yours one day."

Cherish moaned, and he felt her body shudder at the thought. "Yes, sir," was all she said, however.

Glen helped her stand, holding her until he was sure her feet were stable enough to support her, and then guided her back to the counter so she could lean back on it. He then reached for his cup again and took a slow sip as he leaned back on the counter opposite Cherish, his face growing serious. He stared down into his cup as he spoke. "I can handle taking control," he told her. "And I love the idea of dressing you up and taking you out." He glanced up, locking gazes with her. "But, do you want an open marriage? Do you want to explore the way Faith and Selby are?" He held up a hand, stopping her from rushing with her answer. "And please, don't just say what you think I want to hear. We need to be completely open and honest about everything as we move forward." He took a deep breath. "Just tell me what you want."

Cherish didn't answer right away, for which Glen was glad. He needed her to be honest about her wants if they were to make sure to meet each other's needs.

After a lengthy few moments, Cherish finally shrugged. "I don't know, honestly." She shrugged again. "The idea scares me. What if one of us falls for someone else? What happens if one of us really gets into it, and the other one suddenly wants to quit? We could open doors we're unable to close again. To be honest, I'm not sure how I would handle sharing you, even though I know how hypocritical that sounds coming from me right now." She then looked at him earnestly. "Do you want it? Would you want it just to get even with me?"

Glen set his cup back on the counter and walked over to Cherish, taking her in his arms and staring deep into her eyes. "I'm not seeking revenge, sweetheart. There is no getting even or tit-for-tat here. We're not looking at the past, but rather, toward the future. If this is something you want to try, then we try it with our eyes open. We make the rules and trust each other to follow them."

Cherish nodded, sliding her hands up his arms as he held her. This would be their world, and they would make it work for them. Life was about finding the adventures and making the most of them. He had forgotten that, and it took almost losing his family for him to remember. He wouldn't forget them again.

Twenty-Seven

Cherish shoved her phone into her purse, closed the final file folder, and shoved herself away from her desk. This day was over, and she was more than happy to see it go. As she stood, however, she realized the day was not completely over. She stood at the edge of her desk, adjusting her purse on her shoulder, as Mary Overton stepped into her doorway, arms crossed over her chest, looking as if she had a corncob shoved deep up her ass. What Bernie saw in the woman, Cherish would never know.

Cherish sucked in a deep breath as she paused, waiting to hear what had brought the grump of a woman to her door. "Is there something I can help you with?" Cherish asked.

Mary glanced over the room, scowling as she took in the changes Cherish made to the small office. "I see you've rearranged. Making the place more to your liking." Cherish could have sworn the woman gave a disgusted sniff as she said it. "I thought the way Kim had it set up was quite efficient." She glanced around the room with a sneer turning up her lips, obviously not at all pleased with the way Cherish moved things around.

Cherish shrugged as she glanced around the small office as well. "What can I say? Everyone has their own way of doing things." She turned her gaze back to Mary. "I wanted to make it more to my tastes. Bernie said I could do whatever I needed to make it feel comfortable for me."

Mary scoffed. "I just bet he did." She took a deep breath, her back straightening as she did, making her look taller, almost as if she made herself rise above Cherish. "I'll have you know, I was against hiring you. I'm still against it. Bernie says you're the best at what you do. I hope he meant office work and not something else."

Cherish felt her blood boil at Mary's words. "What the hell have I ever done to you?" she snapped, shifting where she stood as she braced against the other woman's audacity. "I didn't tell your employee to get herself knocked up. All I did was answer an ad for a job, a job your husband gave me by the way." She moved closer to Mary, tightening her grip on her purse strap as she did. "I'm damn good at my job, a job where I work very hard, I'll have you know. I'm not interested in your husband or anyone else in this shithole. I've had a bully in my life since I was a little girl, and if you think you can top her, you've got another thing coming. You don't want me here, fire me, but I'll be damned if I'll put up with your snotty behavior every damn day." She shoved past the other woman, pushing Mary out of her way. "Enjoy your evening." She stormed out of the warehouse toward the back door for employees. She didn't even look back to see if

Mary Overton glared at her, which she was sure the woman was. Cherish didn't care. She refused to allow Mary to treat her like some skank just itching to steal Mary's husband.

Cherish shoved her way out the back door, storming down the concrete steps on her way to her car. As she reached her vehicle, she paused at the driver's door, staring back at the open warehouse doors. *Will it always be like this?* She took a deep breath and yanked her car door open. There was no way she would put up with this harassment on a daily basis. She needed to talk to Glen again about going back to work for Rutherford. She took a deep breath as she started her car. Only a week, and she already wanted to walk out of Harbor City Carpet.

~ ~ ~ ~ ~

Glen ran the towel through his hair as he stared at Cherish, who sat on the foot of their bed. He understood her frustration with her job. He wasn't necessarily in the construction field like Cherish, but he still knew how the rumor mill worked at places. Even big corporations had their gossip trains, regardless of what human resources warned against. However, he wasn't sure how he could help her here. She cheated on him, and it wasn't even like people found out about the affair because of carelessness on Cherish's part. She outed herself when she confronted Edwin that Sunday at Rutherford to collect her possessions. After that, there was no way people wouldn't talk about it. Once the people at Rutherford found out, it was only a matter of time before the gossip spread and one person mentioned it to another person at another business who mentioned it to someone else at another business. Soon, the drama at Rutherford was all over Melbourne, and Glen's wife's infidelity was the talk of the town. Well, part of the town, anyway.

Dropping the arm holding the towel to his side, he walked over to where Cherish sat and joined her on the bed. He reached out, placing a hand on her leg and gave her a reassuring squeeze. "I'm sorry you're having to deal with this," he told her. He gave a weak shrug. "I guess we never know the full extent of our actions and their consequences until it's too late." He quickly held a hand up, stopping her from saying anything else. "That wasn't a judgment. Promise."

She offered him a weak smile. "I didn't take it that way." She shrugged. "Besides, you're right. I didn't realize while I was...you know...how it would hurt you or Jordie, and I sure as hell didn't realize how it would follow me to another job. I was too caught up in what I was doing to even think of anything else." She reached out, placing her hand on top of his. "I'm sorry I was such a selfish bitch."

Glen leaned over and kissed Cherish's forehead. When he pulled away, he grinned. "You're my selfish bitch, so it's all good."

Cherish laughed softly as she ducked her head a little. Then, she took a deep breath, straightening her shoulders. "I still hate working at Harbor City Carpet." She shook her head. "Mary will make it her mission to make my life miserable."

"Then quit," Glen said, surprised he even spoke the words. He took a deep breath, realizing he meant them. "Life is too short to work somewhere that doesn't make you happy. Quit. Find something else. We'll be all right until you do."

Cherish turned, staring over at him, her brows pinched as she studied him. "Are you sure? I'm not sure how long it'll take me to find something else."

Glen squeezed her leg again, smiling. "You already know a place that wants you. Call Jed and get your job back. Faith said she wouldn't care if you went back to Rutherford, and she's in Biloxi this week, so Jed might need the help from someone he wouldn't have to train."

"You could handle me working there again?" Her expression told him she didn't really believe him, but Glen could tell she held out hope he wasn't lying to her. The fact that his comfort level was the first thing to concern her assured him he made the right decision. "A couple of weeks ago, you wanted me out of there. Besides, with the personnel shuffles, I may only get part-time work right now."

He leaned over and kissed her forehead again, inhaling her scent as he did. Pulling back, he nodded. "I'm sure. And I already said part-time is fine. It'll give you more time to take care of Jordie." He shrugged. "You could actually be one of those school moms who are always there helping out."

"Me? A school mom?" She laughed softly. "That will shock everyone, I'm sure." She shook her head again, taking a deep breath. "Are you really sure about this? You would trust me to work there again? It wouldn't drive you crazy wondering things?"

He gave her a weak smile. "For a while, I'm sure I'll have my doubts and struggles, trust issues and such, but if we move forward, then I have to trust you. I won't spend my life wondering if you're cheating on me again." He slid his hand up her side and into her hair, taking a fistful and pulling her head back. "You submitted to me, right?"

"Yes, sir," Cherish groaned as she stared into his eyes. "I'm completely yours."

Glen stared into her eyes, searching for any hint of duplicity in her words or expression. Yet, there was nothing there but total surrender. She screwed up and knew it, but that was over, and together the two of them would build an even better life as they explored this new journey.

Glen nodded once. "Then I think you should call Jed and see if he can use you. Keep it part time." Glen winked at her. "I may have other uses for your time."

He watched as Cherish shivered a little, a look of pure passion crossing her face. "Yes, sir."

Leaning down, Glen kissed her, his fist still gripping her hair tightly. Cherish parted her lips as he shoved his tongue into her mouth, tasting her, reclaiming her as his. When he broke the kiss, he grinned at her. "You are mine. Never forget that again."

She smiled up at him. "I won't. I promise."

He nodded again as he released his grip on her hair. "Now, call Jed, and let's see where we go from here."

"Yes, sir," she said, almost with a moan as her head tingled from where Glen gripped it just a second ago.

He watched as she slid from the bed, moving to the front room and her cell phone. His gaze drifted over her slender shoulders down to her heart-shaped ass, a grin pushing up the corners of his mouth.

At the door, she paused, turning back to face him, a small smile decorating her lips as she blushed at the way he soaked in her body. "I love you," she said, her expression softening as he watched her blush even more.

He smiled back at her. "I love you, too."

~ ~ ~ ~ ~

Cherish felt like bursting the moment she left the bedroom, the warmth from Glen's kiss still on her lips. He did it again, just like last time. He saved her when she didn't deserve saving. He stood beside her when another man would have tossed her out on her ass. He loved her, and she would make sure she was worthy of that love.

Entering the living room, she walked over to where her purse sat on the coffee table and pulled out her cell phone. She never thought she would make this phone call or even need to use Jed's phone number again. She knew it would be tough, being back where all hell broke loose, but she could do it. She *would* do it. If

Glen could allow her to walk back into the offices where she betrayed him, then she could handle the snide looks and remarks she was sure to get at first. The people at Rutherford had been her family for eight years, and not the family she deserved. She was sure they would welcome her back, and she would do things right this time. Glen offered her a second chance, and Cherish would not waste it.

She scrolled her contacts until she found Jed's name and hit call.

The phone rang three times before he answered. "Well, this is a surprise. What can I do for you?"

Cherish took a deep breath. "I called to see about coming home."

Acknowledgments

Regardless of my name being on the cover, it takes a team to put these stories in your hands, and I'm surrounded by one of the best. Charleen Cox keeps this team running and organized, keeping our office records, taking care of my swag for each book, and building the things we need for shows and events. Teri Edney is amazing at my book covers and has even started her own graphics business with Beautiful Mess Graphics, which if you're an author, you truly need to check out. She also does my teasers, advertisements, and acts as my marketing manager. Sarah of SEA Creations does all my formatting, which would drive me absolutely crazy. All three of these ladies serve as beta readers, making sure I don't screw up characters or hand you a weak, slow story. Their input and ideas are invaluable in making each novel the best it can be before we allow it to reach your hands. Without these three wonderfully talented and patient ladies, there would never be a Robbie Cox in bookstores. I owe them an abundance of gratitude.

I also need to thank Katie Weisenberger who has been my editor from the start, making sure my tense, commas, and typos are caught before publication. She is awesome, and I appreciate all she does and how quickly she handles the manuscripts, since I'm usually pushing them at her last minute. I also need to thank her husband, Bill, for allowing her to work so many nights to make sure these stories are as perfect as we can make them.

There are so many components in being an Indie Author, and I could never figure it all out on my own, so I want to thank Linzi

Baxter, Gracen Miller, C. L. Roman, and Violet Howe for always allowing me to bend there ear, run ideas by them and ask them questions as to where I'm going off the rails. From marketing to publishing to grammar to trends, these ladies and fellow authors have been a wealth of information, helping me along this journey. Thank you for your time, patience, and valuable advice.

There are more, many more, and each one is important and needed as we strive to bring you the steamiest, most adventurous tales to keep you entertained and returning to see what happens next.

About the Author

Basking along the beaches of Central Florida, R. C. Wynne is a romantic at heart. R.C. loves writing heart-throbbing stories with strong, but sassy heroines, hunky heroes who love their women to have an inner fire, plenty of sexy times to melt your panties and keep your heart racing, romantic happily-ever-afters, and an abundance of emotions to keep you laughing, crying, and even sometimes screaming.

When not writing, R.C. is often found on his back porch enjoying a cigar, a scotch, and some Dean Martin tunes. He derives pleasure from his large family and his crazy group of friends who provide the inspiration for his blog, *The Mess that Is Me*.

His series include, *The Rutherford Series*, *Fangirls*, *The Best of Both Worlds*, and the popular *The Harper Twins*. For more information about his new releases, upcoming events, and sneak peeks into his crazy world, visit R.C. at rcwynnebooks.com.

Connect with R.C. Wynne online:

Website ~ www.rcwynnebooks.com

Facebook ~ https://www.facebook.com/R.C.WynneAuthor
Twitter ~ https://twitter.com/RCWynne2
Pinterest ~ https://www.pinterest.com/robbie9652/
Goodreads ~ https://www.goodreads.com/user/show/128870802-r-c-wynne
Instagram ~ https://www.instagram.com/r.c.wynneauthor/
Bookbub ~ https://www.bookbub.com/profile/1566963280
MeWe ~ https://mewe.com/i/rcwynne

For up-to-date news on R.C. Wynne's latest releases, book signing events in your area, and giveaways, follow his newsletter - https://landing.mailerlite.com/webforms/landing/l7q0q7

You can also join R.C. Wynne's reading group, Wynne's Romance Hideaway, for more updates, extra giveaways, and even more fan involvement - https://www.facebook.com/groups/wynnesromancehideway

Other Books by R.C. Wynne

The Rutherford Series
Losing Faith
Roll the Dice
To Be Cherished
His to Command
Sharing Hearts

Fangirls
Nikki
Lily
Cassie
Olivia
Willow
The Collection

The Harper Twins
Sibling Rivalry
Taming Karla
Always Aimee
The Harper Twins Box Set

Best of Both Worlds
Ribbons & Bows
Under the Wrapping
The Best of Both Worlds

Visit www.rcwynnebooks.com to find out more about these great books by R.C. Wynne!

Writing as Robbie Cox

<u>Warrior of the Way</u>
Reaping the Harvest
Lore Master
The Warrior's Blade
Summerlands

<u>The Cauldron Coven</u>
Death's Shroud
Daughters of Darkness
Chaos Magicians

<u>Halloween Seduction</u>
Come Halloween
Behind the Mask

<u>Life's Moments</u>
Green is the Grass
Waiting Room
Second Light
Saturday at the Inlet
Life's Moments

<u>The Witches of Savannah</u>
Enter the Witch

<u>Short Stories</u>
Circle of Justice

Bull Creek Chronicles
Alpha Rising
Panther Hunted
Bear Necessities

Destined Mates
Magic's Mate
Mate's Appeal
Mate's Touch
My Lover's Mate
My Mate's Wife

Visit www.robbiecox.com to find out more about these great books by Robbie Cox!

THE MESS-Y STORE
Robbie Cox's Books & Merchandise
CELEBRATE YOUR LOVE OF READING ROBBIE'S STORIES

Books. Shirts. Totes. Socks. Mugs. And More.

SHOP NOW TO FIND YOUR FAVORITES!
www.robbiecox.net/merch

Get all your great merchandise at The Mess-y Store, from coffee mugs to T-shirts to laptop sleeves! Visit www.robbiecox.net/merch to order your fun swag today!

Milton Keynes UK
Ingram Content Group UK Ltd.
UKHW020835030424
440506UK00008B/843